AN EXTRAVAGANT DEATH

Also by Charles Finch

The Last Enchantments

The Charles Lenox Series

A Beautiful Blue Death

The September Society

The Fleet Street Murders

A Stranger in Mayfair

A Burial at Sea

A Death in the Small Hours

An Old Betrayal

The Laws of Murder

Home by Nightfall

The Inheritance

The Woman in the Water

The Vanishing Man

The Last Passenger

AN EXTRAVAGANT DEATH

Charles Finch

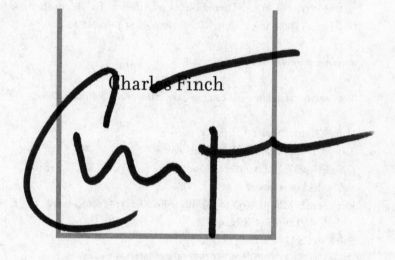

MINOTAUR
BOOKS
NEW YORK

For Emily! With my deepest love.

Published in the United States by Minotaur Books, an imprint of St. Martin's Publishing Group

AN EXTRAVAGANT DEATH. Copyright © 2021 by Hampden Lane LLC. All rights reserved. Printed in the United States of America. For information, address St. Martin's Publishing Group, 120 Broadway, New York, NY 10271.

www.minotaurbooks.com

The Library of Congress has cataloged the hardcover edition as follows:

Names: Finch, Charles (Charles B.), author.
Title: An extravagant death / Charles Finch.
Description: First edition. | New York : Minotaur Books, 2021. | Series:
    Charles Lenox mysteries ; 14
Identifiers: LCCN 2020050029 | ISBN 9781250767134 (hardcover) |
    ISBN 9781250767141 (ebook)
Subjects: GSAFD: Mystery fiction.
Classification: LCC PS3606.I526 E98 2021 | DDC 813/.6—dc23
LC record available at https://lccn.loc.gov/2020050029

ISBN 978-1-250-76715-8 (trade paperback)

Our books may be purchased in bulk for promotional, educational, or business use. Please contact your local bookseller or the Macmillan Corporate and Premium Sales Department at 1-800-221-7945, extension 5442, or by email at MacmillanSpecialMarkets@macmillan.com.

First Minotaur Books Trade Paperback Edition: 2022

10 9 8 7 6 5 4 3 2 1

CHAPTER ONE

I t was a sunny, icy late morning in February of 1878, and a solitary
figure, lost in thought, strode along one of the pale paths winding through St. James's Park in London.

He was a lean gentleman of middling height, with a walking
stick clasped behind his back. Aside from him the park was empty,
its grass frozen a stiff whitish arctic green, and the ruts in its muddy
pathways—made by carriages during a thaw the week before—
hardened into solid relief. For a moment he paused to gaze at these
random tracks where they had frozen in place, and it occurred
to him that human affairs, too, could unexpectedly take decisive
shape just when everything seemed to be in flux.

The person's name was Charles Lenox, and at that moment he
was probably the preeminent detective in all of England, professional or amateur. It was this fact that he had been unhappily mull-
ing during the chilly stroll from his house in Mayfair toward his
destination, which was Parliament. The buildings of Britain's seat
of government rose unobstructed before him, the splendor of their
honey-colored stone lofted above the softly curving flower beds and
handsome empty trees of the park.

He might have come by carriage; certainly it would have been warmer. But he had chosen to walk. He wished to have a clear head before this meeting. Much of the last two months of his life had been dedicated to a dark, violent, and unpleasant investigation, and now that investigation was at its endpoint, and it was his duty to gather its threads into his fingers.

Numerous days had passed during that period in which he saw nothing of his family—not his wife, Lady Jane, upon whose clear-eyed intelligence and unflappable good sense he relied so deeply in the general course of life, nor his older brother Edmund, and never for more than a minute or two in the evenings his two beloved daughters, Sophia and Clara.

Edmund, at least, he knew he would see shortly. For once the prospect brought him little joy.

At one o'clock exactly Lenox arrived at a small wooden door, faded and scored, a humble detail in the vast, imposing design of Parliament. This was the Members' Entrance. Lenox had once been a Member of Parliament himself—a fling of some five years or so with politics, following which he had rededicated himself to the study of crime—and was thereby entitled to use it for the remainder of his days.

It was Canfield, one of the post's familiar old porters, who greeted him.

"Mr. Lenox!" said Canfield, standing up from his stool. "How do you do? Come in."

"Very well, Canfield—how are you?"

"Cold as charity, sir." Canfield smiled good-naturedly. He was an open-faced Londoner, cheerful, tall, and strong. "Though come to think of it, why must charity be cold? Still, my mother always said it on days like this. Cut right along this way, sir, please, and I'll follow along."

Lenox looked at the porter with surprise. "Oh, I know the way."

"Of course, sir, but I must take you."

Canfield's attitude was polite but definite: He would go. Lenox hesitated for a moment, then merely nodded. The porter removed a ring of keys from a drawer and used one to lock the door to the Members' Entrance from the inside; anyone who wished to come in would have to wait in the cold, very annoyed, Lenox thought, or else go round to the public entrance. They would be put out—being a population, the Members of Parliament, who were not as a rule much habituated to inconvenience.

Canfield hooked the keys into the inside of his gray wool jacket, where they hung next to a match safe. They were careful with fire here, Lenox remembered with a quick feeling of both amusement (the recollection of Guy Fawkes might make anyone a little cautious with matches) and of—well, what? Sanctuary, perhaps. It had been an arduous new year thus far, 1878, but after these weeks of hard exertion he found himself taken in by Parliament, and it was a more powerful relief than he would have expected, the large, slow-moving, well-ordered ship of state, as unchanging as the tides, welcoming him home.

He should have known that whichever porter he'd found here would accompany him, of course. For he was at Parliament not on any humdrum business, but to see perhaps the second most important personage in Great Britain, after the Queen: her Prime Minister, Benjamin Disraeli.

With sure footsteps, Canfield led him through the complicated corridors of the building, up a stairwell, and past the bar. It always gave Lenox a queer feeling to be in these halls again, a bit like being back at school. The place very familiar, but no longer quite so intimate as it once had been.

Though Parliament was in recess, a few gentlemen sat here and there, sipping glasses of hot cream whisky and negus, some reading, others conversing in low tones. Lenox spied Lord Whiston and the two exchanged friendly nods. The barman, too, bowed slightly; one remembered a tipper.

At last they stepped into a quiet hallway with shafts of light slanting down across its stone floor from a row of mullioned windows.

"Had a good Christmas, sir?" Canfield asked.

"Very good," Lenox replied automatically. Christmas seemed like an event from years before, though it had scarcely been six weeks. "And you?"

"Oh, yes! Nice for the little ones. They love to decorate the tree."

"How many have you now, Mr. Canfield, if I may ask?"

"Nine, sir."

"Nine! Gracious me. A large family."

Canfield smiled faintly, as if to say that perhaps that understated the affair.

"So it is, sir," he said. "And busy work they make for us, too, but we're happy. Eliza, our eldest, will be sixteen next week. Perhaps you remember her from the staff party, many years ago—though perhaps not. She would have been nine then."

"Of course I remember her. Please send her my regards."

"And I have heard your good news, sir. A second daughter?"

"Oh! Yes. From Edmund, I suppose? I thank you."

The truth was that Lenox barely knew Clara, his new daughter, at all—only as a roly-poly bundle of warm, wriggling, happy life in this wintry world. She was still shy of five months old, awaiting her first summer, full of urgent hungers and curious little cooing smiles. She was sturdy, as he had heard second children tended to be; easily made happy by sleep and milk.

He loved her, of course, but at Canfield's comment he reflected, tiredly, that he would like to know her as well.

They came to the end of the long hallway. It was colder here, with only the calls of a few winter songbirds from the courtyard breaking the silence.

The porter knocked at the door. A smartly dressed young secretary opened it and bowed to them with military brevity. Canfield, his duty completed, bid Lenox good day.

"A pleasure to see you, sir," he said.

"And you. Try and stay warm at your post!"

"I shall certainly try, sir. Now and then the kitchen staff brings down hot irons to keep by our feet." He grinned. "And a tot of rum if we're good. Good day, sir. I hope to see you again soon."

The porter took off back down the hallway, and the young secretary—Jones, was it?—led Lenox into a spacious, well-lit room in which several desks were occupied by a dozen nearly identical young men, all similarly dressed in sober gray twill suits, all with hair smoothed brilliantly down. This seemed peculiar. Disraeli himself was a rather unkempt fellow, respectably turned out to be sure, but with tobacco in his cuffs and usually a day past needing a shave and haircut.

Lenox trailed the secretary toward an imposing arched doorway. The Prime Minister's own office.

"Oh, hell," the detective muttered to himself.

He wasn't intimidated by the setting, but he was conscious of being at less than his sharpest. Lenox was approaching his fiftieth birthday, and though he had managed to keep moving forward on three or so hours of sleep a night for the past several weeks, he couldn't say, as he once might have, that the effort had placed no strain upon him.

The young secretary—Smith?—knocked crisply twice. There was a pause. Lenox glanced down at a handsome demilune table sitting snug against the wall next to the door, its glossy surface covered in neat ranks of calling cards left for the Prime Minister. Presumably all of these people, thirty or so, had tried and failed to get in that day. Lenox saw the card of old Whiston from the bar, sitting between that of a Russian diplomat and a famous essayist for the Saturday weeklies.

Several of the cards had their corners folded down, indicating that their owners would wait upon Disraeli in the building. As he gazed at the calling cards with a naked curiosity that in a less tired moment he might have tried to conceal, Lenox tried to decide why he merited admission on this particular day when they hadn't. There was a catch here. That he much he thought he could scent.

A gentleman in a well-cut black suit opened the door and greeted him. "Lenox, good to see you."

"Good afternoon, Elkin."

The secretary bowed and retreated, and Lord Elkin opened the door a bit farther.

He was a handsome man, with even white teeth and an imperious, impassive expression. His grandfather had made one of the nation's great fortunes in coal and bought a title with a trifling percentage of the proceeds. Elkin himself was masterfully classless, neither too far above his roots in trade nor acceding to any condescension, a dab hand at games and an excellent dancer and shooter, part of the raucous yachting circle of the Prince of Wales. He was also Disraeli's closest and most ruthless political confidant.

The chamber into which he led Lenox was not unlike a college library, large, hushed, and handsome. On one wall there were celestial figures painted in gold leaf on a dark blue background. A quiet fire blazed in the hearth (Fawkes!) and there were decanters of whisky, water, and various other reassuring liquids on the table between the gray armchairs and sofas. This had been Disraeli's headquarters for years; even now, back in power, he used Downing Street less than most Prime Ministers did.

And there, at the far end of the room, he sat. He was turned in his chair so that Lenox saw him in profile, and speaking in a low voice to a third gentleman who stood a few paces back, near a window—and here Lenox realized that he had been wrong, for the gladness he felt at seeing his brother, Sir Edmund Lenox, was overwhelming, nearly physical.

"Charles!" said Edmund, noticing him.

"Hello, Edmund." Lenox smiled. He bowed to Disraeli, who had stood and was patting his pockets for his snuffbox, looking amiable, as he always seemed to. "Good afternoon, Prime Minister."

In truth there were few living men more formidable than Benjamin Disraeli. He was legendarily witty, and a famous novelist in *his spare time*, which gave him an air of genius that intimidated even the usually unflappable. He loved women, tolerated men. There were innumerable rumors about his affairs.

"Lenox!" he said. "Very pleased to see you again." They had met many times, though they had never been particular friends. "I wish it were under other circumstances. The whole thing is extremely regrettable. Still, I'm glad you intervened."

Lord Elkin spoke. "We have been discussing with your brother how we may repay you for that."

"Have you?" said Lenox, who had never liked Elkin. "How kind."

Disraeli picked up a fine coffee cup and gave it a single swirl. "Yes, we have," he said, staring down at the drink. He looked up. "Britain owes you an acknowledgment, Lenox. These have been very great exertions you've made."

"Only my work."

Disraeli smiled and took a sip of his coffee. "Perhaps I may phrase it differently in that case: We hope that you will consent now to do her one additional service." The Prime Minister paused, then sank the dagger. "By leaving her shores at your earliest convenience."

Lenox paused for a moment, taking his time to reply. He made a note in his mind to have something sent to Eliza Canfield that afternoon. A few yards of damask? Lady Jane would know.

In some region of his thought this was what he had expected as he walked through the park half an hour before. Still, it stung. Having feigned an appearance of surprised contemplation for long enough, he hoped, at last he replied.

"By leaving."

Disraeli nodded firmly. "Yes. America, we thought. It would be the Queen's pleasure to give you a knighthood, too, if you want it. But those are merely details to be sorted out."

CHAPTER TWO

After the meeting was over, Edmund and Charles went to find somewhere to talk.

There were more than a dozen places within the Palace of Westminster (as it was formally called, for the building remained a possession, technically, of the Queen) to eat and drink. They chose Kate's, which was named after a beloved barmaid of the '80s and '90s. As far as was possible in such a well-trafficked building, it remained a secret, mostly home to a dozen or two comfortably taciturn older Members who preferred silence to badinage, and were content to let a few nods constitute their day's exertion in the conversational arts.

After old Nupkin, the longstanding barman at Kate's, had inquired after their health and pulled their pints of ale, the brothers made their way to a bow window nook with soft blue cushions lining its benches. Soon Nupkin came out and placed two dishes on the ancient oak table: Welsh rarebit on toast for Charles, and for Edmund a dark fragrant soup, steaming in its tureen.

Charles was starved, and Edmund must have been as well, for they both fell heavily upon the food, until, when a good two-thirds of it was tucked away, Charles finally leaned back, sighed, and took a sip of his ale.

He felt vastly better. He was glad the meeting was over.

A pot of tea and a plate of caraway biscuits arrived when they had finished, and Edmund, always tactful, at last ventured a remark. "You're determined not to accept the knighthood?"

"That's correct," said Charles.

"And I take it you will not leave."

Charles turned and looked at the river through the window, briefly silent. "No. I don't think I shall. I wasn't sure what to say."

"Mm."

"There's Clara to consider—Clara, Sophia, Jane."

The nine months during which Lady Jane had carried their child had been a period of continual apprehension. Being over forty, she had remained in bed for much of the last third of the term, and it had been with a sigh of relief that the doctor who attended the birth—old Sir James Marbury, a distinguished man—told Charles that mother and daughter were safe. Between the two of them, he'd said, he never felt quite easy attending a mother of Jane's age, but now all would be well, all would be well.

Lenox had borne this trial stoically, only a bystander after all, but the constant edge of fear had wearied him. He felt it. The prospect of leaving Jane seemed alarming.

He stared at the Thames, steel colored and calm in the bitter midday light. One or two brave small craft were out upon it; virtual emptiness, by the river's standards.

Lenox didn't want a knighthood. It was reckoned an honor, he knew, but to be called Sir Charles for the rest of his days held no appeal for him—indeed, seemed, when he mulled it in his mind, like a positive encroachment upon his life as plain Charles Lenox.

Was there a time when he would have felt differently? Perhaps. Ambition had never driven him quite so hard as sheer curiosity did, but he hadn't been free of it. He still wasn't. Perhaps, in truth, there was even a trace of snobbishness in his resistance: Let the barristers at the Inns of Court be called "Sir," after a lifetime of work, or the brewers of Newcastle, if it made them feel well in their hearts.

This realization of his own vanity in the matter almost inclined him (as he watched the river ripple toward its banks) to accept. But no. It was a different matter for his brother, who held his title as part of a line of baronets. On Charles the same "Sir" that Edmund bore with distinction would be a clumsy, distracting ornament.

America, though; that was the more difficult question.

It was hard to say how much of his brother's thinking Sir Edmund intuited. Like Charles, he was about an inch or two above average height, but Edmund was larger through his chest and shoulders, with a dark brown beard and dark curly hair. His eyes were kind—stubbornly free of the urban acuity Charles's had acquired, displaying, still, the ingenuity of a country gentleman who happened to find himself in a capital.

This belied his position, which was one of unexpected power. Indeed, Edmund had declined a place in Gladstone's shadow cabinet a few months before. Charles, who had advised him to accept, was still not sure if Edmund had done it out of natural reticence, or because he was as yet enduring the state of awful grief that he had entered after the unexpected death of his wife, Molly, two years before. He still wore a black band on his arm.

"I wonder if they've got any marmalade," said Edmund.

Charles looked at him moodily. "If you never spoke you could be mistaken for someone with weighty thoughts, Edmund."

"I am."

"Do they mostly have to do with marmalade?"

Edmund smiled, looking momentarily ten years old again. "You mustn't take it out on me that you have to become a knight and go to the colonies. I didn't set out to break up Scotland Yard."

"Nor did I."

"Then you've had a jolly troublesome accident."

"Very witty."

Edmund broke one of his biscuits in half. As if by magic, James Nupkin appeared at that instant with a small pot of marmalade; Edmund thanked him warmly and gave his younger brother a triumphant look, his epicurean instinct that the situation called for marmalade having been verified by no less an authority than the experienced barman himself.

"Yet you have broken up the Yard," he said, as he spooned the bright orange chunks onto his plate. He looked up. "I've still only heard it in bits and pieces, you know. Do you have it in you to tell me how it happened?"

"Of course."

The whole business had begun in January, he said, and Edmund replied, yes, Lightfoot, he knew that much. Charles nodded. Then he embarked upon his complicated tale.

Philip Lightfoot was a reputable chemist with a shop in Regent Street. One evening the prior December, after the shop's closing, a man had appeared at the door and requested entry, complaining of dyspepsia.

The chemist had let him in to help, but the man had immediately pulled out a pistol and ordered Lightfoot's hands in the air. He then tied the shop owner's wrists, emptied the till, and left— though not before helping himself to a liberal assortment of liniments and compounds from behind the counter.

It was a simple crime. What the thief hadn't known was that Lightfoot had recently joined a consortium of twelve shops around Oxford Circus that had convened to hire Lenox's detective agency on an annual retainer. And as it had fallen out, Lenox himself had been the one to look into the matter.

He had expected that at most he might run some minor villain to ground in the thieves' dens of Soho. In fact, piecing together eyewitness accounts of the incident, he had discovered that the thief was a police constable named Wogan. Appalled and confounded at being caught—he was built like a cart horse but outfitted with the wits of a bird—Wogan had immediately revealed to Lenox something genuinely surprising: that he had been acting under the orders of one of his superiors, a Sergeant J. Jonathan Clark.

From this relatively benign starting point (a tin of Larby's Foot Balm was one of the most expensive of the missing items), Lenox had followed a dark and winding path toward a series of increasingly unsettling discoveries.

Their final result was declared on the front page of the very issue of the *London and Brighton Star* that hung at a jaunty angle on its wooden dowel by the bar here at Kate's.

Three Chief Inspectors in Detective Branch to Be Tried
Wilde, Didion, Swett Charged for Crime Ring; Corruption
Lenox-Dallington agency responsible for findings;
Questions raised about outside involvement in police affairs

Lenox told his brother the story that had led to this headline, sparing no detail, glad to get it out to a neutral party—someone who wasn't from his own agency or a member of Scotland Yard.

"And so they were all in on it," Edmund said marvelingly, taking a sip of his tea. "Three of the four chief inspectors of the Detective Branch! My gracious."

"Yes. Rotten, the whole place. They had been organizing this kind of thing for more than five years. We found one from '72, in fact. Once we started digging up unsolved robberies, it was hard to stop finding them."

"And now they're to be tried."

"Yes, and barring some historic miscarriage of justice found guilty."

The press was in raptures (*The defective department!* shouted *Punch*, a humor magazine). The government was not quite so well-pleased.

That had been the subject of the day's meeting. It was all to the good that Lenox had uncovered this corruption, as Disraeli had explained; very happy to have the Metropolitan Police begin with a fresh start, a new day; and yet, the Prime Minister had gone on, the embarrassment to several highly placed politicians and aristocrats, should Lenox choose to stay and testify in open court, before the ravenous press in their gallery, rather than providing a written testimony (a dry, thorough, unimpeachable testimony, Disraeli stressed) would be great. Ruinous, in at least a few cases. The Earl of Kestrel himself had overseen the appointment of all three men from his seat in the House of Lords, and he was at Buckingham Palace daily to exhort the Queen—his second cousin—to minimize the damage to his reputation.

"And so your presence in London is awkward to a handful of people with influence," said Edmund. "That was about as I had figured for myself. Neither Disraeli nor Elkin was eager to give me details before you came in."

"Perhaps they spotted that you were my brother."

Edmund frowned. "I doubt it. Common name, and I'm much better looking. Ah, but for this they wish you to go to America! That bothers me."

"Not just that. Kestrel would like an investigation into whether the agency ought to be regulated, perhaps even closed down. The same goes for Sir Peter Blasevick."

This was the head of the Yard, the son of an Austrian count and an English mother, a well-connected gentleman within industrial circles. "That seems a lot of sound and fury."

"Perhaps." Charles frowned, carving up his last pieces of Welsh rarebit with greater delicacy than he had during his famished first encounter with it. "I loathe Kestrel. Wheedling, threats—I think him a scrub, and I should be happy to tell him so to his face."

Kestrel was one of England's most prominent citizens. "Sleep on that, perhaps."

"But it's a dignified way out of the situation—going to America. And it might save the agency a good deal of bother."

Disraeli's proposal had been that Lenox should meet with the police in the major cities of America in order to establish international investigative cooperation and exchange the latest methods. He would travel with the full authority of Parliament: a special decree, a wide latitude, a generous budget, nearly every seal of officialdom and import that a Prime Minister could bestow.

"Your own happiness must come before the agency."

"I would not sacrifice Polly or Dallington's aspirations to my own vanity."

These were Charles's partners, and before that had been his friends. Their business was still a relatively new one; for most of his adult life, Lenox had been an amateur detective.

He dunked a ginger snap in his tea, letting it soften, and then took a bite. He longed for an afternoon of sleep. Even the good taste of the tea made him more tired—for tea always matched whatever mood he was in, its strange magic.

"You should only go if the notion pleases you," Edmund insisted.

"It would look like I was running away."

"I don't know that. Indeed, I think many people would see it as a reward. Particularly if you accepted the knighthood."

Lenox gave a non-committal nod. The truth that Charles had left out, even in his account to his brother, felt shameful to him: the way, when Disraeli had suggested a trip to America, he had briefly glimpsed the journey it would entail, the salty sea, the ship with its creak of timber and taut ropes, the busy shores of a new place—and how, to his surprise, his whole being had leapt with a thrill of ecstasy at the idea of it, down to the last drop of blood in his veins.

CHAPTER THREE

C harles Lenox had grown up on his father's estate in Sussex, then followed in the footsteps of Edmund, his only sibling, first at Harrow School and then at Balliol College, Oxford.

Balliol was the traditional breeding ground for politicians, as surely as Trinity College at Cambridge ("the other place," as Oxonians called it) bred scientists. And indeed, Lenox's first notion as he had started into adulthood was that he might go into politics. It would have been somewhat trickier for him than his brother. It was Edmund, the firstborn, whom they had both known from their earliest sentience would ultimately occupy the seat for Markethouse which their father had—indeed, which some Lenox or other (the most adventurously named of the previous baronets was one Sir Galefridus Lenox, who had borne the burden of this forename for much of the reign of James the First) had held through the lives of nearly two dozen monarchs.

Still, Charles might well have set his sights on an early entry into Parliament if, late in his school years, he hadn't stumbled into an interest in crime. It had begun in the most common and humble way possible: with the penny dreadfuls at down-market bookshops, which offered outlandish tales of old highwaymen and rakes.

Lenox had taken his degree at Balliol—a relative rarity, since most young men who did not wish to join the church preferred to depart Oxford without one after a few years of happy idleness and only the occasional tutorial—and then gone to London.

There, he had set up as a detective, just twenty-one and despite the advice of virtually every human being who could prevail upon him to listen for even a passing moment: aunts, uncles, cousins, second cousins, great-aunts, third cousins, family friends, family enemies. School chums, fourth cousins. In those heady days he had received letters from family acquaintances who hadn't touched English soil in thirty years, prevailed upon to plead with him from comfortable perches in Burma and India and Africa.

The message from these well-meaning people was uniform. Charles was demeaning his family's honor by his choice, they said, and at the same time throwing away his prospects for a happy life. They begged him instead to pursue one of the three traditional careers permitted to the younger sons of the gentry: the clergy, the military, or politics.

It was only those closest to him, his parents and Edmund, who had never directly questioned his choice. Edmund had been staunch from the start. His parents, though filled with doubt, had been too loving, he saw in retrospect, to reject their son for his professional decisions, whatever they might be. For that he was grateful.

He had set about detective work with discipline—when he thought now of the hours he had been capable of working in his twenties, poring over old cases, studying maps, interviewing criminals!—and after a halting start had found a foothold in the job. This had never stopped any snob who wished to cut him at a party for being in trade, however.

In those early years he had been in love twice. The first time had been with Lady Jane. But she had been married when he realized his emotions, and then, when she was widowed, too fragile, or so he'd thought at least, to approach. The second time had been brief, a moment of enchantment with a witty, beautiful young woman in society called Kitty Ashbrook, who had ultimately married a peer named Lord Cormorant (haughty, boorish, but landed) in favor of Lenox.

Only when Lenox was in his late thirties had he and Jane completed their slow circle back to each other. Nearly twenty years lost. He sometimes wondered afterward if he had been too dedicated to his work to have noticed the moment when he might have taken his chance earlier, if he could have spared himself the loneliness and self-doubt of that period.

But he had been working so hard in those years to prove that his choice had been the right one. He had been driven by a nearly mad wish to show that what he did had value, and in this he had at least been moderately successful, he thought. Besides, the world had changed beyond recognition from the slumbering 1840s; Lord Kestrel's own third son was a stockbroker in the City. There were more than three professions now.

In the phase just after his marriage, perhaps out of some instinctive sense of duty to his marriage and to Lady Jane's exalted position in society, Lenox had at last made a bid for a seat in Parliament and won. To sit in that august body had been an experience with great exhilarations and meant hundreds of hours spent among men and women of intelligence and vitality. For this reason he was glad he had done it.

Still, he hadn't felt entirely himself until he had resumed his previous career, as he saw now. First and last, he was a detective.

Of course, the other great dream of his days at Harrow and Oxford, to which he had dedicated nearly as much of his imaginative powers then as to crime, perhaps in truth just as much at times, had been travel.

This dream had faded, but back then he had imagined himself

one of the world's great wanderers, perhaps even an explorer of sorts—not the ascetic kind who uncovers new civilizations, but a person who could be comfortable in different ones, from Morocco to Brazil to China, ranging familiarly among them, adding to the store of knowledge England had of each. In a way it was the same impulse as wishing to be a detective: to know everything; to understand everything; to experience everything.

But the majority of his great planned expeditions had never come to pass; and at home after his visit to Disraeli, contemplating America, he felt the keen regret of that fact—which was usually dulled and distant, unimportant—break over him again. Where had the time gone! He had once intended to see so much.

All this was playing in Lenox's mind as he sat in Lady Jane's private dressing room that evening. Indeed, he was jolted out of deep thought when she spoke, and had once to ask her to repeat what she had said.

"I asked—if not America? What alternative did Disraeli offer?"

"Alternative?"

Lady Jane glanced over at him from the delicate chair in front of her dressing table. She seemed irritated. "Put that down, please, if you would."

"What?" he said, then looked down at a slim glass vial he hadn't realized he was holding.

Lenox rarely achieved admission to this chamber—with some justice, for he couldn't help when he was here but pick up some ivory comb, or smell the flowers in their glass bowl by the window doors, or ask what *this* was as he held up a silver bowl full of powder. But it was nearly seven o'clock, they were going out to supper, and they had much to discuss.

"That bottle of scent. Unless you want to smell like bergamot and lemon all evening."

He put the vial down carefully. "No. Apologies. I have already applied my own rose perfume, as it happens."

Lady Jane smiled, a little grudgingly. She was in her forties now, and as pretty to him as ever she had been, her face filled with bright watchful intelligence. They had been married for eleven years. With variations, she had dressed the same way for the evening ever since her first season in London at the age of seventeen. Tonight she had on a dress of gray and pink that had arrived from Paris in soft billows of tissue paper that morning, with a light blue ribbon at the waist.

"Very droll." But Lady Jane's thoughts were elsewhere. "Perhaps he has just begun a negotiation. Perhaps we might just run over to France. Does he know you have a family?"

"I suppose he must. He has dined here, as you know. He and I were in the Commons. And he will have heard a great deal about you."

Lady Jane occupied a high position in society, higher than her husband's. It was not because she was the daughter of an earl, for there were at least a few hundred of these roaming about London. Rather, it was the ferocious integrity of her friendships, as well as her seeming randomness in forming them without regard for wealth, rank, or fashion: only affection. Besides this, Jane was kind, charming, discreet, and, it had to be owned, of course—the daughter of an earl.

"But does he know about Sophia? Clara?"

Lenox rose and crossed the sparely furnished chamber, with its prints of lilies upon the light green walls. Jane's dress this evening showed off her shoulders, and he approached her and ran his fingers over her soft skin. She looked at him in the mirror. Her hair was up, and there was a net of small diamonds in it, glimpsed only when they flashed in the light.

"I doubt he has given them a single thought. There are not many men in his cabinet with fewer than a dozen children."

"If you went to America it might look as if you were afraid to stay."

"No, it wouldn't," he replied testily, though it was exactly what he had said to his brother.

She looked at him with softer eyes. "We've scarcely seen you since the year turned as it is."

"Yes. I know."

"I only mention it because I can tell you want to go, Charles."

He frowned. "I don't, either." There was a large silver-handled cup with steam rising from it on her table, and he picked it up. "What's this?"

Lady Jane had resumed the careful application of her kohl. "Spiced bishop," she said to her reflection. "Ellie said it was too cold not to make it."

This was the house's cook. "And drank half of it herself. Well, so be it." Lenox took a sip of the concoction and it warmed him straight through, apple cider with wine, nutmeg, and brandy. "I don't know how you can tell I want to go, since I don't know myself."

Her attention had left him. "Because I know you," she said, looking carefully at her reflection.

"And you would wish me to stay?"

Still she didn't look at him. "I suppose so," she said.

There was something rueful in her tone, and in that moment he decided he would not go. "Well, I don't mean to go. I need a break from work anyway. And there's a fearful amount to do at the agency."

"Good, then," she said, ignoring the inconsistency of this reasoning and using the edge of a pinkie to brush away a stray black fleck of makeup.

"Good," he said.

Before they left, they stopped into the nursery. There, as the governess tended to the baby, Sophia jumped onto his lap and made a spot for herself, and they commenced a long conversation in which she asked him to explain (just for example) why horses had tails and whether Dutch people were real; and at the end, just before they left, Lenox was permitted to hold Clara for a few moments.

He was still very tired—very tired—and felt himself succumb to a deep sentimentality for a moment, studying her milk-sleepy face, her lace bonnet. Her curious little gripping hands. Then he roused himself and returned her to Miss Huntington before going downstairs to order the carriage. No, he thought. Better not to go. Disraeli would have to brave the disappointment of it; no doubt, indeed, it was already gone from his thoughts.

CHAPTER FOUR

For the next two days London was layered in a fog so dense that according to the papers no fewer than eight men fell into the river from the West India Docks. All of them had been fished out quickly, fortunately, and none worse off than a glass of rum would cure, but as the papers said—still! A pretty pass things had come to, when men and women couldn't walk the streets of the capital without the prospect of barging straight into a lamppost.

"They add that no doubt the thieves will be pleased by the fog," said young Lord John Dallington, his eyes scanning the print.

Dallington was Lenox's protégé—a young, well-born gentleman with black hair, always impeccably dressed, but with even now a lingering reputation as a bad apple. His friends knew better.

They were seated in the Reform, a gentleman's club in Pall Mall. Outside it was harsh weather—the windows were like long, figureless paintings of swirling gray—but indoors the fire was warm and the chairs comfortable, the smell of tea and old books wafting through the air.

"Won't the thieves be just as befogged as we are?" Lenox asked.

"I don't think that would make up a very interesting article."

"*Thieves housebound.* No, it wouldn't do."

Dallington laughed. "*Said to be engaged in needlepoint by fireplace until weather clears.* I would buy the paper to read that, as it happens."

They were here because Lenox had missed out on a great deal since the Lightfoot case began. Dallington was catching him up.

It was still odd to Lenox to be one of the partners in a detective agency, after so many years on his own—mostly unaided in his work, but mostly unencumbered, too. In the past ten years or so Dallington had become one of his closest friends, however, and the third share of the agency belonged to another, an enterprising, thoughtful, and rather remarkable young woman named Polly Buchanan. She was Dallington's wife—but that was an outcome that postdated their professional partnership. Several years before, a young widow, she had seen a gap in the market and set out to solve all the minor domestic troubles (thefts, dowry arguments, missing husbands) that detectives like Lenox and the police ignored.

Her success had been immediate, and now she was the guiding force of the agency. Under her employment were some dozen detectives, most of them former associates of Scotland Yard and other metropolitan police departments across England and the isles.

Usually Polly would have been present herself at a meeting such as this one (which would have necessitated a different venue—like all the clubs along this regal row of London buildings, the Reform was the province of a single sex) but she was out upon a case herself that afternoon.

Lenox and Dallington ordered lunch, and their food came right where they sat in the comfortable library—part of the charm of the club, that you could remain in one seat the whole day long if you wished.

Dallington had been making his way in his muddled fashion through the cases Lenox ought to know about, but shoved aside the papers with a relieved sigh when the food appeared. He was a bright and intuitive detective—but Polly would have done an infinitely better job at this sort of debrief, thought Lenox with an inward sigh.

They ate in comfortable silence, which Lenox broke only after some little while.

At the very back of the deep hearth nearby was an enormous, roughly cut piece of oak. "Do you know what that is?"

"Wood," said Dallington moodily.

"And they say you'll never make a detective."

"Who says that?" the young lord asked angrily. Then he saw that Lenox had been joking. "Oh. Anyhow. I should like to see them say it to me."

It was no use pointing out Dallington's low spirits, which he was doubtless aware of himself, so Lenox returned to the huge piece of oak in the hearth. In medieval times, he explained, it had always been called the "back log."

"Which is, incidentally, the very thing that has brought us here—a backlog of cases."

Dallington was not quite so enchanted as his mentor by the coincidence, and said why did Lenox always have to know where words came from, and added that nobody liked a know-it-all. Then he said he was sorry, he had a bit of a headache, but still it was a bit much. Backlog.

"I spent the morning trying to read Plato," Dallington added, rubbing his temples. "It nearly did me in."

"Why on earth did you do that?"

Dallington flushed. "No reason."

"You're reading Plato for no reason?"

"I said *trying* to read, in the first place. And anyhow, I was, yes, you would think I'd said I was trying to solve the problem of perpetual motion the way everyone's reacted."

This was a small mystery—Dallington's reading generally extended not much further than the comics in *Punch*—but Lenox left it to the side.

"If you're finished eating, let's get through the—"

"Please don't say backlog, Charles. I don't have the margin."

"The other cases," replied Lenox with dignity.

They spent forty minutes on this task, reviewing the performance of their newer employees as well, and finally discussing the wildly disarrayed state of Scotland Yard. They were just entering into the depths of this particular conversation when a fellow called Killian, a dyed-in-the-wool Tory with whom Lenox had once exchanged heated words in the House of Commons, came into the library. He was a balding, heavy-lidded, paunchy, skewering sort of person.

"Good afternoon, gentlemen," he said. "Lenox, I see that you have broken up Scotland Yard! Well done."

"Thank you, Killian."

"Any word on Wallace?" he asked.

"No," said Lenox.

"Dallington? Have you solved it? No—I imagined not—bad lookout. It won't do, Lenox, a murder on your very own street. Tsk, tsk."

"Two streets over, actually."

Killian smirked at them. "Ah, yes. No doubt that makes all the difference. My mistake. Good day, fellows. I'm due to win some money at piquet. I was only coming in to see if there was a pencil here—and look what I have found, the very stub of a pencil. That will do splendidly. Congratulations again, Lenox."

Killian went on his way. Dallington stared behind him with distaste and, when he was out of earshot, told Lenox to ignore him; nobody had come close to solving the Wallace murder.

"I wish they would," said Lenox. "I keep opening the newspaper and hoping to discover that someone has confessed."

"Who, the butler? Not yet. But it will come out in the end. The last thing any of the three of us needs is more work at the moment." Dallington looked at the papers spread between them. "Particularly you."

"You're quite right," said Lenox. He glanced up at the clock. "Speaking of which, I ought to be going."

"I suppose I should, too."

Yet Killian's comment rankled in Lenox's bosom. For he did feel, after all, that even with the grueling schedule he had been operating by, he should have done better, done *something*, to solve the case that was leading every newspaper in the English-speaking world. What was worse, too, he had fibbed: It had happened only one street over from Hampden Lane, in truth; nearer to his own front door than he cared to admit.

CHAPTER FIVE

Recently, Kirk, Lenox and Lady Jane's butler of long standing, a vast and venerable person of about sixty, had come into his fortune. It had passed into his hands by way of a maternal aunt. This respectable woman, living deep in Buckinghamshire, had succumbed peacefully one November night to the dream that awaits us all (as the lawyer who sent the news had rather impressively put it) and left her nephew nine hundred pounds, a sterling silver tea set, a traveling carriage, and a pair of good six-year-old horses.

Kirk had given his notice not long after receiving the news. Lenox and Lady Jane, though they congratulated him profusely, must have been visibly bereft, for Kirk had hastened to add that it was a conditional departure. He intended to stay as long as it took to find and train a suitable replacement.

That had been before the turn of the year, and when Lenox arrived home to Hampden Lane on this February afternoon, he found Kidgerby, Kirk's much-harassed novitiate, continually in the wrong on matters large and small, holding the inkstand from the front hall table in one hand. Kirk loomed sternly over him.

"What has he done now?" said Lenox, hanging up his dark claret surtout.

Kirk took his gloves and hat. "Nothing serious, sir," he said, though in a tone (intended for Kidgerby) that declared the words themselves laughable—the situation being, rather, serious in the extreme.

"No, please, I'd like to know. These small things can have great import."

Kirk shot poor Kidgerby a significant look. The lad was about twenty-five and built like a beanpole. He had served competently and honestly as a footman in the house for several years, but his sudden elevation had overcome him, and these days he apologized as soon as he entered any room, and grew flushed with sadly little provocation.

Yet once you were a butler to a good family, your fortune was made. It meant higher wages, a different position in the delicate milieu downstairs, and even the possibility of more, for capable butlers were in hot demand. Lenox couldn't count the number of people who had tried to poach Kirk—quite openly, no less; it was considered fair game.

"He's left the inkstand dry, sir," said Kirk. "There is a waste."

Lenox frowned. "Well, Kidgerby, I hope this will be an important lesson. I don't know, Kirk. I suppose we mustn't be too hard on him. I've wasted gallons of ink in my time."

"Certainly, sir," said Kirk stiffly.

He looked as if he wished to contradict Lenox, and indeed Lenox wouldn't have put it past him—his inheritance had gone to his head. The same thing had happened to his friend Gubby, whose younger cousin had died unexpectedly, making him the Earl of Wickham; much above himself for several months before he settled down.

Lenox offered Kidgerby a smile. "We won't put you on the street over one inkstand," he said.

Kidgerby had been getting redder and redder since Lenox entered, as if he was bursting to speak but didn't dare. At last he couldn't help himself.

"Congratulations on the success of your case, sir!" he cried.

"Kidgerby!" said Kirk, aghast.

"It's quite all right. Thank you very much, Mr. Kidgerby. It's kind of you to mention. Kirk, is Lady Jane in?"

"She is not, sir."

"How long until supper?"

"A little more than an hour, sir."

"Very good. Did Graham call round, by the way?"

"No, sir."

Lenox was disappointed; he had been trying to see his old friend for some time, but without success. "No matter. I shall be in my study if anyone needs me."

"Very good, sir."

With a nod, Lenox left Kidgerby to his exacting pupilage, walking about twenty paces up the dark red-carpeted front hallway. He paused at his door when a shout and footsteps sounded from upstairs, but they were followed by a laugh, and he felt a quick joy spring up in his heart. Only the noises of home. He went inside the library and shut the door softly behind him.

This sanctuary of his took the shape of a rectangular room, with bookshelves running all along its two long walls. At the far end was a fireplace with armchairs and a liquor stand in front of it, while here, closer to the door, sat Lenox's desk, near a row of tall, elegant windows overlooking Hampden Lane.

He went and stoked the fire (it wasn't a large enough hearth to have a back log), then went to his desk and fetched a thin stack of papers.

He leafed through them, before, his curiosity piqued, going to sit in one of the armchairs so that he could attend them more deeply.

A glass of brandy, a splash of soda, and Lenox was situated. The fire, laid with warm coals earlier to keep the room at a non-arctic temperature in his absence, had stirred nicely into life, snapping a little here and there as peels of the kindling caught and curled. He contemplated it for a moment, sipped his drink, then turned his attention to the file again. It contained what little he knew about the Wallace murder.

It was the kind of crime that ought to have been easy to solve. More difficult were those that took place on the streets at night, in confused gin-motivated arguments that left someone dead mostly by violent accident rather than design.

By contrast, Wallace—Harold Catesby Wallace, as his full name went—had been killed in his own bed, inside a seemingly secure house, on a pleasant street down which a sober and respectable constable passed every thirty minutes each night, whistling a tune and swinging his lantern.

Mayfair was shaken.

Every account described Wallace, the victim, as a short, stout, irascible person. He was sixty-five at his death. He came from a prominent Warwickshire family and possessed independent means. His two younger brothers were both still in the army, the family profession, both distinguished gentlemen; but Wallace had been born with poor vision and had as a consequence been ineligible to serve.

He had never worked nor married. For society, he had chosen mostly to keep to fellow lovers of whisky, which was his great passion. He belonged to two private clubs dedicated to the appreciation of the potable, and once a year traveled from London to the peat bogs of Islay, where he had shares in a distillery and enjoyed, by all accounts, the prestige that the investment bestowed upon him.

Among the unlikeliest of men, in other words, thought Lenox as he flipped through his notes by the fire, to meet a violent death.

Yet he had. One evening a month before, Wallace had entertained two fellow whisky aficionados in his study between eight and eleven o'clock. Both were family men of good reputation, and both had been home within half an hour of leaving Wallace's house according to their servants.

After they had departed, Wallace had asked his butler, one George Colmes, for a candle, and taken himself upstairs to bed. It was the last time he was seen alive.

Colmes had noticed at around nine o'clock the subsequent morning that the master was lying in unusually late. He had gone to the door and inquired from outside if Wallace required anything. A maid, Harriet Warner, tidying a guest room nearby, had witnessed this.

There was no response. Colmes had then noticed that the door was ajar, he said. This was unusual; Wallace, who feared burglars, generally locked it from within when he went to bed. The butler had pushed the door open slightly, and, according to everyone in the household, not just Miss Harriet Warner, immediately let out a blood-curdlingly loud cry.

In fairness, the sight that had greeted him was a grim one: his master, stone dead, eyes wide but lifeless, bloody bedsheets clutched with iron force in his hands.

Scotland Yard had acted swiftly. They interviewed the staff, turned the house inside out looking for the knife which the medical examiner had concluded must be the weapon—going so far as to dismantle and inspect the lavatory pipes—and put together a picture of Wallace's movements in days preceding his demise.

This was the publicly available information, at least—which was all that the file Lenox perused, glass of brandy in hand, held, for he had been shut out from the case from the start. His recent investigation had still been near its outset when Wallace died, and though he had inquired, Scotland Yard by then had been entirely closed to him.

Whether or not he could have helped, what was certain was that the Yard's great effort had produced no commensurate result. Immediate suspicion for the crime had fallen upon the staff, who numbered six, but as it happened all except Colmes had been permitted to attend a servants' ball in Twickenham on the evening of the murder, and all had stayed until the last omnibus home, at five o'clock, well after the hour of the murder.

This left the butler himself. He became the obvious target of the Yard's interest. Finally, in the absence of all other plausible explanations, detectives had arrested him on the strength of two facts. The first was that, besides Wallace, he was the only person with a key to the bedroom. (He had given it up without protest from his breast pocket to the first constable who arrived on the scene.) The second was that there had been a shirt in his closet with a dark, much-scrubbed stain upon one arm, which certainly looked like blood.

Yet there were doubts. From the start Colmes had denied his involvement in the crime with passionate vehemence, and while that was not surprising, circumstances were inclined to support this denial; he had been in Wallace's service for more than twenty years and was well paid. Beyond that, he was himself a whisky drinker, and by most accounts on this score something like an actual friend of his employer.

Of course, friendship could not exclude the possibility of murder. But the butler's behavior on the morning of the death had been unexceptional, and he was known within the household as someone who fretted over disruption, a very regular sort, put out by a late milk delivery—temperamentally unsuited to concealment.

And, Lenox reflected, each of the two points against Colmes was fatally flawed. For a start, why keep the bloody shirt? He would have had the whole night to get rid of it. And then, why would the butler have used the key to murder Wallace and then *left the door open*, knowing this would lead directly back to him?

He wondered whether these questions—which seemed so self-evident to him—could really be lost on the (remaining) detectives at Scotland Yard. He supposed it was possible. Of course, the issue remained of who had actually done the crime, but in the absence of an answer to this, the butler remained the Yard's sole suspect. His trial was set for late March.

It did—bother Killian—affect Lenox after all, he found. Both the injustice of it, should this Colmes be innocent, as he suspected, and the faint uneasiness of knowing that such a murder had occurred a thousand yards from his front door and might go unsolved.

He was just on the verge of pouring himself another drink when he heard the front doorbell ring. There were muffled voices in the hallway and heavy footsteps, followed by a knock at the door.

It couldn't be Lady Jane, obviously, since she would have come straight in. Lenox rose from his seat just as Kirk appeared in the doorway, a figure trailing behind him. Kidgerby?

No. "His Excellency, Mr. Benjamin Disraeli," announced the butler.

CHAPTER SIX

"Thank you very much, Kirk," Lenox said. The butler withdrew, and the detective inclined his head formally to Disraeli. "You are most welcome, Prime Minister."

Even to Lenox, a veteran both of politics and of London society, it was no mean matter to welcome a sitting Prime Minister into his home. Not just that, either, but a Prime Minister by himself—a rare informality, a rare solicitude.

"I hope I am not interrupting you, Mr. Lenox."

"Not at all, my lord. I am sensible of the honor of your visit."

Disraeli glanced around the study, and Lenox took the chance to look out through the window. He saw the Prime Minister's carriage outside, the unmistakable seal on its doors, a second carriage behind it, and four footmen lined at the side of the first, shoulders high. The bulletin of this visit would already be cast up Hampden Lane, and from there would escape to every part of London— Benjamin Disraeli, whose cozy weekly visits with the Queen herself were legendary by now, calling at Charles Lenox's house.

The Prime Minister was too intelligent not to be aware that he was thus bestowing some of his status on Lenox. It was a generous gesture. But generous to what purpose? By what calculation? Lenox was considering these questions as he guided Disraeli toward the chairs by the fire.

"One never stops looking for the books one has written upon other people's shelves," the Prime Minister said, scanning Lenox's as he walked. His tone was rueful. "And their absence always causes a greater pang than their presence does happiness. Ah! But I see my *Vivian Grey*! Capital, capital."

Lenox's mind was moving rapidly, but he had the uneasy feeling that the mind with which he was engaged was moving more rapidly still. "What may I offer you to drink, Prime Minister?"

"Do you know, a cup of tea would set me just to rights—I would be infinitely obliged for a simple cup of tea with lemon. I must dine out after this, you see, and the drinks flow so very freely when Lady Coulter is one's host."

"Of course." Lenox rang the small gold bell on the mantel—he rarely used it—and asked Kirk, who appeared after the barest instant, to bring tea.

Disraeli was dressed in a plain black suit and wore, as was his custom, a gentleman's silk around his neck—little more than a flat black silk ribbon. This was his typical attire, and savvy. Unlike stolid old Gladstone, Disraeli was known for his love of fripperies. He enjoyed the company of extravagant and gossipy women, salon chatter, and the free spirits (literal and figurative) at a house like Lady Morgan Coulter's. He kept peacocks at his estate, walking them each morning like pups, it was said; and he had famously won over a reluctant Victoria by bringing her a primrose to their weekly meeting—for some Prime Ministers, a very brief meeting indeed—and declaring it "the gift of the fauns and dryads who would ever be her subjects."

Such excesses of character demanded a counterweight if one wished to be taken seriously, and Disraeli had placed it in his person: the quiet suit of clothes, the plain black ribbon, the gentle side sweep of hair over his fine, intelligent temples, and his direct, thoughtful gaze.

"I have had your very considerate letter," the Prime Minister said. "Considerate, intelligent—but hardly satisfying."

Lenox lifted his hands from his lap a few inches to express his regret. "I can only apologize that our interests should lie in different directions upon this particular matter."

For just an instant something flashed in Disraeli's gaze. Not malice, but a private sort of enjoyment. "Perhaps they do not. The trial will commence next week. We have time."

Kirk knocked at the door and entered. The hot water must have been on from the second the carriage approached for tea to appear so quickly, and the pouring of the two cups gave the detective a moment to think.

"Unfortunately I have various commitments in London at the moment that make it impossible for me to go abroad, Prime Minister," Lenox said when it was done.

"Yes, I read the letter."

There was a first edge in Disraeli's voice. His time was valuable. "While I am most appreciative of your visit, then, I—"

"Stop there, if you would be so kind." Disraeli took a sip of his tea, closed his eyes for an instant of pure happiness—it was admirable, his apparent ability to set apart a second or two of the present for himself—then put the teacup down and leveled his stare at Lenox. "Let us play it straight with each other, Mr. Lenox. I could send you all over town, to your brother, for instance, or your many other acquaintances in Parliament, to discover why I am so exceedingly eager that you should be away from London during the trial."

Lenox merely nodded. "Mm."

"You might find out; you might not. The simple fact is that there is an unhappy amount of tension within my party at the moment. If

Lord Kestrel is embarrassed at the trial, my membership is prepared to demand his resignation from the cabinet."

"I see."

"And should *that* happen, the numbers might just—might just, mind you, for it would be a close run, and I would fight it very hard—go against me."

Ah. So here they were at the crux of the thing: Disraeli was in Hampden Lane because he was anxious that he would lose control of his party. It had little to do with Lenox himself. This was Dizzy's second term as Prime Minister, and he was now in his early seventies—not old, for he was quite fit, but no longer in the first blush of even political youth.

"Indeed?" said Lenox.

Disraeli—or the First Earl of Beaconsfield, really, since his elevation to the House of Lords a few years before, but nobody, not even *Kirk*, Lenox realized, called him anything but Mr. Disraeli—said, "You are a liberal, of course, and I am a conservative. You might welcome such confusion in my party—indeed, might see it as an incentive!"

He chuckled at this and Lenox said, murmuring, "No, no."

"Of course! And why shouldn't you? I am under no illusion that my position inoculates me against such considerations—the opposite, if anything. Yet I think on some matters, Lenox, you and I are rather close in opinion; and I wonder if you would prefer Mr. Cantwell to hold my office."

Disraeli looked at him shrewdly; and it was a shrewd point, well scored. For in many respects the Prime Minister was, like Lenox, in favor of what most would have considered liberal policies, particularly the extension of the vote to a greater number of people and protections for the poor. It was primarily in matters of foreign activity (Disraeli was a fervent imperialist) that their beliefs diverged.

By contrast, Cantwell was a hard-liner. He came from business and considered the interests of business first in all matters. Just recently, indeed, he had led the bitter conservative opposition to the reforms that made it illegal for children under the age of ten to work in factories and mines.

"Would my absence make such a difference?" Lenox said.

Disraeli smiled. "With the very greatest respect, can you imagine that I would be here if it would not?"

"I shall rephrase—I would be glad to know why my testimony should make such a difference, Prime Minister."

"Because you are our former colleague, because you are Sir Edmund's younger brother, and in particular because you are Lady Jane Lenox's husband. The embarrassment to Lord Kestrel would be too intense if you were to testify in person. We may just skate by if you write out your testimony. And it will make no odds whatsoever to the outcome of the trial. They're all guilty as Judas. But if you are there in person—if the gallery of journalists should get hold of your image, your words, your tone—things could be up for us. For me. I need Kestrel."

"I see," said Lenox.

There was a famous cartoon of Disraeli and Gladstone. "Can you fight?" Disraeli asked Gladstone in it, to which the latter replied, "No." Following which Disraeli said, putting up his fists, "Then come on!!!"

Lenox was conscious that his interlocutor had considered every outcome of this meeting, his tremendous acuity studying each shifting angle of leverage. In the same way, when he sat down at Lady Coulter's table in half an hour's time, the Prime Minister would know exactly each guest's practical and social power to a fineness—without ever, Lenox knew, being less than perfectly engaged, perfectly convivial.

He was not quite sure what to say. Fortunately, at that moment, there was a bustle in the front hall. "That will be my wife," he said.

Disraeli rose with a certain keenness in his eye. "I shall be very happy to see her." He set down his teacup again. "In addition to what we discussed the other day, I can offer you this sweetener: You shall travel under the Great Seal."

Lenox's eyebrows rose. "Oh?"

Disraeli nodded firmly. It was a meaningful offer. The seal would elevate Lenox's trip; the Queen and her representatives were conscious about using it as rarely as possible, and there were diplomatic convoys, whole ships full of gentlemen, who did not labor under its imprimatur. It would be like traveling by special passport, and guarantee, if Lenox wished it, a retinue, a meeting with anyone he chose, up to the president himself.

At that moment Lady Jane came in, and Disraeli, his offer made, turned his full attention upon her for the space of three minutes.

Though taken by surprise, she fought him, with her immense capacity of sweet reserve, to a standstill. For his part, Lenox merely stepped back and observed: two great artists of society in furious civil combat. By the end of it, Disraeli had extracted half a promise that Lady Jane would dine at his house within the next few weeks, while she had put forward the case for a friend of hers, Adeline Snow, whose divorce from a conservative politician had left her isolated from London society.

Disraeli looked very satisfied—far more than he had during his conversation with Lenox, which in the end was only a matter of politics, not supper—and after making himself profoundly pleasant, truly pleasant, even Lenox unable to resist smiling at his confidential murmurs about the people he would shortly meet at Lady Coulter's, not least her infamous sister, Kristin Coulter, the widow of Ruritania, he bade them both a good evening. On his way out he thanked Kirk for the delicious cup of tea; and finally, knowing, with the instincts of a great man, that nearly every encounter he had would stay in other people's minds for the length of their lives, touched his hat and offered a few kind murmured words to Kidgerby. This young gentleman had been standing stock-still in the hallway ever since Disraeli's arrival, as rigid as a post, bright red, probably hoping to remain unnoticed, but now, after the door had closed, wore the expression of someone who would, without an instant's hesitation, have followed the Prime Minister into the very jaws of death.

CHAPTER SEVEN

Five days later, a lurch awoke Lenox from a dream. For an instant he couldn't place where he was, until another sharp roll reminded him: in his snug cabin aboard HMS *Selene*, bound for New York harbor.

He lay there with his eyes still closed for a moment, then blinked them open and glanced over at the small shining brass barometer his friend Thomas McConnell had given him before he left London. The needle was dropping. Wet weather. Lenox checked his pocket watch by the light of dawn and saw that it was just past four in the morning. It was an hour when things aboard the ship for the past three nights had been quiet, but at the moment he could hear the concerted effort of numerous men above him.

Still, he could tell, through some intuition, that the hands were about ship to make it safe, not because it was in real danger. Sinking back into his small groove of bedding, he went over the events of the last week in his mind, contemplating them—and wondering, for the hundredth time, whether he had chosen this path wisely.

Not long after Disraeli had departed Hampden Lane on that evening of his visit, Lenox and Lady Jane had sat down to supper.

Since he had first mentioned the notion of going to America there had been some distance between them, which was unusual. But at supper she had been full of questions about the Prime Minister's visit, listening carefully to Lenox's minute description of it. When the second course came—a fine roasted pheasant in a sauce of mushrooms, wine, and walnuts, with green peas surrounding it on the salver, like green hillocks around a village—she spoke her mind.

"You must ask for more."

"More? More what?"

"More!" The word lingered, and it was only then that he realized her opinion of the idea had changed. "The trip to America, made under the seal, the knighthood—but what more do you want? It is a rare state of affairs to have a Prime Minister desperate to answer your wishes. You must seize it."

"That only applies if I go."

"Oh!" she said, taking a slotted spoonful of peas. "As for that—of course you must go."

"But you cannot expect me to go?"

"Yes, Charles," she said, glancing up at him as if she had never said otherwise. "You have my blessing. It was ill-natured of me not to give it from the start."

"But the girls, Jane, and you, of course—and the agency."

"We shall keep." She reached across the table and touched his hand. In the changing shadowed golden light of the candles, arrayed down the spine of the table, she had looked lovely. "And you will regret it if you don't go see America. I cannot have that on my conscience."

Lenox was about to protest when he realized it was true. He had already been regretting it. He paused for a long moment, hands resting, with knife and fork in them, on the table, then said, "It would be infernally selfish of me."

She shook her head. "You have stayed close to London for a long time. Now you have this chance. Will there be another like it? Not likely. And then, if you go it shall give us all a chance to miss you.

"While to decline the chance might poison your heart against us—me, Sophia, Clara."

"Never," he said.

"Not seriously, I know, Charles, but I should be very sorry if even a small part of you came to resent us." She took a sip of the cold white wine she liked with most foods and looked at him. "That means the only question remaining is what you shall ask for in exchange for going."

In the days that ensued, even as he made plans to follow her counsel, he was caught between a longing to believe what she said and guilt about it. His thoughts kept returning to little Clara. What if something happened to him? Of course he was just as likely to fall victim to an unexpected fate in this teeming city; it was superstition to think of travel as the more dangerous option. Wasn't it?

But in a deeper part of himself, which corresponded, obscurely, to the sound of wind flooding itself over the water outside, to the creak of the rigging above, he knew that it had been a balm to his soul to embark on this journey.

Selene was a frigate, a good sailor, which moved under a combination of steam and sail. Lenox was her sole civilian passenger; the rest, aside from her crew, were marines. They were bound for New York, where they would provision the ship, then on to San Francisco, before voyaging toward their final destination, Hong Kong, where they would serve eighteen months in a convoy of guard ships.

Because of the length of this prospective trip, Lenox barely existed to the men of the *Selene*. He would be gone from their lives for good after eight days, and some eight hundred that would pass before they saw England again. The exception to this polite indifference was the captain, a decent chap named Christopher Heller with whom Lenox dined each evening. Yet of course the captain was much occupied in the sailing of his ship, and so the detective had long hours to himself, which he passed either on deck or reading happily in his cabin, with its elegant sweep of starboard windows.

He got up now (carefully—the ceiling of the cabin was perilously low) and went over to these windows.

All was froth and darkness outside, creamy waves rising just visibly out of a black-gray sea. Lenox put on a tarpaulin jacket and stepped into the galley before moving cautiously up the steps to the deck. He poked his head out—he dreaded being in the way, since, being too high ranking to be told to move, he could so easily disrupt the ship's management unintentionally—and only when he saw that it was clear went up to the quarterdeck.

The ship's third lieutenant, a cheerful, open-faced, rather stout young person in a sealskin slicker, greeted him. "Morning, sir! Salty, ain't it?"

Lenox, who had just been smashed by a hard spray breaking over the side of the ship and was staggering in a roughly westward direction, holding his hat down, managed to say, "Hullo, Winterson. Yes. A bit."

"If you look to starboard, you'll see something that might interest you, sir."

Once, a decade before, Lenox had spent many happy weeks—enough to know which side starboard was, anyhow—aboard the *Lucy*, as it sailed for Egypt. He moved in what he hoped was a credibly seamanlike way to the starboard side of the quarterdeck, and when he arrived he was glad he had—for next to the ship was a pod of dolphins, breaching in beautifully asynchronous motion out of the water.

"Dolphins!" cried Lenox.

"Ain't they?" said the lieutenant, shouting over the noise of the rain and wind. "They normally fetch up more toward Scotland and the north—but this time of year, with the cold, you do see 'em."

Winterson returned to his business after a moment of respectful silence for their aquatic convoy, but for a long, long time, as the sky grew slowly lighter, Lenox stood at the gunwale, staring, rapt, into the water below. There were perhaps ten or twelve of the creatures. They were surprisingly long and slender, sleek, muscular, their coloring a beautiful pearlescent gray on top, paler beneath.

Though their motion seemed effortless, they were going at a blinding speed. The ship must have been hauling ten knots. But the dolphins showed no sign of leaving her.

"Do they often do this?" asked Lenox at last, when Winterson had circled back toward his side of the quarterdeck on some errand.

"Oh, yes, sir," said the lieutenant, stopping.

"How very beautiful," he murmured.

Lenox had passed a busy few days before leaving England. On the first he had dedicated twelve exhausting hours to setting down his testimony for the trial of the three corrupt detectives—anticipating every conceivable defense he could and striking it down preemptively, caging them as tightly as possible into their crimes. It had been a matter of intense concentration, sunup to sundown and beyond, motionless at his desk, rewriting over and over.

Only when he had completed this task to his satisfaction (and thanked the heavens that he was not a writer by profession) had he send a note to Disraeli, accepting his offer.

He requested a variety of things, which he and Lady Jane had devised over the course of the previous evening. Some were outlandish; for instance, he said straight out that he wished Disraeli's direct assurance, in writing, that he should himself be able to bestow that knighthood which had been offered him. He asked for a budget far in excess of what he should need, and he withheld the right to determine his own itinerary and pace completely—without the slightest interference.

And, he'd said finally, he wanted the Wallace file from the Yard. Every word of it. He would send a clerk from his agency to copy it, along with someone of authority from Disraeli's office so that it could not be interfered with before it came to him.

He'd sent this letter off to the Carlton Club, knowing it would find its way from that Tory game preserve to the Prime Minister more quickly than through even Parliament or 10 Downing Street.

He and Lady Jane had dined with McConnell and Toto that night, much of the talk taken up with America—and with what they could expect Disraeli's response to be. None of them were prepared for its brevity, however, when it came back only a little over an hour after Kirk had dispatched it: *Done. Beaconsfield.*

The ensuing days had been a whirlwind of preparation, goodbyes, and then the travel to Plymouth, with its mazy cobblestone streets, romantic to walk through with Lady Jane beneath the lamplight, the sense of separation before them, their hands clasped a little more tightly—and finally his departure.

And now, in what felt like ten minutes since he had been in his own home, he stood watching the dolphins, a feeling of awe and momentousness in his spirit. This was why he had come. Let no one say that even at his age, he could not see the world afresh again.

The storm intensified and all at once the dolphins disappeared. That was how they always departed, the lieutenant told Lenox in his clipped naval drawl, "very sudden-like." Three bells rang then; and Lenox, watching the water where they had been with no less satisfaction than when he had been watching the creatures themselves, realized he was soaked to the bone, and decided to go down to his little cabin, ask for some coffee, eggs, and bacon from the galley, and set about untangling the mystery of who had murdered Harold Wallace.

CHAPTER EIGHT

My dearest Jane,

My first thought as I sit to write you is how much I wish our positions were reversed, for you would do a far finer job than I shall be able to of describing this strange, yet marvelous city, quite unlike any I have visited. How very much I should value your perceptions of it!—for mine are so crowded in upon with novelty that I can scarcely catch up to them before new ones arrive, demanding contemplation.

This is my third morning here. After taking a day to learn the customs, I've grown quite comfortable among the retired colonels and generals here at the Union Club, smoking their pipes in peace and reading the papers, just as if they were in Pall Mall. There's a billiard room (always empty) and a card room (always full), besides the reading room and lounge. The food is better than people warned me it would be in America. A young Irishman brought me eggs on toast and some surprisingly decent tea just ten minutes ago. A cup of it is in my left hand as I write from my desk, which overlooks the street they call 5th Avenue, mostly numbers here, very modern, and a row of blossoming pear trees, just coming into a ruddy pink.

I hope you have already had the letters I sent on my first evening, but now, whether or not they have reached you, I can give a chronological sketch of my trip so far.

Upon arriving in New York harbor, *Selene* was greeted by a large jolly-boat containing about a dozen men with grave faces. The entire crew of our ship gathered on the rail to see why—I heard the forecastle gunner speculating that perhaps Watkins, of the foretop, was wanted for horse theft. I was curious too and wondered aloud to the ship's chaplain if perhaps there was a deserter aboard.

It was only with deep embarrassment that I realized the boat was for me. Or for the Queen's seal, really—it emerged, later, that anyone traveling under it is met by such a party. It was fearfully awkward, however; you would have laughed to see me realize that I was not quite so ready as I should have been, sprint down to my cabin, shove my books and clothes into my trunk, and then try to make my way down the side of the ship without putting a foot wrong, all in front of 300 men desperate for the entertainment of seeing a lubber (me, in this case) fall in the water. I didn't, thank the Lord, but they did have the gratification of seeing one of the men in the boat trip and drop my trunk as he was receiving it, then stumble backward in his full bright red uniform and plunge into the harbor. Poor fellow—I very much doubt whether he has recovered from the shame. He was not present at supper that evening anyhow.

My days since have been occupied with calls. I sent my card to the dozen or so acquaintances we discussed, and have since been gratifyingly sent various invitations. The embassy settled me here (the Athenaeum had wired ahead just as they

said they would, good souls), gave me the young valet who
brought my breakfast (he is called Fergus O'Brian—nearly
all the servants in America are Irish, apparently because
their democratic hearts cannot abide the idea of a son or
daughter of the land of liberty answering "*yes, sir*" and "*no,
ma'am*" to them, and the Irish emigration during the famine
having made them plentiful here), and a guide, an American
of English birth named Wyatt. I like him. He is conscientious and thorough. If I were forced to level a complaint
against him,

Here Lenox paused, his pen above the sheet, and frowned. He
sat back in his chair and took a sip of the warm tea, then chewed
ruminatively on a crust of toast. Wyatt was a career diplomat. He
was very friendly, bald but for a rather long white fringe of hair that
encircled the nape of his neck.

Lenox did not quite know how to say to Jane that, while indeed
conscientious and thorough, Wyatt had an alarming habit of falling
asleep any time he went unobserved for more than the space of a
minute or two, no matter the situation. Nor was he quite sure it was
fair, because it had only been two days, two very full days, that they
had spent together—and so, after swallowing his toast and taking
another sip of tea, he went on:

I should be hard-pressed to do so.

 Shall I tell you something of the society in America? Last
night Lord Eddings brought me to the opera, which he tells
me is the main public crossroads for the upper class of this
city. America has improved him, by the way. Or marriage,
perhaps. Less of the pinch-faced worry and envy you will no
doubt remember from the ballrooms in which he was seeking
to marry without a penny, and more of his wit, which I always
liked. His wife is thirty years his junior, twice as pretty as he

ever was, and he dotes on her absolutely, could be her footman. Her father is in cattle. He is never seen, I understand;
not genteel. Personally I should like very much to meet him.

It sums up the great divide here between new money and
old, which will sound familiar, but is much rawer in New
York than at home. There are the "Knickerbocker" families,
you see, on the one hand, and they are descendants of the
Dutch who settled this place, and on the other a variety of
the usually much richer but unpedigreed men and women
trying to buy their way into society, some very successfully.

We met both types at the opera. The Knickerbockers
were dressed somberly and had fewer jewels; but the brighter
sparks of the place, Lady Eddings for instance, eyed them
anxiously the whole time.

The two sides meet in Caroline Astor, whose name I could
hardly have helped knowing from our own society pages,
but whose influence here I didn't properly appreciate. As I
understand it, her rule is absolute. Her box was dead center;
she arrived in the second act, a discreet, dark-haired woman
of 40 or thereabouts, her dress nicely split between tact and
resplendence. There was a ruby on her finger that might have
paid for a union regiment 20 years ago. She is opening the
spring season in Newport next week with a ball, and there
was a polite crush to get near her; the last invitations apparently remain in her hands, and they are not insignificant to
anyone in this city. Only 200 of them, and by Eddings's estimation 3,000 people who are hoping for one.

The Astors themselves, he said, after looking around very
carefully for eavesdroppers, are jumped-up fur traders, rich
but unlettered. Yet Mrs. Astor herself is descended from your
Livingstons, Backers, Schermerhorns, Melyns, and suchlike,
and it is she who decides what the word "society" means,
both here and in Newport.

She was perfectly indifferent to my existence when we briefly met, which seemed a diverting sort of farce to me—as social discriminations abroad always are. But of course Eddings took it very seriously. He hopes to go to the ball himself. He is not optimistic, however. He suggested I visit Newport. I won't have time to go, though the descriptions—opulence beyond belief, they say—make me curious.

Today I meet the mayor of New York and then his commissioners of the police, and I may say that these appointments will be of more curiosity for me than the society rounds.

Above all, I am pleased because today shall bring me again into the lower parts of Manhattan, through which we passed when we arrived. I have never seen anything quite like those streets—the variety of languages, the closeness of the buildings, the roughness of the cobblestones, the extreme friendliness of the people, familiarity, even, the scent of hot chestnuts and cut flowers, everything to be sold "uptown" to the rich, every form of enterprise, rowdy public bars, small entertainments . . . it seemed much livelier to me than the poor parts of London. In Delancey Street, or so was my impression, each person seems to wake up sure that this is the day their fortune will be made. And every so often no doubt they're right. Such is the undeniable charm of America.

There has just been a knock at my door—there, I've answered it, you can see I have had to refill my pen. It was Wyatt. The carriage is waiting. I have more to tell you, but all I can do if I wish to get this letter off before I leave is send my love to you—my love, and my gratitude for your encouragement of this trip, which has already—oh, what's the use, better to say it in person, four or five weeks hence, but it has made me a happy fellow; except I miss you and the girls desperately; even Kirk and Kidgerby. I am fearfully jealous when I imagine everyone who gets to see you, now that your husband's unceasing demands upon your time have been temporarily suspended. But I shall overcome my envy so long as you promise to remember that I remain, across however many oceans you care to name,

Your faithful and loving husband,
Charles Lenox

PS: I am not close to deciphering the truth of the Wallace matter, but there are certain features of interest in it. Tell Polly and Dallington I will wire them if anything occurs to me, if you please. And love to all. Rushing to enclose this letter now—forgive handwriting—awful scrawl, I see. Love, Charles.

CHAPTER NINE

The mayor of New York was a small man in round spectacles by the name of Smith Ely Jr. He was extremely civil to Lenox and utterly indifferent to the subject of crime and its detection. After a stilted fifteen-minute meeting, he formally offered the Queen the full offices of the city of New York, should she ever need them, and said good day.

"Your luncheon will be better," Wyatt assured Lenox, walking alongside him to a waiting carriage. "You'll see the real New York at Delmonico's."

"Who are these commissioners?"

"There's a passel of 'um—five or six. One's old Baldy Smith, who ended up out of the war as general. He's a hard-nosed gentleman. Won Antietam by himself, if you believe his account, but lost Fredericksburg in the same company, if you believe others."

They each took a bench in the spacious carriage. It was a mild, sweet day, with sun slanting across the avenues. They were by a river, which Lenox knew must be either the Hudson or East, and discreetly he withdrew the pocket-sized book of maps that Lady Jane had given him just before he embarked. They were heading south, and the river was on his left, so it must be the East River, he supposed.

He looked back up at it from his little book. It was very pretty here. There were small orchards running along the avenue, and a few small houses here and there, nothing much really, mostly fields. They were all the way at Seventy-Fourth Street, though—the distant north.

Delmonico's was on William Street. It was more impressive than Lenox had expected. At eleven o'clock there was already a line of carriages outside the tall, triangular building, whose two sides sloped away from a curved prow. The door was kept by an enormous mustachioed man in a green frock coat. If Lenox wasn't mistaken, the coat had gold coins for buttons.

"Party, gentlemen?"

"The commissioners," said Wyatt, with more direct bravura than Lenox would have suspected the long-serving diplomat of possessing.

"Follow me."

"There are several of your higher-order criminals here," Wyatt told Lenox in a quiet voice as they entered. "The doorman's their lookout."

Lenox might have queried the wisdom of police commissioners meeting in the same place as the criminals—but it fit in with New York, where everything seemed to happen inches from everything else.

It was raucous inside the establishment, with a strong, not unpleasant smell of sawdust and beer. At the center of the room at a round table was their party, a group of ten gentlemen.

They rose to meet Lenox, and they were all extremely courteous, the four commissioners and their various supernumeraries. The luncheon was delicious (it was here, at Delmonico's on William Street, as one of the commissioners proudly told him, that the notion of ordering *à la carte* had been invented), and served with the best dark bread Lenox had ever eaten, each stacked piece spread with butter. The wine was good, too. As the bottles passed around the table, the commissioners more and more happily shared information about their department and asked Lenox several intelligent questions about London's own system.

At dessert, the somewhat dusty old general ordered several additional bottles so that they might salute the Republic. There was quite a streak of patriotic pride in many of the gentlemen Lenox had met, he reflected—not surprisingly, with such a significant war, won at so high a price, so recent in the country's past.

As the new wine was being poured, the least prepossessing member of the party found his way to Lenox's side. He was a small, dark-haired fellow of perhaps twenty, with round black glasses and a weak chin. There was a much scarred and battered walking stick, joined together by a dingy silver ring, leaning against his leg.

"My name is Blaine, Mr. Lenox, Theodore Blaine. My friends call me Teddy."

"I'm pleased to meet you, Mr. Blaine."

Blaine pushed his glasses up his nose. He seemed out of place in the company. "I wanted to express my sincere admiration for the monograph you published about madness and homicide in the *Forensic Journal*. I read it twice. Your interviews from Bedlam were especially informative, if you will forgive me the forwardness of saying so."

"Ah!" said Lenox, who was not much better at withstanding flattery than the average man. "How very kind of you. That was a long while ago, but it did take a great deal of labor."

"Tell me, do you really believe that there are murders without any cause, yet with premeditation?"

"Do you not?"

Blaine's shoulders rose a little. "In America, we begin with money, revenge, and love, and find that answers for most of them."

"To be sure, those are the three great motives," said Lenox earnestly. "But I do believe, after these many years of observation, that there are rare instances—increasing, perhaps, as the size of cities increase, with the inevitable pressures of such an environment—in which murders are the work of the purely mad, driven only by their terrible instincts."

"We had a case here in '71," Blaine said. "A Mr. Josiah McIlhenny. He was a—"

"I know the case well!" cried Lenox. "I followed it from across the sea with great interest. Yet perhaps you have details that I do not know."

From here on out, the luncheon became a more definite pleasure. Blaine was, however diffident his initial appearance, a bright, open young chap, and eager to learn, with a surprisingly detailed knowledge of Lenox's own history, dating as far back as the very tricky Thames murders of 1850.

They chatted for a good hour. "You found the plum in the pudding," said Wyatt as they left. The young Irish servant climbing onto the box of the carriage, O'Brian, was carrying a silver bowl and a proclamation bound in leather, both presented to Lenox at the end of the meal by the (at that stage deeply intoxicated) general. "Blaine, I mean."

"Yes, I liked him."

"But do you know who he is?"

"I took him for the assistant to one of the commissioners."

Wyatt laughed. "Blaine! Oh, no, no. He is altogether an amateur."

Lenox was curious. "Then how did he come to be there?"

"You have heard of Arkansas?"

"I have."

"Then you may conceive of the wealth that accrued to Blaine's father when he bought most of it thirty years ago and sold it piece by piece in the last ten," said Wyatt, chuckling to himself as he packed the bowl of a bright cherry-wood pipe with tobacco. He glanced up at Lenox. "It must surely be the third or fourth richest family in New York City, people say."

The detective frowned. "Yet surely it's not pronounced that way."

"Blaine? I scarcely see how else it could be."

"No, no—Arkansas. The case of Kansas, with that emphatic "*ziss*" at the end, seems very definite evidence."

"No. It's Ar-kun-saw. Come, Mr. Lenox, you cannot cavil at poor Arkansas, having come from the country of Godmanchester."

Wyatt sounded each syllable in the town's name, and Lenox laughed. "Gumster," he said, which was the proper pronunciation. "And there you defeat me, Mr. Wyatt. I have no standing."

Wyatt lit his pipe, and they fell into a pleasant silence. Lenox was surprised at this information about Theodore Blaine. He had been uncommonly respectful. Most single young gentlemen of large fortune he had known were drunk with their own high valuation of themselves, knowing it was held by others too; few Mr. Bingleys to be found anywhere, at any time.

"The Astors, though?" Lenox said when they had driven either time. "The Flaglers?"

"The Blaines are reckoned as rich or richer than either of them." This was the kind of sentence you would never hear in Lenox's circles in England, but which was uttered here as nonchalantly as news of the weather. "The Vanderbilts may come into it."

"So Theodore Blaine holds no official position?"

"The son? No. He must have heard of your luncheon and asked for an invitation. He is a very odd duck, yet he would hardly have been refused." Wyatt looked at Lenox. "You are surprised at his character? But you did not see him walk."

"Walk?"

"He is badly lame in one leg, I'm afraid."

Lenox frowned with sympathy. "Ah. I saw his cane. Poor chap."

"The worst of it is that he has an elder brother who is quite different—tall, handsome, athletic. Their mother dotes on him, and I don't know that she's quite so fond of young Teddy. Perhaps she is. But it's the brother that she brings everywhere with her, for her husband, the father, doesn't go out much. Yet the father has a tender spot for the younger son, I believe. They play cards together, at least. A penny a hand. In a house on Fifth Avenue whose paint-work alone must have cost a hundred thousand."

"What a very interesting country."

"Yes. Teddy was at Deerfield but declined to go to Harvard. His brother would have been ahead of him there. In fact, if I am not mistaken the brother went to Andover, but Teddy needed a gentler schooling. He is an unworldly sort, as you saw. I am not quite sure what he means to do with himself now."

The answer became apparent in the short term, at least; that afternoon, Lenox received a card from Blaine (a very plain card, by New York standards, cream colored with navy-blue borders and no other decoration) asking whether the detective might be free for breakfast or lunch tomorrow. It was with some regret that Lenox replied that he would be traveling to Boston early in the morning by train.

CHAPTER TEN

That afternoon, Lenox put on his dinner jacket and checked his appearance in the mirror of his room at the Union Club. He had received a shave and haircut that afternoon from a man named Paul, who had been enslaved in Texas until the end of the war, then wound his way up to New York through various parts of the South, a journey he had described to Lenox in the course of a long, absorbing conversation.

Afterward, having heard this story, it seemed somehow slightly obscene to Lenox how dazzling Park Avenue looked in its first spring motions, lazy early butterflies fluttering around the bright pink dianthus that grew toward the softening sun.

O'Brian was holding a cab at the ready, conversing with the doorman at the Union Club. The young Irishman was handy but bashful, only about fifteen, a leggy boy with coal-black hair.

"A fine evening," Lenox said to him and the doorman, nodding his thanks as O'Brian held the door of the carriage for him.

"Yes, sir."

The door snapped shut after him. Lenox was accustomed to a certain ease with his servants, which he had so far not managed to cultivate here. Another difference.

He was due to dine at seven. It was only just four, however, and in the minimal free time he had, he had asked to be taken to the striving lower parts of Manhattan again, the better to explore them on foot.

They arrived at this neighborhood, far downtown, after a brisk drive, and Lenox alighted on the corner of Orchard Street, near Grand Street.

His initial impressions were confirmed; strengthened. The narrow boulevards hummed with activity, people crowded in, heavy-laden carts of textiles creaking up the cobblestones, junk shops, hat shops, grocers, watch repairmen seated at small carts, apple sellers, theatrical beaks.

With O'Brian at his side, he walked down Essex Street. "Tell me, how much crime is there here?" he asked.

"Sir?" said the young lad uncertainly.

"Were I alone, should I certainly be assaulted—dressed as I am?"

They had attracted several looks. A few touches of the cap to accompany those looks, but more of the stares furtive—calculating.

"I should say perhaps so, yes, sir."

"What is that little place?" he asked, pointing to a low doorway.

"A chowder shop, sir."

Lenox felt in his pocket for some of the unfamiliar American coins. "Would you care for a bite?" he said.

O'Brian flushed red. "Oh! Thank you, sir. If you like, of course, sir."

"Then let us go in. But you seem hesitant."

"There is a better one a street over. Oysters in every bowl."

"Lead on," Lenox said.

O'Brian took him to a dismal-looking brick tenement. A baby was shrieking nearby, and O'Brian apologized. But once they were seated, Lenox saw that he had been wise. The room was tiny but clean, and the smell inside rich and delicious. They ordered two

bowls of chowder and two glasses of beer, which came in short order, along with a great mound of crackers.

Lenox didn't know what sort of supper the night ahead held, so
he tucked ravenously into the savory stew. After a few careful bites,
O'Brian forgot his manners, eating furiously, happily, the way only
a young man still half child can. Or one who has known hunger.
While he was looking away Lenox signaled the young woman who
had brought their orders to fetch a second bowl for his companion.
O'Brian, after a moment of consternation when she did, twigged
what had happened, thanked Lenox, and set about this second
helping no more gradually than he had the first.

As they were walking the streets afterward, Lenox convinced the
lad to open the door to his life just ajar. No, sir, he had not been in
service long, not above six months; oh, his father—he had died on
the voyage over; O'Brian was the eldest of seven; lived with them
all not far from here, as it happened; had gotten this job by waiting
at the embassy every day from four in the morning for two months,
collecting string and newsprint to sell after each day's failure.

Now he was "fearful well paid," in his own words. Something
like pride appeared in the way he looked angrily at the ground as
he said them. Since he had gone into service, two of his younger
sisters and one of his younger brothers had been able to start school
again. The next-oldest child to O'Brian himself swept streets. Between them they supported the family. Not forgetting, he added,
the washing and sewing their mother did.

What a contrast it seemed when, a few hours later, Lenox found
himself in a drawing room on Washington Square, at a table laden
with silver and crystal dishes.

There were twenty people present. O'Brian was outside, with
the other servants—and if he wanted to know what fearful well
paid actually looked like, he had missed his chance by staying out
there.

The evening's host was one Abram van der Leyden, an imperious gentleman in a monocle. Lenox had accepted his invitation from among the many he had received on the strength of Lord Eddings's advice, and he did not regret it. This was the true Knickerbocker society, he found, and he had been curious about it, after the relative freedom of the opera; indeed, an oblique joke was made about Mrs. Astor, one that he hardly understood but which evoked great mirth in the room.

For all the superior airs of these old New Yorkers about their quieter taste, they did themselves pretty well, it seemed to Lenox. There were bottles of champagne in a pair of silver stands at the entrance of the room, beneath layers of rock salt and ice, and van der Leyden went about himself, refilling glasses. There were caviar and ices; soft quinces sliced into fan-shaped half-circles; and when they sat to dinner, the finger bowls were of solid gold.

"Mr. Lenox, you must tell us how we compare to London society," said Mrs. van der Leyden when they were seated. Apparently the conversation was to be general. "I know your wife is a famous woman of society."

"I hardly know where to begin," Lenox replied, smiling. A soup was being laid before them. "I may begin by saying that I have rarely eaten better, and we are only at the first course."

His hostess—a plump, middle-aged woman, rather beautiful—smiled. "You ought to come to Newport, sir—you really ought—for it is there that we outdo ourselves. We have a cottage there. You should be most welcome."

Lenox was briefly confused—the cottages on his brother's property rarely extended to a third room—but merely inclined his head. "Alas, my time is not my own while I am here, or I should be very grateful to accept the invitation, ma'am," he said.

A jaunty young fellow in a pale blue suit, with a white flower in his buttonhole, said, "Perhaps if Teddy Blaine were to invite you?"

"Mr. Blaine?" said their host.

The young man turned to the table. "Young Blaine showed up at Delmonico's today—harassed poor Mr. Lenox, from what I understand."

There was a reaction in the room, something between a titter and a tut. "His brother pulled a decent oar at Cambridge, however," said a large, theretofore silent young man at the end of the table, to general agreement, and the discussion moved on to rowing.

It was past midnight when Lenox walked home later that night, exhausted, trying to calm his whirring mind, his eyes turned up toward the sky. He loosened his collar. A strange sky it was, too: dark lavender, nearing black, starless, yet somehow suffused with light. Looking back down to pause at a cross street, Lenox glanced at the row of handsome limestone houses to his left. They were similar to the ones he knew from London but unmistakably different.

And all at once he felt a sort of soaring within himself. A very strange sky! For the first time in an awfully long while he was far, far from home. He thought of what his brother Edmund must be doing—well, sleeping, of course, since it was nearly morning in London, or perhaps even awake, having a first cup of tea, the papers strewn over his quilted bedclothes, the familiar songbirds awakening in the birch trees outside his house.

And Jane, Jane too would be sleeping, but the day ahead of her would comprise the usual, comfortable rounds; Polly and Dallington might discuss the agency's present cases over their breakfast before too long, mysteries to be solved.

Thomas McConnell—if Lenox knew his friend—would likely have been up all night at Great Ormond Street Hospital, where he passed more and more of his time, sometimes twenty-four hours without a stop. And of course Graham: Graham, in some ways his oldest ally, was no doubt already at work in Parliament, setting about his day.

But Lenox was *here*. How peculiar. He took in the unfamiliar shape of the streetlamps, the slightly odd faces of the houses. Funny, those van der Leydens, with their plump rosewood sofas and thick wallpaper, the eccentric nutmeg-creamed nesselrode they'd served him for dessert, even the cut of their shirts and cuffs.

Yet to them it was the center of the universe, New York! Lenox knew this feeling: the traveler's thrill, a mixture of novelty, adventure, and a slight tincture of homesickness, too, welcome homesickness, a reminder of all the happy things that home held in wait for one's return. It had been a long time since the emotion stirred in him.

He walked on. In a way this was the first time he had drawn a real breath since arriving in New York and seeing his things bundled over the side of the *Selene*, and he regretted it extremely that he should have to leave so soon. He understood how Eddings could make a life here, and his mind drifted to the other cities that deserved a lifetime—St. Petersburg for instance, he was sure; Paris, Copenhagen, San Francisco, each with its own customs, its own snobberies, its own artists, its own version of the distant sky . . . But here was the Union Club. He touched his hat to the porter and went upstairs to his room.

Lenox slept too well that night, and the next morning had to rush to the Grand Central Depot, with O'Brian harrying people to the side to make way for him. He arrived just in time for the 9:22 train to Boston.

As he was about to board, though, he saw a familiar face.

"Mr. Lenox!"

It was Theodore Blaine, and now that they were on the train station's platform Lenox saw that he did indeed have a limp. He was again carrying his battered black walking stick with the silver ring around it, an object that gave such a misleading sense of his place in the world. It must have had sentimental value.

"Hello, Mr. Blaine," he said. "What good fortune to be able to say goodbye to you in person."

"Ah! Just so, except—well, it seems my manners are badly out, sir. In fact I am here because I had hoped I might accompany you some of the way to Boston."

"Accompany me?"

Blaine nodded. "I think I would like to be a detective, you see, sir, and there are so few opportunities in New York for serious conversation on the subject. But perhaps you were looking forward to a solitary journey."

Lenox suddenly noticed a retinue behind Blaine: no fewer than five men, each of them dressed much more finely than the young gentleman himself, in his rumpled navy suit and black glasses, and certainly all of them stronger. Something between bodyguards and footmen, Lenox decided.

Only a royal would have commanded such an entourage in London—a second son, never. He knew, for he was one himself.

"I am glad you took the initiative," he said. "I should have thought of it myself. But I understand it is a very long trip to Boston, some eight or nine hours."

Blaine smiled, face filling with relief. "I have made it many times. I have an overnight bag in case"—he looked behind him vaguely, and one of the men was indeed holding a valise—"in case there are delays. But I promise you that I shall not impose upon your time more than is necessary."

"Not at all," said Lenox, smiling. "There is a case that puzzled me all the way across the Atlantic, though it happened in the street next to mine in London. Perhaps we may solve it together."

CHAPTER ELEVEN

It would have been impolite to refuse Theodore Blaine's request, but in the event Lenox had no cause to regret his politeness. Blaine was quiet, respectful, and, in a haphazard but enthusiastic way, knowledgeable. He had little of the entitlement one might have assumed he would from his background. Perhaps it was his leg—the way that sometimes early hardship, if not too profound, could salvage a person from his own privilege.

Still, money never quite hid. Without being asked, one of the men with Blaine had produced a wealth of food and drink: peaches, salted cashews, lemonade, sparkling water, and, though it was not yet ten o'clock, two bottles of cold Rhenish wine, packed on ice.

Over these mostly untouched refreshments, they spent an engaging two hours piecing together the facts of the Wallace murder. It took both of them a moment to look up from the absorption of the study when the train made its first stop, at a small town whose railway signs marked it as Stamford, Connecticut.

"Am I in a new state, then?" cried Lenox, staring through the window with intense satisfaction. "My second one."

"Many congratulations," said Blaine, sharing easily in his companion's happiness.

Lenox took out the little book of maps from Jane, which had a checklist naming all thirty-eight states, and placed a tick next to the pleasingly inscrutable word *Connecticut*. "Do you know the origin of the state's name?" he asked.

"I don't, now that you mention it. I suppose it must be the name of a local tribe. I can tell you that it's called the Nutmeg State."

"Is it? Why?"

"The spice trade."

Lenox was still studying the small soft leather book, with its richly detailed, delicately colored maps. "I had nutmeg last night. And soon enough I shall be able to add Massachusetts. Tell me, Mr. Blaine, have you traveled much in the western part of your country?"

The young man replied that he had—he was particularly fond of St. Louis, he said, Chicago too—but just as he was warming to his subject, the train, which had pulled away from Stamford, stopped.

As the delay began to lengthen, people in the car started to murmur. They weren't at a station.

"Some congestion on the tracks ahead, I suppose," said Blaine.

He looked back toward his small battalion, and one of them stood, in his handsome blue uniform coat, with its shining buttons almost military, and said that he would look into what had happened.

But he was saved the trouble—at that moment, the door to the train car opened, and an imposing figure in a police coat stepped on.

"Is there a Mr. Charles Lenox aboard?" he said.

The gentleman making this inquiry was fifty or so, something near Lenox's own age. He had dark, coarse hair, pale skin, and a rather handsome face, which was, however, marred on one side by the aftermath of a terrible wound, crossed with scores of small white scars, one eye permanently half-lidded.

Lenox recognized that kind of scar. After Crimea you had seen them. Their sad tale wound its way back to 1784, when an imaginative lieutenant in the Royal Artillery had swiped a spare cannonball from the arsenal and started to tinker with it, looking for improvements. Eventually, he hollowed it and filled it with gunshot, small lead balls, until it was just heavy enough to fire like a solid cannonball.

The invention was a devastating success. It scattered hundreds of fiery-hot shards of metal into enemy lines, causing terribly painful injuries as often, or even more often, than death. It was hard to know what the lieutenant would have made of his invention. Whatever it might have been, his name—Lt. Henry Shrapnel— lived on in the weapon he had created.

The tall, forbidding person who had stopped the train to speak with Lenox was one of Shrapnel's latter-day casualties. The telltale signs ran down one side of his face.

Lenox's eyes went to his lapel, where he found what he'd suspected he would—a Union army rosette. There had been innumerable shrapnel wounds in that war.

This whole series of observations took the space of a few seconds. The detective stood. "I'm Charles Lenox."

The gentleman turned. "Ah. I have a message for you, Mr. Lenox."

He held out an envelope, and Lenox had an awful swift emptying feeling down his spine, his thoughts flying to Sophia, Clara, Jane, his brother.

He took the envelope and tore it open.

March 14, 1878
The Cove
Newport, RI

Mr. Lenox,
There has been a murder here—an unforgivable murder, a girl still not yet 19. I beseech you to come to Newport . . .

Lenox exhaled. He looked around the carriage, suddenly remembering himself. Wyatt was a few feet behind him, all curiosity. Blaine had stood too. The train's conductor was nearby, staring with naked interest at the gentleman with the scarred face.

Lenox took in the fellow's dress more carefully and saw that it was private livery, though it ran near to looking like a police uniform. Like Blaine's attendants.

"May I ask your name, sir?" he said.

"James Clark, sir. I am an employee of Mr. William Stuyvesant Schermerhorn." Lenox must have looked blank, because he went on: "The author of the letter, sir. If you are amenable to coming with me, there is a special waiting on the adjoining track."

"A special train?"

"Yes, sir." Mr. Clark gestured toward Blaine and his men. "It will comfortably accommodate your party, should you wish them to accompany you."

Lenox, baffled at this invitation, said he thought that he had better read the letter in full, and sat down again, conscious that all eyes were on him and slowing down to read carefully in reaction to this pressure.

> March 14, 1878
> The Cove
> Newport, RI
>
> Mr. Lenox,
> There has been a murder here—an unforgivable murder, a
> girl still not yet 19. I beseech you to come to Newport imme-
> diately. You may name your fee. I remit this letter by special
> dispatch with a private car, which shall certainly meet you in
> New Haven if it misses you in New York. You cannot possibly
> come too quickly. As I say, you may name your fee.
>
> In haste, your servant,
> *William Stuyvesant Schermerhorn IV*

Lenox read this letter twice. At its foot was a coat of arms with what looked like a tulip in a field beneath a sun, and underneath it the phrase *Indefessi Favente Deo.*

Did Americans have coats of arms? He supposed they must. He turned to Blaine. "Do you know anything about this person, Schermerhorn?"

"Yes, to be sure. I have known him most of my life. A very respectable gentleman."

"I would appreciate your opinion on this letter."

Blaine took the letter and read it. As he did so, his expression was overcome with a quick-dawning consternation. "Oh, no," he said. He looked up. "Yes, I know him—a respectable gentleman, Mr. Lenox. He would certainly not make sport of you."

"No, the efforts of Mr. Clark"—Lenox nodded to the private guard here—"have assured me of that. Mr. Clark, do you know anything of the contents of the letter?"

"I do not, sir. My instructions were to find you and accompany you to Newport, if you should be willing to come."

Lenox turned to the conductor. "Is it quite customary to stop the train for private messages like this?"

The conductor, a small, cheery, round-headed fellow with small bright eyes, looked suddenly guilty. "No, sir."

Suddenly Lenox put together the heavy weight of the letter he held, Clark's uniform with its silver buckles, Blaine's words, the name *Cove Court*, the private car, and realized this was a matter of money. There was probably a jangle of silver in the conductor's pocket.

He bridled against the impudence of this stranger beckoning him to Newport.

"I'm sorry you have wasted your efforts, but I must decline," he said, handing the letter back to Clark. "I have plans to keep in Boston and beyond."

"May I represent to you, Mr. Lenox, that Mr. Schermerhorn was desperate that you should come. He enjoined me to mention that no fee you name could be too high."

"Yes, he mentioned the fee in his letter as well. I shall have to forfeit it."

Why was he reacting so severely to this invitation? He couldn't say himself, as he stood and met Mr. Clark's gaze. Perhaps because there was an echo of an old slander here, the scorn he had faced for taking up work when he became a detective, the shame he had fought against in himself at the time, the parties from which he had been excluded, the fat-faced fools from Oxford who had cut him dead in their clubs merely because they would never have turned their own hands to any work more arduous than preparing a drink.

"I am sure Mr. Schermerhorn intended no offense," Clark said.

"Undoubtedly not," said Lenox. "Nevertheless, you have my answer."

"And it is final?" said Clark.

There was nothing angry in his tone—only professional. Lenox observed with neutral interest that this was a highly competent emissary before him, James Clark.

Blaine, just over his shoulder, said, "Mr. Lenox, if you like I could wire to—I have known the Schermerhorns for many years, socially. Hello, Mr. Clark. I believe we have met."

"Mr. Blaine," said the private guard, inclining his head in a bow.

Lenox hesitated. "Is there a telegraph office in the New Haven station?"

This was the next stop. Lenox could tell there were none at Stamford, from the little engineer's shack that had been the only building near the platform.

"Oh, of course," said the conductor. "It's one of our busiest stations."

Lenox paused, then nodded. "Is there a later train to Boston from New Haven?"

"We change engines there, so you shall have half an hour. Else there is the 2:49. It follows the same route but stops more often because it has a refrigerated car."

Lenox checked his watch, thanked the conductor, and then told Clark and Blaine he would be happy to wire for more information from New Haven.

It took just about half an hour to get there. New Haven's train station was a beautiful, airy structure, with a high pale green half-dome of a ceiling and a line of handsome benches where various respectable-looking passengers sat, waiting for their departures. Lenox looked it over with great curiosity. A busy place, with carts selling hot pretzels, doughnuts, and cider; Yale College pennants and glasses at a little stall (he bought one of the pennants for Sophia); a newsstand with papers.

He realized that these same newspapers must be how William Stuyvesant Schermerhorn the Fourth had thought to seek him out. His appearance (*Celebrated London Detective Arrives for Visit to States*) had been remarked in the headlines. He sighed to himself. Some accident or misfortune, no doubt, nothing like a murder, and he would lose half the day by it.

He left Wyatt on a bench as Blaine and Clark went to the telegraph office, and decided he would take a turn outside, where he smelled the familiar scent of horses and carriages, heard various happy conversations. In spite of his annoyance, in spite of his relative conviction that it would all prove a wild goose chase, a faint curiosity about this murder—this *unforgivable* murder—was building in the back of his mind.

CHAPTER TWELVE

I f it had not been in motion, the solitary train car puffing its way
from New Haven toward Newport two hours later—the "special,"
as such privately owned train cars were called—might have been a
drawing room on Fifth Avenue. It was furnished with sofas and
chairs, a liquor stand, a shelf of books bound in morocco leather,
and there were even, rattling just slightly on the walls, a series of
three handsome oil paintings depicting the Battle of Brandywine.

Riding in the car were Lenox, Blaine, O'Brian, and Mr. Clark;
Wyatt had gone on to Boston, where Lenox promised to be the
next day. ("Is Boston the last stop on the train?" he had murmured
to the conductor before leaving Wyatt behind. "Yes, sir." "Good,"
he'd said, "thank you," his anxious visions of Wyatt slumbering into
the northern reaches of Canada assuaged.)

The rapidity with which Blaine had received his replies from
William Stuyvesant Schermerhorn had quite astonished Lenox,
until he learned from Clark that Schermerhorn had a private telegraph office in his house in Newport. It was a privilege that so far as
Lenox knew only the Queen and one or two others had in England.

In the first telegram, Blaine had asked for more information about the murder, signing with his own name. That information had arrived within five minutes.

> Hello Blaine STOP Death near the 40 Steps STOP
> Regret very much to say it was Lily Allingham STOP
> Spotted early this morning by fishing boat STOP Body
> in situ for now STOP Please represent to Mr Lenox that
> we wish him to come with all possible dispatch STOP

Lenox had listened as Blaine read this aloud, standing in the New Haven wire office.

"You've gone pale," he said when Blaine was finished.

Blaine looked up. He had been reading it over again, to himself. "Oh! I suppose I probably have, yes. I'm sorry. I know Lily Allingham. Knew Lily Allingham."

"Oh no. I'm terribly sorry." Blaine looked dazed. "You must—sir, could you fetch him a cup of tea with plenty of sugar?" Lenox said to one of the young heir's cortège.

The fellow nodded and walked purposefully away. Sweet did well against shock. "She was a beautiful girl," murmured Blaine, staring at a spot on the floor about ten feet from them.

"What are the Forty Steps?" Lenox asked.

"Eh?" Blaine looked up, still clutching the wire. "Oh! They are a famous landmark in Newport."

"Do you know the town well? Where?"

"I do. The finest houses there are along the Cliff Walk. That is a promontory at some height above the water—twenty feet, say. The Forty Steps are built into the Cliff Walk. They lead down from the height of the houses to the shore. Anyone may use them, by long tradition. The right of way along the Cliff Walk is always unobstructed, though many of the wealthier people in Newport should like to have the shore to themselves."

"I would like to know whether there is a chance it was an accident before I go there. Would you prefer me to compose the response?"

"No, not at all," Blaine had said. "I am quite myself again."

Again the answer to Blaine's query had come very rapidly.

No chance of accident STOP Cause of death blow to head STOP Please transmit Lenox that police here unfit for murder investigation STOP Small town STOP

And that had been the moment that decided Lenox, the reference to the local police. He had no doubt of the veracity of it.

Now they sat on the train. Clark, with sunlight playing over the unblemished side of his face, was staring quietly ahead, accustomed to sentry duty. Meanwhile, Lenox's young Irish valet was toward the front of the car, where the engineer had his booth. The two of them were sharing some sort of snack. Perhaps something from the otherwise untasted delicacies laid on a table against the right side of the car.

Blaine was seated, gazing through the window. All but one of his various aides-de-camp—to their obvious displeasure—were following in a different train. The cup of tea at the station in New Haven had steadied him, but he was very quiet, very still.

As for Lenox, having observed his fellow passengers discreetly for some time, Clark particularly, he was reading.

The delicately inked little book of maps that Lady Jane had given him before his departure had a glossary, too, in part stocked with brief descriptions of significant places in the States. The entry for Newport was illuminating.

Port city of Aquidneck Island, in Narragansett Bay, Rhode Island. Notable for its summer population, drawn earlier in its history primarily from the large southern plantations,

*but since midcentury more broadly, and in particular from
New York society. Founded in 1639. Housed Jews fleeing
Spanish persecution in 1658, and consequently still home
to a large Jewish population; boasts the oldest synagogue in
the United States. Known for its cottages and the striking
views from the Cliff Walk. Recreations: Sailing and fishing, April–October. Recommended lodging: Mrs. Berry's,
Bellevue Avenue; Bradley House, Thames Street. Recommended dining: The Paul Revere Tavern, The Old Black
Horse. Plentiful shops located in and around Bellevue
Avenue. Attempts to gain access to the island's private
homes not advised.*

"Mr. Blaine," Lenox said, "I wonder if I could impose upon you
for whatever information you might have about Miss Allingham.
Mrs. Allingham?"

Blaine drew his stare from the windows only after a beat. "Miss—
Miss Lily Allingham."

Lenox could feel Clark's attention, though he hadn't moved in
the slightest. "And?" he said.

"I cannot say that I knew Miss Allingham well. She was a year
or two younger than I," said Blaine. The scenery blurred past them
in the windows, and unconsciously the young fellow reached for the
lower part of his leg, massaged it for a moment. "The first thing you
are bound to hear is that she has been considered one of our great
beauties. The diamond of the season, one of the columnists here
has taken to calling her. So she has had a taste of fame this year."

"She was a member of Newport society, then?"

"Oh! Yes, certainly. I should have said that first. And New York."
Blaine shook his head clear. "Let me see. Lily Allingham. Yes. Only
child of Mr. Creighton Allingham and his wife."

Lenox was taking notes. "Do you know her name?"

"Cora, I believe, though I wouldn't swear to it. I suppose you would say that they were socially of the—the middle tier, of the group here that cares for such things. That sounds bad."

"You must speak as frankly as possible."

"Miss Allingham's beauty gave them a heightened social significance. They were perhaps not of the first rank until she was noticed. Now they go everywhere. They were on the Flagler yacht in Monaco over Christmas. Lily herself has been much courted, needless to say. I do not know whether they have a house in Newport. I don't believe that they do. There aren't many. But it's no surprise at all that they were guests there, if indeed that's why she was there. She would have had a dozen invitations. Many of the hostesses like to have the season's darlings stay with them."

"How does someone like Schermerhorn come into it?"

"I'm not sure."

"Is his wife one of these hostesses?"

Almost reluctantly, Blaine said, "No. She's abroad. But there were rumors—well, that Schermerhorn's son and Miss Allingham might be married."

That changed the complexion of things enormously. "An engagement?"

"Not that I know of." There was a long pause. They both looked at Clark, but he stared steadily on, silent as the grave. "When I told you I was interested in crime, I did not imagine—I could not have foreseen—"

"No, of course not," said Lenox.

"I didn't know Lily well."

"If you should wish to return to New York, Mr. Blaine, I understand. Indeed, you have already given me a great deal of help."

A strange stubbornness passed over Blaine's face. Perhaps something of his father in it or, who knew, his mother. "No. I—my family—I have a convenient place to stay, in Newport, as it happens. With your permission, I should like to come."

Lenox inclined his head. He reflected that in all probability it was the sort of case that would be over in two hours, perhaps even solved by the time they arrived. If not, though, Blaine would be a useful ally. He knew the terrain.

"Then follow my lead," said Lenox.

"Of course. And I hope you shall stay with us."

"Thank you, but I will find lodgings," said Lenox. "I shouldn't like to impose."

More to the point: It was better to have independence. He had no real conception of what kind of little world he was entering— only the knowledge that the word *Newport* was freighted with a certain magic here in America, denoting to the more humbly blessed enormous parties, breathtaking costumes, the most concentrated and intensely enjoyed wealth in all America, perhaps. At least, that was its reputation.

The train was passing by a gray, serene stretch of water, very close to the tracks. "We're nearly there," said Clark, the first time he had spoken in an hour.

Lenox felt a flash of weariness; of being a long way from home. In truth he *hoped* that the matter had been resolved already, that he could spend the night in Newport, visit the sea for half an hour's walk, and be on his way to meet the Poe Society in Boston, a group of retired professors who solved crimes together. He had been looking forward to it particularly.

To their east, the town came into view: charming New England spires, white clapboard houses, a densely populated place. Beyond it the rough choppy white waves of the bay were visible, gulls wheeling above, the sight of all that open water tugging at Lenox's heart.

He still didn't see any of the great mansions for which Newport was famous. The other side of the island, perhaps.

When they arrived, Lenox gave O'Brian (who had evinced no special surprise at the sharp change in their plans) money. "Could you please take a hansom cab and find us two rooms for the night?

Mr. Blaine, shall he try Mrs. Berry's first, or Bradley House—or some third option?"

"Mrs. Berry's," said Blaine without an instant's doubt. "You shall be very comfortable there. If she is full, Mrs. Clumber's will do. Bradley House at a pinch."

"Thank you. O'Brian, look at the rooms yourself before you take them, if you would, thank you, and make sure they are suitable. The only thing I mind is any very active animal life or visible dirt. I am sure there shall be no difficulty with either. An uncomfortable bed I can stand. And leave word of where you have landed at—well, where?"

"The Horse and Foal," said Blaine. "It is two doors down from Mrs. Berry's."

"O'Brian? You have that?"

"Yes, sir."

The train was pulling to a stop. "Very good. Let us see, then, what we shall see."

It was scarcely twenty minutes later that Lenox found himself near the summit of the Forty Steps.

Beneath them on the beach, a small crowd of people, perhaps a dozen in all, stood around a white sheet that was pinned to the ground at its corners with heavy stones. One by one, they looked up at the new arrivals, shielding their eyes against the sun and the furious wind, their faces all filled with dismay and fear, along with perhaps a trace of hope that whoever was on the steps had come to rescue them. A few must have recognized either Clark or Blaine, for they waved up in the direction of the trio. Lenox took a deep breath, situating himself mentally, and then started toward the steps with the other two men at his side, Blaine fighting, it was obvious, to walk without a hobble.

CHAPTER THIRTEEN

Lenox had been at innumerable crime scenes over the years, and if the last several days had been a whirlwind of new impressions, the scene that awaited him at the bottom of the wooden staircase was oddly familiar. As he descended the steps, he felt a ready calmness.

It was a rocky, windswept beach, the shore curving gently inward for about a mile's length until it suddenly jutted out, forming a striking green cape at the end of the island.

But it was the houses above that stood out.

They sat about twenty or thirty feet higher than the water, just as Blaine had described. They were immense, most of them blindingly white, though a few were stone, and one halfway down toward the cape was painted in an eye-catchingly hideous black-and-white checkered pattern. Some sat quite close to the cliffside, others farther back, but each was on a large expanse of close-shaven grass.

Lenox had known grand houses, to be sure, but he had never seen anything quite like this. Castles and manors in England were generally ensconced within woodland, far from other inhabitants.

Here, though, the houses sat nakedly visible to one another, serried in stark, handsome formation, some close enough that you must have been able to see quite clearly into fourteen or so of your neighbors' bedrooms. It was disorienting, as if fifty castles dotted around England and Scotland had all been relocated brick by brick to the same small peninsula in Cornwall.

"Are the cottages farther inland?" Lenox said to Blaine.

"Excuse me?" said Blaine, next to him on the steps.

"Schermerhorn mentioned his cottage."

Blaine looked at him blankly, hand on the wooden rail. Then he said, "These *are* the cottages, Mr. Lenox."

Lenox stopped. "These houses?"

"Yes. These are the cottages of Newport."

Lenox stared at the houses for a moment. "That one with the marble columns must have thirty bedrooms in it," he said, nodding toward a house a quarter mile away. "You call that a cottage?"

Blaine reddened. "That is my family's cottage, as it happens."

Good lord. "My apologies."

"None required."

"The word *cottage* is an affectation, then. Not in your family's case, that is to say, but in—"

"Yes."

Like Marie Antoinette playing milkmaid, to call such an edifice a cottage: an enticement to fate. He wondered, not for the first time on this voyage, since it was a great subject in the American papers, whether there would be a second revolution in this country before the century saw itself out.

At that moment a large, officious-looking gentleman in a wool suit approached the bottom of the stairs, anticipating their descent.

"Good day, sir," he said, stepping onto the lowest stair. "Good day, Mr. Blaine. Mr. Clark."

"Please allow me to introduce you to Mr. John Welling," said Clark, stepping forward. "He's the mayor of Newport. Jack, this is Charles Lenox, the detective Mr. Schermerhorn has hired."

"Consulted," said Lenox.

The mayor put out a hand and Lenox shook it. "It is a very sad scene, Mr. Lenox, very sad. The quicker we can see to justice the better, as far as I'm concerned."

They had reached the beach. Lenox said he was pleased to meet the mayor, and asked to be introduced to the dozen or so men standing around, trampling things hopelessly, blast their eyes—two local constables, the police chief (a reedy fellow named Partridge, looking utterly overwhelmed), and various other busybodies.

He asked if he might have the scene cleared. Welling said certainly, of course, though in the end it was Clark who began the job, not the mayor.

No one questioned Blaine's presence there, or even remarked on it, somewhat to Lenox's surprise. He stored this away to remember. Money: That was what counted in Newport, Rhode Island. Of course, it was what counted in most places, but in some more bluntly than others.

"Mr. Blaine, perhaps while these gentlemen are taking their leave of each other you would be kind enough to give me an overview of this town—what we can see of it—so that I have my bearings."

"Of course," said Blaine. "We might go back up the steps for a moment. It would be easier from there."

Lenox wondered if this was a good idea for his young companion's leg. "Certainly, if you choose," was all he said.

From the top of the steps they stood level with the cottages, a biscuit's toss above the men slowly shuffling away from that eloquently motionless white sheet on the shore.

Blaine pointed inland, directly ahead of them. "Do you see that crowding of masts across the island?" he asked.

"Yes."

"That is the harbor, which you saw from the other side as we rode on the train. It's a fifteen-minute walk west from here, no more. The wharves are very active. Some of the fishermen still live there. Between here and the docks lies the chief part of the town, including Bellevue Avenue."

Lenox looked at the sweeping shoreline to their left, the beautiful cottages. "So the summer residents stick to this side of the island."

Blaine nodded. "Mostly. There are forty cottages or so, I suppose, and another forty houses that would not be deemed cottages, perhaps, but are fine enough—this side of Bellevue. More of both kinds of houses are going up every day. The price for the existing ones has gone all out of proportion, too—absurd. But you know how fashion is."

Lenox studied the grand houses for a moment. He saw now that there was, indeed, a small explosive commotion of construction every so often, new houses being squeezed on to the Cliff Walk. He wondered what Blaine considered an absurd price. Lord Eddings, his transplanted friend, had told him that a row of particularly eligible seats at St. Bartholomew's Church had fetched $320,000 the year before, an amount of money so large it was hard to imagine for a non-American. For a moment Lenox felt almost intimidated by the fortunes that surrounded him—but that was only atmosphere, he remembered, and shook it away.

"How long have these houses been here?"

"Southern families have been coming here since before the war, mostly from Georgia and South Carolina," Blaine replied. "But it is only in the last five or ten years that New York has taken to Newport. Now there is nowhere else to be, however."

"Five or ten years!"

Lenox, coming from England, was accustomed to villages that hadn't seen a new family in the squire's house since the time of Edward the Second. "Yes," said Blaine.

"All of them look as if they have been standing there since before Rome fell." Lenox's eyes swung across the south point of the island. In the distance, there was a lighthouse. "How long would it take to walk there?"

"Twenty or thirty minutes, I suppose," said Blaine.

Lenox turned right, in the opposite direction of the lighthouse. Up there, past the picturesque little village where they had made their arrival, the island ended in a rocky outcrop covered with small houses, boats bobbing in the water.

"Another part of the village?" he said.

"Yes," Blaine replied. "Most of the servants who don't live in the cottages live there. Locals, too, and the majority of the men who still make a living by fishing. A handful of retired whalers. There are several boardinghouses, too."

It couldn't have been farther than a mile or two, but it sounded like a different world. "Does anyone from these cottages ever go up there?"

"Once in a while. There is gambling there and other . . . other vices."

Lenox nodded, staring hard at this little agglomeration of dwellings, barnacled to the cliff at a safe distance from the imperious cottages. "It is a small place, Newport."

"Oh, very small."

"And what of Mr. Schermerhorn?" asked Lenox. "Which is his house?"

Blaine looked surprised yet again. "Why—you are standing on his land now, I believe. I'm sorry, I assumed Mr. Clark had told you. That is the Cove."

All of Lenox's internal alarms went off. "You mean to say that Miss Allingham died on Schermerhorn's own property?" he asked.

"The beach is a public way," said Blaine, frowning. "But yes— just in front of it."

Lenox gazed at the nearest house—the Cove, evidently, or Cove Court more formally. It was both less grand and somehow also more substantial than many of those around it, a handsome clapboard structure set forty or fifty yards back from the cliff, with numerous small outbuildings of matching design. Two handsome chestnut horses were grazing near one of them.

A dead young woman, found next to the family house of the young man who had been courting her. Lenox was highly conscious that such a circumstance usually turned out in just one way.

"Mr. Lenox," a voice called behind him from the steps. Clark. "The area is clear."

He looked, and indeed the beach was empty now but for the mayor, the police chief, and a single constable.

"Tell me," said Lenox to Blaine, "this walking path along the top of the cliffs here—does it not intrude upon private properties?"

"It is the Cliff Walk," said Blaine. "It runs across the properties to be sure. But by ancient tradition anyone may walk here. The townspeople are fairly biddable, but they would revolt were that to change."

"I see," said Lenox. He spared one more moment to survey Newport, finishing with a glance toward Cove Court, where someone moved behind a window. "Very well. Let us descend. The time has come to inspect the body."

CHAPTER FOURTEEN

Lily Allingham lay on her right side. Her fair hair was spread out in an accidental halo on the sand around her; she had met eternity in a gown of fragile pink lace, with pearls sewn carefully into its bodice.

There was a single large wound on the left side of her head. Lenox saw why Schermerhorn had been so definite: plain murder, it was clear. There could be no other explanation. On a different part of the beach he might have suspected an inebriated fall, but where her body lay the shore was soft and sandy, with none of the great jagged rocks that began a few hundred feet south of the steps.

No, the wound had come from a human hand, or else the body had been moved *after* it fell—itself a sign that at a minimum, someone had been present at her death. There was also a livid mark on one of the girl's wrists. It might have nothing to do with the murder, but Lenox's best guess was that it did. A violent grip. He was looking for someone in the hold of an awful passion, another argument for the idea that it was one of Lily Allingham's suitors who had killed her.

Lenox's practice at scenes such as this, one he had carefully developed, was to walk in gradually increasing concentric circles around the body. He started now by gently inspecting Miss Alling-ham herself. He found nothing, but he did note a scent of gin on her body. That surprised him—not a lady's drink, unless America was different from England.

He began to walk his outward circles, but there was little to see. The body had fallen cleanly into the sand and stayed there, and there were no objects nearby. Nor were there any useful markings—hundreds of footprints, but that was hardly a surprise, given how many people had been around the area.

When he had finished his inspection of the area, Lenox crouched by the body one last time. He would not have another chance to see Lily Allingham. She was beautiful indeed, even in the repose of death, at once ethereal, in the fine shape of her eyes and her fair hair, and sturdy, of the world, slim but substantial. He studied her right wrist, her left temple. What kind of weapon? He tried to think like McConnell. Something small and hard, he thought the doctor would have said. A rock. A pistol.

Then he noticed something else: a faint discoloration where a ring must have once been on her third finger.

Had it been removed recently, or several lifetimes ago, at least in the world of a young woman? She might have been engaged before and broken it off. He asked Welling if there was a ring missing from her hand, but no one present could say, and no one knew whether she had been accustomed to wearing one, includ-ing Blaine. They would have to ask someone closer to her. Her parents would know. Though that was a conversation Lenox knew would be grim.

He started his careful circles again, just to be sure, stopping only when, still having found nothing, he reached the sheer face of the cliff.

He looked up, and it was then that he realized that of course he must inspect the cliff top too. After nodding that he was done to Partridge, the police chief, Lenox took the stairs again, Blaine and Clark behind him. The rest remained below to wait for the coroner.

Up on the Walk (as Clark called it) Lenox carefully surveyed the trampled-down path two or three feet from the edge of the cliff. The vista from here was almost coldly stunning, a vast expanse of sea and cliff, indifferent to human activities.

Finding nothing on the path, Lenox stalked in among the knee-high grasses closer to the precipice. "Has this area been searched?" he called down to Partridge and Welling.

"No, sir," the police chief said. "Not by myself or my men, least-wise."

Lenox knelt down carefully and combed through the grass with his hands. He moved forward in a low stoop, no doubt resembling one of the lesser primates, but after ten or twelve feet, he had his reward—or at least, saw something unexpected.

He brushed the grasses aside to reveal the object, glinting dully in the daylight. He picked it up with his handkerchief. It was small and weighty, but despite this Lenox scarcely dared to believe it was their weapon—until he saw, on its shiny golden surface, a smear of what could only be dried blood.

A thrill of discovery in his heart.

"What is it?" asked Blaine, who had stuck to the walking path.

Lenox held the object up. "A flask," he said. "Do you recognize it?"

Blaine stepped cautiously closer to look. The flask was an expensive object, gold, with a large inlaid ruby in its center and a grooved top that was attached by a little arm to the body.

Blaine shook his head, disappointed. "No."

Lenox opened the flask and smelled. "Whisky," he said. "Still a few drops left."

He closed the flask again and squinted around. Not gin, he observed, despite the scent on Lily Allingham's body.

Nevertheless, the circumstances seemed clearer. If he were putting together the story of the previous evening, he would hazard that the murderer had never even been down to the beach. No, he had killed Miss Allingham on this cliff top. Then he (or she, Lenox supposed) had rolled the body off the cliff to delay its discovery, and perhaps somehow, in this progression of events, lost this weapon in the dark. Even in broad daylight Lenox hadn't spotted it immediately. Late at night, possibly drunk, the murderer would have had a very difficult time recovering the weapon, even with a good hunt.

"Mr. Lenox. Mr. Lenox!"

Lenox turned and saw a small, well-dressed man striding across a great expanse of lawn to him from the nearby house, waving to get his attention.

"Mr. Schermerhorn," said Blaine.

"I had deduced as much," said Lenox.

He quickly folded the flask into his handkerchief and placed it in his jacket pocket.

As Schermerhorn neared them, Clark materialized. Clark's employer ignored him, however, his concentration set upon Lenox. Schermerhorn was handsome, with salt-and-pepper hair and high, prominent cheekbones in a small, neat face. The chief impression Lenox had from his bearing was of pride—pride in his house, in his person, in his name—and of wealth, a watch chain glittering with tasteful jewels (inasmuch as jewels could be tasteful), a suit of clothes clearly cut to Schermerhorn's frame by an expert tailor.

"Thank you for coming, Mr. Lenox," said the American, fixing Lenox's hand in a hard handshake.

"Yes. It's a terrible crime."

"We are shaken—extremely shaken. A fine young woman, Miss Allingham."

Lenox murmured something sympathetic. Schermerhorn, looking around with a rattled grimace, began to racket on rather pointlessly—good family—charming girl—most attached—good works.

The suit was well cut, but it was a sober gray, and Lenox spotted in him the same kind of old Knickerbocker, ostensibly allergic to the new fortunes flooding New York, that he had met at supper the night before.

"May I invite you inside for a drink?" said Schermerhorn at last.

The detective was by no means sure that the man in front of him was an impartial party to all of this.

"I had planned to call on you after breakfast tomorrow, with your permission," Lenox said. "The first hours are vital in an investigation such as this. I must discover what I can now. But I should very much like to speak to you in the morning."

"Oh! Of course." Schermerhorn looked nonplussed. "I should have thought you would want to hear the details of last night as soon as possible."

He did. "Of course," he said. "I think official courtesy requires that I seek them through the proper channels first, however. I am here in America as the Queen's representative, as you may know."

Schermerhorn looked indifferent to the claims of Newport officialdom, but more alive to the claims of a Queen.

"Of course," he said. "Mr. Clark will take you wherever you need to go. Clark, any of the carriages is at your disposal."

Lenox put up a hand. "Thank you, Mr. Schermerhorn, but I have Mr. Blaine here—besides which I must settle myself wherever my valet has found rooms."

Schermerhorn noticed Blaine for the first time then, standing off to the side. "Oh, hello, Teddy. I didn't know you were in town."

"Hello, Mr. Schermerhorn."

"Terrible, isn't it? Miss Allingham." He paused fractionally, thinking something private—Lenox would have paid good money to know what—before turning his attention back to the detective. "I was sure you should stay at Cove Court, though, Mr. Lenox."

Lenox was only able to extricate himself from this invitation, and from Clark, with more words than he cared to spend, but at last he and Blaine went free. They did accept an offer to drive them into town from the mayor, Jack Welling, who happened to be leaving the coroner and police chief to their business on the beach. It was in his small barouche that at last Lenox and Blaine heard the details of the case.

At four o'clock that morning, around first light, Welling said, a small fishing yawl with three men aboard had spotted Lily Allingham's body. There were several witnesses who had been on that part of the beach as late as midnight the evening before; that added up, Welling said, because Miss Allingham hadn't left the ball at Cold Farm—some eight or nine houses down the Cliff Walk, he said, when Lenox inquired—until nearly midnight.

"Did she leave the ball with anyone?" asked Lenox.

"She left alone," Welling said. He looked momentarily uncomfortable, but principle won out. "There is a report from the party that Mr. Schermerhorn the Fifth went after her, though. Mr. Partridge and his men are investigating it. They spoke to him briefly this morning."

They had taken two turns and were driving down a series of streets lined with enormous oak trees, which towered over a variety of handsome old New England houses, trim saltboxes with manicured gardens and American flags hanging from their front porches. Very different from the cottages, as he supposed he must call them, but in their way just as pleasing, or more. They looked beautiful in the falling spring sunlight.

To Welling, Lenox said, "How does the younger Mr. Schermerhorn account for his leaving the ball?"

"He says he went to look for Lily Allingham but couldn't find her."

"He was interested in her romantically, I understand?"

Welling nodded, his large, reddish face, with its bushy mustache, in what looked like an unwonted attitude of worry, concern; he was a man who preferred to be on easy terms with the world.

"So I understand."

"There is O'Brian," said Blaine.

They had stopped in front of a tavern with a pair of small cannons outside its door. O'Brian was sitting at a table in front but leapt up when he saw Lenox.

"I shall wish you good day, then," said the detective. "Mr. O'Brian, where are we staying—Mrs. Berry's? Mrs. Berry's. Gentlemen, you may find me there. For now I must get some food and drink into me or I shall shatter. Good day, Mr. Welling. Mr. Blaine, I will see you in the morning, if not before?"

CHAPTER FIFTEEN

Accoording to O'Brian, Mrs. Berry was the granddaughter of a modest farmer who had risen to the position of lieutenant in a Rhode Island regiment during the American Revolution, when he had been captured and held for two years in Canada. In the spacious front room of her house, there was a portrait of him and his wife above the fireplace. Between them was the framed, tattered "stars and stripes" that the wife had sewn into his uniform coat for warmth, and which her husband had used as a blanket for the whole of his internment.

This front room was where Mrs. Berry sat by a small stove and supervised the complex inner workings of her busy house. She had inherited her ancestors' discipline: Her establishment was in shining, beautiful condition, far cleaner than the cozy but dusty Union Club. Its wooden floors were polished, its windows clear.

Yet in spite of this aggressive cleanliness there was something comfortable about the place as well—every single object well loved and very well worn, from the butter dish in the breakfast room to the coal scuttle in the hall.

Mrs. Berry herself was a tall, bony woman in her sixties, with a severe but not unkind face. She welcomed Lenox in practicalities:

who to call for fresh water, when he could expect tea, nothing beside the point.

In his fatigue, he was very grateful for this—and not forty minutes after leaving the Cliff Walk, he was sitting on the sweetest little balcony the village in Newport could conceivably have offered, he thought, with an immense view open in front of him of the sea, sun dipping down toward it, spreading golden light over a widening wedge of gray water. Along the coast, the vast houses perched upon the cliff, each of them large enough to contain dozens of secrets, hundreds.

He had two spacious rooms to himself. Their furnishings were spare compared to the thick curtains and heavy wooden furniture of the last English inn he had seen, in Plymouth, but comfortable—and on the shelves, most thoughtfully, a whole variety of intriguing books, novels, compendia of local history, poems, epics. Mrs. Berry must be a reader.

There were boxes filled with pink and white flowers on the rail of the balcony. Sitting on the table was a teapot, and resting near it a collection of small plates and dishes, which held scones, strawberry jam, sandwiches with cucumbers, and a very decent sort of savory cracker he had never tried before, and which he supposed must be local, with hard white cheddar cheese sliced at its side. Like all Englishmen he had snobbish feelings about cheddar cheese, but it had to be owned that this was a very credible version. Even his chair, with soft cushions on its seat and back, was eminently comfortable.

As he sat, shaking off the attentiveness of a day spent in the company of strangers, receding into himself, he experienced a certain evening melancholy. He would have liked to have Jane alongside him, or his brother, or Graham. Even to be in his study alone.

But he set these feelings aside and let his mind float upon the cool breeze, let his eyes soften. There was a red, white, and blue knitted blanket over the arm of a matching chair, and he laid it unevenly over himself, settling back then, holding his warm teacup in both hands . . .

When he awoke, the sun was all but gone. Only twenty or thirty minutes could have passed, but it had nonetheless been a deep, restorative rest, the kind of nap to put away a strenuous day.

He let his eyes fall gently closed again and lived for a while in the soft space between sleep and wakefulness. When at last he reopened them, it was in time to see a sunset of sublime purity, pink and gold beneath the immense soft clouds, the great houses underneath lost for a moment to nature. He watched it in silence, interrupted only occasionally by a muffled shout or conversation from some nearby street, until the sky was slate gray, all color gone.

He rose at last and stretched himself. "O'Brian!" he called.

After a moment the lad appeared. "Yes, Mr. Lenox?" he said.

"Would you be willing to do me a favor?"

"Of course, sir."

He fished an unfamiliar dollar note and some coins from his jacket pocket. "What I would like is if you could go back to the tavern where you were waiting for me—or any tavern you choose, really."

"Very good, sir."

"You may say you are here as my servant. That should excite some interest. Buy yourself supper, stand a round if you like. Then, if you can do it naturally, find out what the locals think about Miss Allingham's death."

"Very good, sir."

He was extremely young. "Do you think you can do that?"

O'Brian scorned the question. "Of course, sir."

"You are comfortable in a tavern?"

"A day hasn't passed since I turned nine that I wasn't in one, sir."

"No pressing them, please—they'll get suspicious of an outsider asking questions, even you—but if in the normal course of things . . . but then, I'm giving you a lesson you don't need, if you have been inside taverns since you were nine."

"No, sir. Yes, sir," said O'Brian.

"Thank you, Mr. O'Brian."

The eager young fellow sloped off, and Lenox sat down at the desk. That might rustle a few answers out of the people who knew Newport from a different angle than your Schermerhorns and Blaines and Wellings.

He thought of the flask sitting where he had placed it in the little iron safe beneath the bed, then reflected for a moment on Schermerhorn. One of your bantamweight despots, Lenox decided, king of his cottage, and no doubt of some segment of Madison Avenue, too; but Lenox had almost as little doubt that the fellow's son was guilty of a murder, and no amount of localized power could change that fact.

Having just left, O'Brian returned, heralded by the stamping sound of him taking two stairs in a swinging rhythm.

"Before I go, sir, Mrs. Berry instructed me to tell you that there's a lady waiting upon you in the lower salon."

"A lady? Who?"

"I did not ask, sir."

"I see. Please tell Mrs. Berry I shall be down directly."

"Yes, sir," said O'Brian, and went.

When he went downstairs, Lenox found Mrs. Berry sewing a quilt by her comfortable stove, from which she could survey the door of the large parlor and the foot of the stairs. She directed him to the visitors' salon. He thanked her and walked the few paces to this small room overlooking the street.

Sitting there, reading a copy of *Blackwood's*, was a woman with her back turned to the door.

"Good evening," Lenox said.

The woman turned. He recognized her, but there was a frozen

moment in which he couldn't place her, couldn't even identify what period of his life she came from.

She, however, broke into a smile of unfeigned joy at seeing him. "Charles," she said. "How long it's been. Yet how little you've changed!"

"Why—Lady Cormorant!" Lenox said, flushing with real happiness. "It has been many years since I saw you last!"

"Dreadfully many," she said, though still smiling. "Impolitely many. Yet when I heard you were here I came without delay."

"I'm so very pleased you did," he said. It was the pure truth. He took the hand she offered, bowing slightly. "You must let me offer you a cup of tea—a glass of wine, or sherry. Or anything that can be fetched. What would you like?"

"I would very happily accept a glass of wine."

"Of course."

He busied himself in finding the boy who helped Mrs. Berry, ordering a half bottle of sherry and a half bottle of hock and something to eat—anything, he responded rather wildly, when the timid lad, covered in pimples, asked what he meant. His mind was altogether elsewhere.

Kitty Ashbrook! How very strange. Once, long before, she had been the human of all those hundreds of millions on the planet with whom he was sure he would spend the rest of his days.

He returned to the front parlor, stoking the fire to brighten the room before he sat so they would be comfortable, then asked her rather inadequately how she had been.

She must be nearing fifty, he supposed, since he was, but she looked a decade or more younger. She still had the same glossy chestnut hair, elegant small shoulders, and large bright eyes, good-natured, warm, and intelligent, that she had at twenty. Indeed, there was still something youthful in her movements, the conscious grace left over from once having been the most beautiful young woman in every room she entered. Her small, pretty features had not grown pinched; instead, the lines around her mouth and eyes were, in that unmistakable way all faces take on the general disposition of their owners, kind ones, reassuring ones. Her gentle, lived-in face. It reminded Lenox a little of Edmund.

"I cannot tell you how pleased I am to see you, Lady Cormorant," said Lenox.

"You may call me Lady Cormorant, of course, but I am only a dowager, you know. Lord Cormorant died of a fever in Calcutta ten or so years ago."

"I had not heard. I'm very sorry."

She inclined her head to thank him, but added, "My second husband is an American."

"Your second husband! My sincere congratulations."

She blushed, and he felt his heart jump out to hers. "It has not been so long, in fact," she said.

"He must be a very good man."

"He is. His name is Thomas Hunter. I certainly hope you shall meet him while you are here. But Charles, how came you to be in Newport! I have seen your name in the papers over the years, and now, within hours of Miss Allingham's death, you appear. It seems like magic."

"Far from it, alas," said Lenox. "Shall we have a drink, and I can tell you what has brought me to America? I hope you are in no great rush?"

She smiled. "For you, none at all."

The wine arrived, and first they discussed the circumstances that had brought him to Newport, then those that had brought her, and then they brushed up on mutual acquaintances, some of whom neither had thought of for many a long year.

Lenox was, unaccustomedly, grateful for his glass of wine—for being with Kitty once more was an odd feeling. He could see why he had loved her. The emotions were not the same at all now, his feelings toward her ones of goodwill, of pleasure in her company.

Nevertheless, recalling those old emotions affected him. If he tried, he knew he could bring to mind every detail of the two passionate months when he had been sure that Kitty Ashbrook held his future in her hands.

He had been—what, twenty-five at the time? Around the period of the death of a young American on a train, as it happened. His first case involving the death of an American.

At the time, Lady Jane had been married, and Lenox had been under increasing pressure to make a family for himself. He had ignored this with some success, at least until he met Kitty; her quick ways, her silvery laugh, had fast won his heart.

But in the end she had chosen the dreary, arrogant Cormorant—had chosen a title, which, as Lenox could see with the benefit of hindsight, was what nearly every woman would have done, perhaps *ought* to have done, in such a perilous world for women.

Lord, though, how it had stung at the time.

The years fell away; they drank their wine and shared in the food the boy had brought. If Lady Jane could have looked into her husband's heart, she would have found nothing at all there to trouble her—but it was also the most at ease, the happiest, Lenox had been since arriving in America, a genuinely welcome surprise.

"But I am quite out," she said at last. "I had come here to invite you to a tea tomorrow—a champagne tea."

"A champagne tea! I will come if I possibly can. Where is it to be?"

"My husband's first cousin lives in one of the cottages, Greystone. We generally spend the first part of our summer season there before moving on to Cape Cod, where it is quieter. Everything grows rather repetitive in between here, as we discovered a few summers ago, and Mr. Hunter likes to work."

"May I ask, Mrs. Hunter, do you not miss England?"

"I do! Yet I think I should miss Newport, were I there. For I do like it. And then, I return once in a while and stay with my brother and his wife in Derbyshire. It's very peaceful there. Our mother lives with them. She and I write daily—though it is not the same."

"I remember her very fondly. Anyhow, forgive me, it was an impertinent question," Lenox said.

She smiled. "There can be no such thing from an old friend," she said. "Can I count on you to come, then? All of Newport will be there, if that is an enticement—there are people who would cut you to ribbons for this invitation."

"Are there?"

"Partly because Mrs. Astor may stop in, and while there have been parties here for a month, her ball, of course, is the one that will officially start the Newport season and end New York's—and there is still a day or two left in which one might receive an invitation, though I have given up hope for myself."

"Given up altogether?"

"Mostly. I like Lina, but it has become a rather cutthroat place these days, Newport, and I have lost my taste for that game."

He hesitated. "I wonder if it would be bad form to ask you about that. You see, as it happens, you are the person I most need at the moment—someone who understands the town, and whom I can trust."

She glanced at the clock. "I am due to supper at eight o'clock. Until then I am at your disposal," she said. "What would you like to know?"

CHAPTER SIXTEEN

It was around a quarter past eight when Lenox left Mrs. Berry's, half an hour or so after Kitty had departed. He had spent the intervening time nursing a last half glass of wine and making notes from the day at his desk.

He went into the streets of Newport with a lively curiosity to explore. It was dark out, but well lit. He walked briskly through the town for thirty minutes, from Bellevue Avenue to Bannister's Wharf, until at last he felt tolerably knowledgable about his new environs. A cheerful place, on the whole. The streets were narrow and roughly cobbled. Barks of laughter here and there—fishermen's taverns, he speculated. There were lanterns at some of the houses, and on the larger thoroughfares kerosene streetlamps, all of it looking no doubt much as it had been a hundred years before, during the country's rebellion against the British.

How far, and how close, from the great houses as they lay upon the sea, each containing its own complex history. According to Kitty—or rather to Catherine, Lady Cormorant, as it was her right by courtesy to be called, though perhaps here she simply went by Mrs. Hunter—the upper classes of Newport made up a tiny community, which was run as regularly as a medieval court. Carriages went out at the same hour every afternoon. Hostesses made up the same parties on the same days each week, and outside, noses pressed against the window, hundreds yearned for admission.

The most helpful part of the conversation, though, had been Kitty's description of Lily Allingham.

"They are all named after flowers here," she'd said as they sat in the parlor at Mrs. Berry's. "Lily, Daisy, Rose, Pansy, Violet."

"We have some of those in England."

"I don't know if it is quite my taste." She smiled to soften this judgment. "Yet I confess I admire the girls here very much."

"How so?"

"They don't regard themselves as second-class to the men. For one thing, they're extremely well educated. England—now that I have traveled a little, it seems terribly backward in that regard. These girls know how to ride, play piano, speak French, paint, talk history, and dance. Most of them could fix a horse's shoe in a pinch. They know how to reject a proposal and how to accept one. They know their minds."

"Interesting."

"Whereas English women—they will sacrifice anything, live upon the merest pittance, *starve* themselves, to see their brothers go to Eton or their fathers in a new hat at church. Meanwhile the brothers and fathers never think of it twice."

Lenox could have cited counterexamples, but he knew there was truth in what she said.

"And Lily Allingham was of the new type?"

"Oh, most decidedly—something even beyond it."

"Beyond it?"

Kitty looked sad for an instant. "She was so very beautiful, you know. Ah! Anyhow, yes—she knew her value."

"I understand she was to marry the fifth William Schermerhorn."

"So one heard. The old white heads had gotten together and settled it. A good match for him, a spectacular one for her. Her family is not much, though quite comfortable by standards outside of this island."

"From what I understand, his family has the money for ten such marriages."

"Yes. And for a girl as beautiful as that, a good family does almost better than a famous one."

"What is he like, the Schermerhorn son?"

"Small, indignant. Handsome."

"He sounds like his father."

"Very much. Mind you, they carry a good deal of weight here, the Schermerhorns and their various cousins.

"But listen, Charles, you are quite wrong if you think that Lily Allingham was settled to be married to Willie Schermerhorn."

Lenox looked at her curiously. "Oh?"

"There was a chance of it. But it was her first season. I would guess she had a dozen proposals. The young gentlemen in New York will propose to a girl as soon as look at her."

"That complicates matters."

"If you believe the gossip, she was also entertaining an offer from Lawrence Vanderbilt."

"Vanderbilt! Son of the famous one? Cornelius?"

Even in England nearly every living soul knew of Cornelius Vanderbilt. He had been one of the richest men in the world at the time of his death the year before, which had been front page news in London—the person responsible for half the railroad tracks in America.

"No, his nephew. The son of the Commodore's brother. Wildly, wildly rich, all of them—not in the way you and I are accustomed to, Charles, not *land*, but what they would call *cash*, money that flows out of the hand like so many kisses."

"I have seen the cottages."

She smiled ruefully. "Before you go I hope you catch a glimpse of the real heft of it—how little they think of buying five oils by

Rembrandt from some fallen duke, when the same duke's wife herself might tarry over ordering a second loaf of bread from the baker's."

It was the same story across all of Europe. The wise men in Parliament could explain it: Several bad harvests in Europe, combined with the advent of refrigeration, had annihilated the income of the great landowners in England and abroad. Earldoms a thousand years old were destitute; Polish counts were ten a penny.

One result was that the young men of these families had started marrying Americans. Another was that the Americans had started to buy up the contents of country houses full stock, libraries, tapestries, paintings, furniture—often the only things aristocrats were allowed to sell, since the land and house, even the timber, remained entailed upon future generations. The Duke of Kilcallon's own bed, built by hand in the 1200s, now sat in a financier's mansion in Utica, New York; so Lenox had read in the *New York Times* on his first day in America.

"What is Vanderbilt like?" he asked.

"The opposite of Willie Schermerhorn, as they call the son. Lawrence is tall. Not especially good-looking, but well dressed, and charming enough."

"How so?"

"You'll see." She paused. "He knows he is a Vanderbilt."

"Will he be at the tea tomorrow evening?"

"I should think so. Perhaps not, if he is in mourning for her."

"What is the opinion of Newport, then?" he asked. "Who do they think killed this poor girl?"

"Half of them don't mind who—the aunts, the old gentlemen with their cigars. They think she deserved it." Kitty had thrown up a hand, a gesture he suddenly remembered from earlier days. "Madness. But she was so strikingly beautiful, Lily, and not modest either."

"It sounds as if you knew her fairly well."

"I did. I believe I was one of the few people who liked her. She was a girl with a *mind*. I admire that above anything. At any rate, the other half of the population here is quite certain that it was either Willie, which would make the most interesting story, or else a vagrant, a townsperson. Someone from the village."

"It seems unlikely that anyone in the village would have had motivation to kill her."

"Perhaps, but everything about it seems so improbable! I still cannot quite believe it myself that she has died."

Lenox ruminated over this last observation as he walked through Newport. Finally he ducked his head into a tavern, which he discovered upon entering was the Paul Revere, a place that no less an authority than Lady Jane's little book had recommended. Over the bar was a handsomely painted mural of a man in a tricorn hat, face fierce, riding a horse at a gallop. The anachronism of the lanterns jangling from the horse's saddlebags in the painting could be forgiven. It was Paul Revere; lanterns ought to figure in somehow.

The tavern was bright and calmly noisy, occupied mostly by men of rough-spun but amiable appearance who nursed pewter mugs of beer, looking extremely comfortable as the tavern's small fire blazed against a night growing cold.

Lenox took a table with that morning's newspaper on it, ordered a chop, some potatoes, and another half bottle of wine, and polished them off in good hunger, reading as he did.

For dessert the Paul Revere offered something called "hasty pudding," according to the tall, lean barman, another laconic Yankee.

"What is hasty pudding?" Lenox asked.

"Pudding made fast, I b'lieve."

"I see."

In the event, hasty pudding proved to be a thick boiled corn flour, sweetened with a top of crusted brown sugar, and hiding in its warm depths a dozen plump raisins. Lenox ate it with enchantment. Then he paid, returned to his room, changed into his nightclothes, and tucked into his bed. A sea breeze whispered into the room from a cracked window. He had time to think—*How very far from home I am!*—and smell the lovely scent of cold water. Then he was asleep, nine dreamless hours of total absence, a pure and rejuvenating slumber after one of the longest days he could remember.

CHAPTER SEVENTEEN

I t was time to interview Schermerhorn.

Lenox slept so late that he didn't have time to query O'Brian about his scouting from the night before. He just had time to eat a piece of toast and swallow a sip of tea, and then he was on his way, in a carriage whistled up to the front door by Mrs. Berry's carbuncular boy (a grandson, it turned out), to the Cove.

Accustomed to Dallington's friendly shadow, Lenox felt a pang of compunction over proceeding without young Blaine. Still, he had told the lad that he would be leaving from Mrs. Berry's no later than nine o'clock. Likely Blaine was ensconced at home. Few people wanted to be a detective for longer than it took to see their first body, Lenox had found. Far more agreeable to sit on a train discussing crime as if it were an abstraction.

In the carriage, he studied his notes, wanting to be sure his command of the facts of the case was complete. It was a short drive, and it proved to be the old soldier Mr. James Clark—the shrapnel scars on his face limned by the weak morning light—who awaited Lenox at the grand doors of Cove Court, two heavy oak slabs with a stylized tulip carved deeply into each.

"Good morning, Mr. Lenox. Mr. Schermerhorn is in his study, if you'll follow me."

The house through which Clark led Lenox was plain by the palatial standards of this town, but sturdy to its last nail. The floors of the broad, airy hallways never once creaked; the alabaster walls, hung with portraits of sober old New Yorkers of a different epoch, seemed to whisper a quiet word of remonstration against all things modern, all things adorned, anything but plain wood and white paint.

Yet this plainness was a show. Lenox could read a house, and he knew when there were difficult choices to be made about the cost of maintenance. Here, a hundred hands were at work; the garden alone, its quiet, colorful flower beds (no topiaries, unlike many of the cottages—the more solemn Knickerbocker spirit again, he supposed) occupying half of them.

Schermerhorn's study confirmed Lenox's impression. It was the largest room he had yet seen in the house, a cavernous chamber with a view of the gardens through tall glass windows. All the latest newspapers—twenty, at least—were fanned out on a table easily twenty feet wide, along with a hundred magazines and journals from all over the world. The tulip in its field, and that family motto, *Indefessi Favente Deo*, were embroidered in an intricate tapestry on the wall. *Unwearied by the grace of God*. Well, no, it didn't seem a very wearying life. There were gentlemen's clubs in London with less polish and profusion in their lounges. It smelled like a gentleman's club, too, furniture wax and something else Lenox couldn't quite catch until he realized what it was—hair pomade.

The family patriarch, no doubt the source of this minor vanity, had risen from his desk when Lenox and Clark entered. He removed a pair of reading glasses and held them in one hand, which made him look rather like a headmaster.

"I am glad to see you at last, Mr. Lenox."

"Good morning," said Lenox, approaching the desk.

Schermerhorn waited for more—perhaps even for an apology?—but at Lenox's silence, went on. "We must discuss your fee."

"Ah, yes. I fear I must decline to take one. As I mentioned, I am in America on the Queen's business."

Schermerhorn paused. He seemed discomfited. "Certainly from the perspective of Welling and Partridge, it would be better were you in my official employ. Indeed it is why I sent for you."

Lenox bristled against the phrase *sent for you*. Perhaps he was not so immune to vanity himself. "I came because I thought I might be of some use to the local constabulary," he said. "I suppose we shall have to see whether that is the case."

Schermerhorn seemed to sense that he had struck the wrong tone. "Clark, give us a moment, would you?"

Clark nodded and left. Schermerhorn pushed a silver cigar box toward Lenox.

"Thank you, no," said the detective.

"Surely you will sit, at least?" said Schermerhorn, managing a smile.

Suddenly Lenox placed the smell that lay underneath even the pomade and the soap and polish: spirits. Gin? Whisky? It was too vanishing a scent to say, but Schermerhorn had been drinking that morning. Lenox scanned the desk and the table to its left. No sign of a glass.

"Of course—thank you."

"Can I offer you anything to eat or drink? A cup of coffee? A glass of wine?"

"I cannot drink alcohol in the morning," said Lenox, with a face that said he regretted it.

"Nor I. If I have plans to sail I take a glass of port with an egg beaten in it, but never more. We are a very enthusiastic sailing family."

They were seated across a desk from each other. "I had hoped to speak to your son," said Lenox.

"He's ready to speak to you whenever he is required. I hoped we might have a word first."

"As you please." Lenox pulled a notebook out of his pocket. "You were quick to call me here, Mr. Schermerhorn."

"Yes. It was evident right away that we needed someone from the outside."

And indeed, in the same morning light that had shown Clark's scars so clearly, Lenox saw that Schermerhorn himself was, though he concealed it well, full of agitation and concern.

"You were fond of Lily Allingham?"

"I knew her socially."

"And her parents?"

"Socially," said Schermerhorn once more, stiffly.

Lenox nodded, writing in his notebook. He didn't need it for a meeting like this one, but a notebook often had a strange effect of authority on witnesses.

"How long has your family been in Newport, Mr. Schermerhorn?"

"The Cove was built in 1822. We were one of the first families from New York to come here."

"The town must have changed a great deal since then."

"More than you could possibly understand."

"From what I understand, Lily Allingham was something of a new type?"

Schermerhorn frowned. "I suppose. She was a very sweet girl."

Clearly Schermerhorn disliked questions. Lenox knew he would gain no points for subtlety, and so, after a lingering pause, he said, "I understand she was likely to become a member of your family."

Schermerhorn stiffened, then flushed pink.

"I knew it would come to this!" he burst out. He stood up from his chair. "My son would never have touched a hair on Lily Allingham's head. It's up to you to prove it. And if you will not take money to do it, you shall do it out of honor!"

Lenox's reaction to this explosion was silence. Finally, it was Schermerhorn who broke off their mutual gaze.

"I apologize," he muttered.

Lenox glanced down at his notebook. "So you have heard that your son is a suspect."

Schermerhorn, still standing, turned away and walked toward the window. "It is the ordinary gossip," he said. "They were intimate. Willie was contemplating a proposal, you may as well know. And people are only too happy to bring up that foolishness about the yacht club last year."

Lenox knew nothing about the yacht club. "I see."

"But one knows one's children," said Schermerhorn, staring out the window. "Willie could not have murdered anyone. Let alone a woman."

"Where was he last night?"

Schermerhorn turned back to him. "That's the trouble! He followed the—he followed Miss Allingham out of the ball they were attending. She was in some sort of a temper. He has no idea what it was about. Nor did he ever find her."

"What did he do after his search?" Lenox asked.

"He came home. I wish he had returned to the ball."

"Did anyone see him come back here?"

"I don't know. He has his own keys of course."

"I imagine that in a house of this size, there are always servants about."

"Yes. They are giving their reports to Mr. Clark's people now," Schermerhorn said curtly.

"And you, Mr. Schermerhorn? Where were you last night? Not at the ball?"

"Certainly not. I was here in my study, of course. My wife is traveling. I stayed up and read."

"What did you read?"

It was a truly innocuous question—Lenox tended to ask it reflexively when anyone mentioned reading, in criminal circumstances or otherwise—but Schermerhorn stared at the question from his British guest. "You cannot possibly think I was involved in the murder."

"No," said Lenox gently.

Schermerhorn went on staring, until at last he said—after having had time to think about it? or honestly?—that he had been reading a sailing journal. He couldn't recall any of the articles— perhaps one about how far to stay off a lee shore. He'd been tired. He supposed he had gone to bed at eleven o'clock or so. No, he hadn't heard any noise; no, the servants hadn't either. They had all been informed there was a reward to be had from the head of the household for helpful information, but none yet emerged.

All Lenox knew with certainty as he listened to this was that someone was lying. He knew it as surely as he knew his own name. But he couldn't say anything about who, or why; intuition took you only so far.

"Perhaps I could meet your son," he said at last.

"Of course," said Schermerhorn, and Lenox observed the peculiar perfection of the American's clothing, the sharp crease in his collars, the perfect pleat of his jacket, as he went over and rang a silver bell.

CHAPTER EIGHTEEN

The bell fetched a servant, who fetched a servant, until at length Willie Schermerhorn strolled into the room, gave his father a tight nod, and then stood near the doorway through which he'd arrived, staring openly at Charles Lenox.

He was just as Kitty Ashbrook had described. In height he was perhaps six inches over five feet, not more, but he dressed well and carried his chin high, showing off a fine profile. He was much of a piece with his father, Lenox thought, though with fair curling hair that must have come from his mother.

They were introduced to each other.

"How do you do?" Lenox asked.

"Miss Allingham was in a group of us that had lunch on my boat the day she died. I can hardly believe she is gone." He sounded sincere. "My father tells me that you are the best detective obtainable."

Obtainable! Only the tenacity with which good manners had been instilled in him kept Lenox from saying anything. "I doubt it very much, but I am here."

"Yes, you are."

The three men filled an awkward few seconds by staring at each other. The door came to their rescue: The younger Schermerhorn had brought with him a cup of coffee, and wordlessly, two maids appeared, one to refill the coffee, the other to replace the monogrammed silver ashtray on Schermerhorn's desk with a fresh duplicate.

"I understand that you saw Miss Allingham two nights ago."

"Yes, that's correct."

"And followed her out of the ball."

Willie Schermerhorn looked at his father, then back to Lenox. "Yes."

"Did you find her?"

"No."

"Or see her from a distance, perhaps?"

"No, I didn't," he said.

"It's peculiar, then, that she was killed so close to your family's house."

"Yes, beastly odd! Listen here, whoever you may be—I didn't kill Lily."

"No?"

Willie Schermerhorn stopped his pacing and looked Lenox directly in the eye. "No. I would sooner have slit my own throat than do anything so dishonorable. I would never have harmed her. Never."

There was real passion in his voice, and his father looked satisfied. "Even if she had rejected your proposal?"

Willie Schermerhorn stopped. "Who told you she did that?" He waited for Lenox to reply without his effort being repaid. "It's a damned lie. We were engaged, as it happens. I loved her and she loved me."

This last line he delivered with less vigor than his defense of himself. Lenox wondered why—wondered if perhaps it had not been quite so settled. "Did you have plans to announce the engagement in the papers? I don't know what the custom is here, but in England such things are announced."

A look was enough to tell Lenox that it hadn't been. "Not yet."

"You don't know of anything about her and Mr. Vanderbilt?"

To Lenox's surprise, Willie gave a short laugh. "I do. I know that every—listen, did you see her?"

"See her? I did."

"She was the fairest creature on earth."

"She was very beautiful," said Lenox evenly.

"She was more than beautiful. You must know that if you are to capture her murderer. She was the prettiest girl New York has seen in a century. McCallister himself said so, and he has seen every girl since the '30s with his own two eyes. Yes, I know Vanderbilt proposed to Lily, along with every scrounger and cripple who could find his way within shouting distance of her. You do not surprise me there, Mr. Lenox."

"How many proposals?"

Willie threw a hand up, as if to say Lenox was missing the point. "Pick a number. A dozen? One or two a month since the fall, I'm sure. Men here aren't shy."

This seemed intended as a sneer at England. If it was, Lenox ignored it. "Did she wear a ring on her right hand, Miss Allingham?"

"I think so—at least, she often had some kind of jewelry on, and I remember that she sometimes wore rings. Why?"

"You don't recall a specific ring?"

Willie Schermerhorn looked puzzled. "No."

Lenox made a tick in his notebook. Though it hadn't been his intention, he didn't mind the irritation it induced in this princeling of New York. "How long had you two known each other?"

"She came out in September, and we grew close over the course of the winter. It was at a benefit for the fire department that she was graceful enough to tell me that she reciprocated my regard for her. Since then we have been planning to marry."

"Can you tell me why she left the ball two nights ago?"

"She was tired."

The father chimed in. "The start of the season is very busy here, Mr. Lenox. Miss Allingham was in an archery competition a few days ago, a pastime many of the girls here enjoy, and she would have been out every night. There was also Mrs. Astor's ball to come. The official start of the season. She and my son were scheduled to dance."

"You are attending?" Lenox said.

"Of course," Schermerhorn said off-handedly, though without managing to entirely camouflage his pride that his attendance was past doubt. "As for what my son says about their engagement, he is too reticent. I can say that I regarded Miss Allingham nearly as a daughter."

Lenox nodded gravely. "Then I am not surprised her death has so upset you."

The father nodded, looking a little happier. "Yes."

He turned back to the son. "Did Miss Allingham tell you she was leaving the party?"

"She mentioned that she wanted to walk back home. It was very busy, and I'm not certain we said an actual goodbye, in so many words. I wish we had."

"Had you argued?"

"No."

Had Willie Schermerhorn hesitated infinitesimally? Lenox would have to play the scene over in his mind later. For now, he said, "I understand Wales House is the cottage where she and her parents were staying?"

"Yes. It would only have been a ten-minute walk or so."

"And safe?" asked Lenox.

"Women regularly walk here at night."

"Alone?"

The younger Schermerhorn frowned. "Perhaps not alone. But I did not think anything of it at the time—I offered her my company, of course, but she said she was planning to catch up to a friend."

"What friend?"

"She did not say. It could have been one of half a dozen girls with whom she was close."

Or one young gentleman.

Lenox was debating whether to ask something: Why, if Lily Allingham had been headed to bed, was she found at the opposite end of the Cliff Walk from Wales House, where she was staying—here, near Cove Court.

Instead, he said, "Do you carry a flask?"

"Sometimes, certainly, like anyone. Why?"

"Did you have it two nights ago?"

"I can't remember. No—I do. I did have my flask with me."

"May I see it, please?"

The young man looked at him with a trace of haughtiness. "Why?"

"Get it, Willie," said the elder Schermerhorn.

He, at least, had cottoned on to the fact that Lenox was not here to exonerate anyone out of hand. The young man frowned, rose, and called out ("Hey, there") in a fashion that produced three people—a butler, Clark, and a footman.

"Dillon," he said, evidently addressing the butler, "fetch my gray cloak with the warm lining."

"Yes, sir."

The butler reappeared a moment later and handed over the cloak. Willie patted the pockets and produced a small flask. It was made of bright silver encased in pebbled light-brown leather. His initials, WSS, were monogrammed in the leather.

"Would you like to inspect it?"

Lenox shook his head. "No, that's quite all right. Do you have another?"

"Should I?"

"A gold one? With a ruby?"

The young man seemed to scoff at the notion. "No."

"Does it sound familiar? Do you know anyone who carries such a flask?"

"I do not."

In situations like this, Lenox's mind calculated very rapidly, discarding options one by one. For a few minutes he had been contemplating a question, and now he asked it.

"Did you kill Miss Allingham?"

Willie Schermerhorn's reaction was made up of an unsatisfying blend of confusion and anger at Lenox's effrontery. "Of course not," he spat at last.

"You know I must ask."

"Father, is Clark—listen, whoever you are—"

"If you didn't kill her, who do you think did?" Lenox asked.

Willie Schermerhorn stopped in the midst of his appeals and considered the question. "I don't know," he said at last.

Lenox studied the boy for a moment. There was something odd in the way he spoke and carried himself—a mixture of grief, Lenox thought, and bewilderment. Yet with it, also, whether it related to Lily Allingham or not, some strangely hidden triumph gleamed in Willie Schermerhorn's eyes.

CHAPTER NINETEEN

Lenox declined the offer of a carriage to take him back to town. Instead, he left Cove Court and walked straight across some five hundred yards of lawn toward the sea. Beautiful lawn—the grass springy, close shaven, a jewel-like green. When he reached the Cliff Walk, he looked down. Nothing was left but sand where the body of Lily Allingham had lain the afternoon before.

He looked south at the long range of cottages. The Schermerhorns' was the third closest to the village—Wales House (where Miss Allingham had been staying) closer to the end of the island, and Cold Farm (where the ball at which she had spent her last evening alive had been held) between here and there.

His feet turned south, and soon he was gliding down the Cliff Walk, the sea to his left, the grand houses to his right, each its own study in American taste. He passed Greystone, where Kitty Ashbrook had invited him to tea that afternoon, and which looked, indeed, as if it had been hewn from a single colossal piece of rock, a tremendous edifice loaded down with crenellations and towers, in every appearance more suited to a French knight of the twelfth century than a robber baron of the nineteenth—except that it had a telegraph wire running from its battlements.

By contrast, Cold Farm must have once been a real farm, its buildings rather modest at a glance, but with closer attention more impressive—a century or more old, but updated to modernity.

The last spot of interest that he reached on his walk was Wales House, and to some people it would have seemed the finest of the lot. It was a light-colored stone and had a row of enormous rounded windows facing the water.

Who was the owner? He must find out as soon as possible; in a sharper frame of mind, he would have asked the Schermerhorns. Still, he was less inclined than usual to think that it was someone in the victim's household who had killed her—he had seen for himself that upon leaving the ball, she could have taken a right down the strand and been back here in ten minutes, home and in bed.

Instead she had turned left, apparently, and ended up near the Cove. The decision determined her fate.

Lenox was soon nearing the headland, the water whipping up white over its boulder-strewn shore. It was a stirring sight, and he stopped and appreciated it for a moment, hands in pockets. The air was a balm, he had to admit; in London, where one could return home with skin literally darkened from the soot swirling in the air, so pure a breeze was unimaginable.

He circled the headland and turned up-island. This course took him past the lighthouse, and the wharves with their crowded masts and not altogether unpleasant smell of freshly caught fish. By the time he had made his way back to Mrs. Berry's he had compassed much of Newport—and found himself with more questions than he had had before.

The walk impressed upon him, for one thing, that Lily Allingham had died so far from home. And then, the smell of gin on her had been unmistakable. What could that mean? Had she been drinking in her last hours? Above all, he wanted to ask Kitty Ashbrook a host of things: whether women here carried flasks, for instance, whether they were truly free to walk alone at night, and who from Lily Allingham's last ball might conceivably have noticed the circumstances of her departure . . .

O'Brian was waiting for Lenox when he came back to his rooms. He looked as if he was having a hard morning—one of those enviably mild malaises the young endure after a night of drinking, which seem so unfair at the time, and in retrospect so easy.

"Good morning," said Lenox. "How did you fare?"

"Well enough, I hope, sir. I tried in at the Ducks and Drakes first, sir, which it was Mrs. Berry's grandson who said that was a locals' tavern. But it was very quiet. The chap there was Irish, though. So we fell into talking, and he told me it livened up only in the late mornings—fishermen coming in—and that I should try the Seagull. So that was where I went."

"And where is the Seagull?"

"On Thames Street, sir. Well, I went there, and explained to the bartender who I was, and asked if I could stand anybody a round—because I was devilish curious about this case my master had taken on—I explained who you were, but they all *knew* who you were, they had all been talking about it, and the long and short of it is I didn't need to buy a drink—the drinks were bought for me, and supper, too," he added triumphantly.

"Good." Lenox suspected he knew what was coming. "Did they all think Willie Schermerhorn killed her?"

O'Brian nodded. "Some of them, sir, to be sure. We talked about every possibility, sir. There were a great many rounds of ale. I lost count. But most of them don't think it was Wee Willie. As they call him, sir, not me."

"Who do they suspect, then?"

"Most of them think it was Mr. Clark, sir."

"Clark!" He had taken Clark's presence for granted—had certainly never considered him having anything to do with the young girl who had lain beneath the Cliff Walk. "Why?"

"That's what I asked, sir. They only said he was a hard horse. And raised their eyebrows. Tellingly, like, sir."

"I see."

"But I didn't leave it there! I kept asking."

"Well done," said Lenox.

"Eventually a fellow told me more. Newport fitted out a regiment for the war, he said. Clark was a sergeant-at-arms. They sent out twelve hundred men, and a little more than three hundred returned. Clark was one of them."

"Does that count against him?"

"No, sir, not at all—but he was a fearsome taskmaster, the fellow said. Violent-like, sir. Brutal in battle, and near as brutal in camp. He once shot a fellow guilty of desertion on the spot, sir."

Lenox absorbed this. It might have been an exaggeration. It might also be true. "Did anyone say he'd been violent since he's been back here from the war?"

"No, sir—only they said, if old Schermerhorn—they called him Horn—if old Horn needed dirty work done, it was sure to be Clark who did it. I asked how they knew, and they said there's all sorts of tales, sir."

"Such as?"

O'Brian thought for a moment. "The cottage next door to them—one of the fellows at the Gull worked there as a gardener for a while. He said the owner had been planning to add to the house. Architect plans all laid out, like, sir. Well—Clark went over one day, and there was a row, and the man came out painful pale, said this fellow."

"I see."

"And the construction was never mentioned again after that. Not once."

They talked for several more minutes, Lenox inquiring more closely about the specific claims. Mostly gossip, but not insignificant for that. Nobody had brought up Lawrence Vanderbilt. A handful of the people in the Seagull had seen Lily Allingham in person, O'Brian said—uncommon pretty, they agreed.

The young man tried to return the money Lenox had given him, but the detective told him to get himself lunch; he would be going out, if O'Brian could find him a carriage as soon as possible. Of course, the lad said, and sprinted downstairs, his morning head forgotten.

Unhappy though the meeting must be, Lenox had decided that he must attempt to introduce himself to Mr. and Mrs. Creighton Allingham.

Riding down Bellevue Avenue twenty minutes later, the detective reflected, a little sadly, on what both Blaine and Willie Schermerhorn had implied about the Allinghams—that they would not have had a place in Newport society but for their daughter's beauty.

Where did that leave them now?

"Do you know who owns Wales House?" he asked the man driving the carriage, a stout, grizzled old fellow with a cigar champed between his teeth.

"Vanderbilt."

"Which one?"

"The real one," said the man, apparently considering that answer enough.

Interesting to know that she had been staying at the residence of one of her suitor's relatives. "Frequent parties?"

"Not so far. The whole lot of them are in France for the spring. They'll be back by June, always are."

Lenox frowned in the back of the carriage. "So the house is empty?"

"Someone or other is usually staying there," the driver said.

Lenox withdrew his notebook from the inner pocket of his jacket and looked at the notes he had set down after his conversation with Kitty.

Lily Allingham—Wales House
Willie Schermerhorn—Cove Court
Lawrence Vanderbilt—Sea Cloud
The Ball—Cold Farm

Confusing names to have to keep straight, he thought with some irritation. "Sea Cloud is close to Wales House, isn't it?" he said to the driver.

"The next house down!" said the driver, full of his own irritation apparently, and clamped his teeth down on his pipe, as if he had said enough for his own tastes.

In the entrance hall—where he waited, having relayed his request to see the Allinghams first through a footman, then a butler—Lenox was reminded of what Kitty had said about the great cultural riches slowly making their way from the stately homes of Europe to the mansions of America. They were all in evidence here: a gilt hall table that would have stood out at Versailles, a portrait of an open-faced young soldier by Ingres, and a dozen other treasures strewn between them.

It was a queer feeling. Britain was so central to Lenox's image of the world—yet here, behind Britain's back, America had a different future in mind. Just before he'd left London, Lenox had run into the poor old Duke of Marlborough, whose line had brought enough disgrace to the name *Churchill* that many thought it could never recover its luster—they had sold van Dycks, the Churchills, diamonds practically by the yard, a perfect jewel of a library with twenty thousand books in it, the most famous Rubens in the world. Gone from England's shores forever now in all likelihood.

The splendor of the hallway was almost uncomfortable—and Lenox was secretly glad when the Vanderbilts' butler, in his starched blue livery, returned to say that the Allinghams had left for New York that morning, to see to the details of their daughter's funeral service.

CHAPTER TWENTY

It was a short walk to Sea Cloud next door, smaller than the imposing Wales House but finer to Lenox's eye, closer to an actual cottage, with perhaps as few as six or seven bedrooms—minuscule, by the standards of Newport. Like some of the whaling houses in town, it was shingled in a patchy gray, its roof unevenly and rather picturesquely discolored by salt and wind. These cadet Vanderbilts didn't do badly for themselves.

Lenox strode toward the house with his hands in his pockets, eyes straight ahead. He was deep in thought. A spectator standing at some distance might have mistaken him for a much younger man—still lean, still fluid in his motions. Someone who knew him intimately might have gone so far as to venture that perhaps it was because he was on the trail of a case; whatever physical hardiness had diminished over the years, his youthful energy stirred back to life when he was doing what he loved. Apparently that didn't change depending upon which country he was in.

When he arrived, a servant led him into a drawing room whose large windows showed a splendid view of the water.

Sitting on a divan, with a book of poems in his hand, legs crossed, was a young man. He wasn't actually reading. He was dressed in a sack coat of light tweed, with a college tie, Princeton, if Lenox was guessing correctly, and an emerald watch fob. He had a long, rangy frame, and while, as Kitty Ashbrook had said, he was not notably attractive, there was something appealingly easy in his manner and dress. The detective—in a frock coat that fell to just above his knees, such as he generally wore—felt himself rather old-fashioned by comparison.

"Lawrence Vanderbilt?" he said.

The young man rose and they shook hands. "That is I. You are Charles Lenox? I heard through the grapevine that you were investigating."

"The grapevine?"

"The rumor mill."

"I've never heard the term."

Vanderbilt had stood to shake Lenox's hand, and they faced each other. "Before my time, but during the war there was a tavern in Greenwich Village where officers met to catch up on information. Not a few Confederate spies, too. It was called the Old Grapevine."

"You sound as if you're a student of history."

Vanderbilt invited Lenox to sit. Only the watch fob and the loose jacket differentiated him from Willie Schermerhorn. Yet Lenox's eyes lingered on that emerald.

"No, I always liked reading, that's all. I've sometimes thought I might burden the world with a novel myself before my days are up."

"I am surprised you have heard I was here," said Lenox.

"Newport is not a large place. You may be assured that your presence has not gone unnoticed." His smile was wan as he said this. "Have you found anything out? I have not been able to do anything but sit and stare into space since it happened."

"I understand that you were close to Miss Allingham."

Vanderbilt laughed bitterly. "Yes, you could say that. I was going to marry her."

Lenox was quiet for just a moment. "Had you come to an agreement?"

"With our eyes."

"So you believe she felt as you did."

He turned on Lenox angrily. "I know she did, damn it." He waited for the detective to react but, met with an impassive gaze, slumped back and lit a cigarette he pulled from a chased silver box on the side table. "Excuse me. I withdraw that—that oath."

"It's all right."

"It's impossible to believe it's real, Lily being dead. Lily Allingham, dead!"

Lenox had heard people say this precise phrase so often that he had finally accepted it must be true: that when you lost someone, it genuinely seemed impossible; did not seem as if it were a part of reality that they could be gone, could be no more, could come no more at your call.

"What I heard," Lenox said gently, "was that you and Willie Schermerhorn were the suitors she favored among many candidates."

Lawrence Vanderbilt didn't reply for a moment. Then he said, "Yes, I suppose that's true. But I am quite sure I knew her mind. I am sure of it. And she had chosen me."

"Did you see her on the last night of her life?"

"Certainly. We danced."

"Did you exchange fond words?"

"Yes," said Vanderbilt shortly, as if he just barely acknowledged the validity of this intrusion into his private memories.

"Did you see her leave?"

"No. I searched for her everywhere. Then someone said she had gone, so I walked toward Wales House, hoping to catch her."

So she hadn't told Vanderbilt that she was leaving, only Willie Schermerhorn. "And you didn't find her, obviously."

"No." The young man looked miserable. "I suppose she was already up at Cove Court by then."

"Do you have any idea why she walked toward the Schermerhorn house? Did she have friends there? Or know anyone in town?"

The first edges of the town (where Lenox was staying) began not long after Cove Court, and Lenox was almost persuaded that this could have been the victim's true destination.

"I don't know. I know that she would have felt herself bound to tell Willie Schermerhorn that their understanding was over. That was my first reaction to the news. I wish she hadn't."

That was the motive Vanderbilt suspected, then: Willie's violent anger at being rejected. Lenox had thought it over; for him, the question remained why she would have walked to the Cove in the dead of night to speak to him rather than doing it at the ball. Moreover, just that morning she had gone out on Willie's yacht. It would seem they were on very close terms. Unless something had happened.

"What did you do after you couldn't find her? Return to the ball?"

"I went home. I was quite tired."

"I suppose a servant can confirm that?"

"I would imagine so. I didn't know at the time to look for an alibi. Ask Carver, though. He'll find someone who was awake and heard or saw me coming in, I'm sure."

At that moment, a young woman in a mauve dress came into the room. She was elegant, with a collected manner, and wore a loose, expensive-looking gold bracelet.

"Lawrence?" she said. "I thought I heard you call."

"No. Just a momentary—Mary, this is Charles Lenox, who is visiting Newport from London. Mr. Lenox, my sister. Mary Vanderbilt."

Both men had stood, and Lenox bowed. "How do you do?" he said.

"Very well, thank you."

She sat down next to her brother, and while Lenox would have liked to speak alone with Vanderbilt further, it was clear that she had no intention of leaving. Indeed, soon a father and a mother emerged as well, two well-dressed but rather more rugged, sun-weathered specimens. They also seemed determined to wait out Lenox, who had the distinct sense that Lawrence Vanderbilt was being encircled for his own protection.

After a prolonged and tedious exchange of courtesies, he thought he might at least try to get a last question in. "Can you tell me about young Mr. Schermerhorn's incident at the yacht club?"

Mary Vanderbilt shifted uneasily. Her parents exchanged looks. Distaste passed over Lawrence's face. "Heard about that, have you? Yes—he struck a member of the wait staff with his cane, a Negro. Shameful thing."

Lenox was taken aback. He'd had no idea the episode, mentioned as a minor annoyance by the elder Schermerhorn, had been of a violent nature.

"Why did he do that?"

"Insolence, he said."

"Was there action brought against him?"

"No."

"I'm sure he paid the man something," Mary Vanderbilt said. "I hope he did. There was no permanent injury."

"Is he a violent person in general?" Lenox asked.

"Willie?" Lawrence shook his head. "Perhaps he has something of a temper. I wouldn't have described him as violent."

"Lawrence," said his sister.

"I'm not going to exaggerate, Mary! Lily is dead. He's a vile snob, Willie, and a bully, and treats no one with respect who can't do him some kind of good turn, but I've known him all my years and I never thought he was particularly violent. It may be that I'm wrong. Maybe he killed her!"

Lenox absorbed this. "Did you ever give Miss Allingham a ring, Mr. Vanderbilt?"

"A ring? No."

"Did she wear one?"

Vanderbilt frowned. "Not any specific one that I can recall—jewelry, to be sure. Mary, do you remember?"

Lawrence's sister said that she thought usually Lily Allingham wore a gold ring, but couldn't swear to it. Lenox thanked her, then said to Lawrence, "Do you have a flask?"

"A flask? Yes. Why? What is this—a ring, a flask. What happened? Was she drinking? She barely drank, Lily. Never to excess."

"Lawrence," said his father, chidingly.

"What! It's been put about by that lout Welling that she had too many glasses of champagne and fell from the Cliff Walk. I cannot credit it."

That was interesting about Welling. Lenox waited to see if any of them would continue, then said, "At the moment I'm searching for a gold flask with a ruby in it, if you should know of such an object. No monogram."

"Oh." Lawrence paused. "I've never seen it."

"Pity," said Lenox—but he was answering automatically, for he was sure that someone had reacted when he described the flask, one of the four people in the room, and he was trying his best to discern who it had been.

He looked at them in surreptitious turn. The father had a broad mustache and a weathered, western face. The mother was of the same type, both of them contemporaries of the great Cornelius, both with at least some years' experience of life before the enormous tide of wealth had swept them here.

By contrast, Mary Vanderbilt was all polish, and Lawrence the rather flash, melancholic young cove, temperamental and entitled, that Lenox had already seen.

Next Lenox asked what Lily Allingham had been like, and this drew forth Lawrence Vanderbilt's least guarded answer. According to him, she had been brilliant, tender-hearted, poetic, thoughtful, enigmatic—and Lenox saw loaded onto the poor girl, as if she were a beast of burden, all of Lawrence Vanderbilt's dreams for what a woman should be, added now to Willie Schermerhorn's austere and calculating vision of what it would mean to his own pride to marry a generational beauty.

Through the purple clouds of Vanderbilt's answer, however, Lenox did sense some truth in the description—particularly when he said that Lily Allingham could be cutting, usually with men (she had apparently rebuffed one of the richest bachelors in New York with two simple words on the back of his letter, returned to him: *Too old*) but a moment later soft and kind.

At last Lenox ventured to ask about the flask again. But this time there were four sturdily blank faces, or at least one that went along with three looks of real ignorance.

Experience told him it was time to go. He had gleaned all he would. He thanked the family politely and went outside, where he stood for a moment and thought. Neither of the young men could account for their whereabouts at the time Lily Allingham had been murdered. Willie Schermerhorn was apparently violent; Lawrence seemed unbalanced, choleric, fitful. Either of them might be guilty. But was he overlooking a motive other than love?

CHAPTER TWENTY-ONE

There were two telegrams tucked under a wooden fastener on Lenox's door when he returned to Mrs. Berry's house. For a brief instant it took him back to Harrow, where one's demerits had been posted in the exact same fashion. He smiled, shaking his head at the distant memory, then pulled them out, tearing the first open as he went into the inner of his two rooms.

It was from Wyatt, and thus from a different version of Lenox's trip; one in which he had never heard Lily Allingham's name.

Shall I remain in Boston STOP All here still most
eager to accommodate STOP

Laying it aside—he would have to answer—Lenox stooped to the basin and gave his hands, chest, and face a thorough wash in the cool water, rinsing away the sweat and exertion of the walk back from the cottages.

Still patting himself dry, he took the second telegram to the balcony. With the experience of the morning behind him, he could make out the various houses, including Greystone, where he was due for tea in a few hours, and the Cove, where a team of gardeners stood near the cliff's edge, mowing the grass with great scythes. He studied them for a while. Could they have been sent there to search for something? That would heavily implicate someone at Cove Court. He made a note to find out their usual schedule.

The second wire was from Edmund, handed in at eleven that morning at Charing Cross.

> Detectives convicted STOP Diz very pleased STOP
> Was just in Hampden Lane STOP All happy there
> STOP Hello to the yanks STOP

Lenox smiled at the last line, then read the whole message again. So the detectives were convicted. He felt lightened, and realized he had been waiting for news about the trial. No matter how scrupulously he had arranged his testimony, it would have weighed on him if they had gone free. Six weeks of hard, dangerous work—when he thought of the bitter overnight cold he had experienced lurking around Westminster, this mild Newport day seemed like an impossible luxury.

He'd like to know if they would go to prison, but the American papers would tell him tomorrow. And no bad thing if, as Edmund said, Disraeli was pleased.

He put the telegram down and searched the row of cottages again for the gardeners at the Schermerhorn residence, shading his eyes. So, everything was safe at home; and he felt a settling of his wild impulse from a few days before to find the next ship sailing to London.

He wondered about these conflicting emotions. In his childhood and his twenties, Lenox had planned in such exquisite detail the lifetime of travels that awaited him. His work, and later his family, had curtailed those plans. It was a trade he would make again. Yet the reverence one felt for those earliest dreams of life, he thought, never died.

But did he still have that initial impulse, the yearning to see the world he had experienced so intensely during those days at Harrow, poring over maps and reading tales of other lands? Or was he merely paying allegiance to a person he had once been?

No, he thought, looking at the strange, serene lawns of Newport and the masts crowded around the island's cape: He felt it still. A thousand fine differences made this place (still farmed and fished within living memory by the native tribes, however many masterpieces and marble fountains found their way across the Atlantic), distinct in every glance from England, a thousand imperceptible novelties. It was the same way a person transported to Salzburg would be able to tell instantaneously that she was not in Liverpool, with no information beyond the place's atmosphere.

Anyhow, he was here. He was determined that it should be worth it: that he should find his mind stretched in new directions, his stock of experiences larger and more diverse when he returned. He got out of the chair, dried himself off a final time, dressed for a summer afternoon tea, and had O'Brian whistle up another carriage to take him to his first social gathering in Newport.

An hour later he was standing on the rolling lawns of Greystone, which swept like the backs of a great Cambridge college toward the sea.

"There is something irrepressible about your American," Kitty Ashbrook, standing next to him, holding a glass of champagne, observed.

"What do you mean?" asked Lenox.

She swept a hand out in front of her, as if to say *just look*.

And it was a remarkable sight. Not far off, there was an enormous table, fifty or sixty feet long, which held a feast that would have suited a royal ball better than an afternoon tea: pink-frosted shortbreads, fountains of liquid chocolate, cool sherbets and ices, pheasant and fowl and fish, elaborately carved melons, plump oranges and quinces, champagne, cakes, ale. And everything between.

When he had arrived, the mood had been sober. But Kitty was right—people had relaxed quickly, as if the bounty of the food and the spaciousness of the blue sky prevented any mourning from becoming too serious, lasting too long. American optimism, perhaps; or perhaps human nature.

"The servants are dressed as if they were at Versailles," said Lenox.

Kitty laughed. "I believe that's the first doubtful word I've seen you pass about Newport, Charles. I admire your restraint."

"Look at the poor boy by the wine." They both glanced at a fourteen-year-old in a blue jacket frogged with silver lace, who was, with quiet wrath, wrestling a huge bottle. "He looks like a Hungarian general on the eve of battle."

Kitty laughed involuntarily and covered her mouth. Lenox felt an absurd delight.

"There are some of Lily Allingham's friends, by the way," she said, nodding toward a different part of the scene. "Playing croquet."

Lenox followed her gaze. The young set were mostly involved, and as they watched, one whooped with delight. "Slightly callous, perhaps," he observed.

"Perhaps," said Kitty, looking thoughtful. "They had the war here so recently, you know. Death is quite familiar. All of them lost fathers, uncles, grandfathers, relations, family friends—quite early in life, poor souls."

In fact, the owner of the cottage, Mrs. Elijah Greer, was herself a war widow, just forty or thereabouts, which meant she must have been in her very youth when she had lost her husband at Bull Run. She mourned him still, a black silk ribbon threaded through the left sleeve of her pink dress, though she seemed lighthearted, even gay.

She was first cousin to Kitty's husband, Mr. George Hunter.

Lenox had taken an immediate liking to this gentleman—a contented, intelligent soul, good-humored, open, and friendly, but with the confident bearing of someone who had served well in the war himself. He was an accomplished jurist. The two men had political acquaintances in common from both sides of the water and had immediately fallen into an absorbing conversation.

The rest of the party was leerier of Lenox. Several people had offered stiff greetings, some making a pass at mentioning mutual connections, and he had answered politely—but in general felt no great warmth emanating from them. He wondered why.

"Which of these young people were Lily Allingham's particular friends?" Lenox said.

A string quartet had just begun to play, and a few of the group busy with croquet cut humorous steps over the lawn. Kitty was watching them. She looked very lovely, in a gold and white gown with sheer sleeves. Indeed, she was beautiful; yet for Lenox the pleasure in her company was in visiting with the person she had once been as much as in being with her now, or perhaps in resolving a minor old wound. He supposed that she felt the same way.

But her mind was elsewhere at the moment. "Lily was probably the most despised girl in Newport, unfortunately, Charles. Too beautiful. Not mild enough to be anything else," Kitty said. She held her champagne glass lightly in her ten fingertips, assessing the group. She nodded toward a young woman holding a croquet mallet. "But there is Rose Bennett. She was close to Lily."

This was a striking girl, tall and imperious, with long dark hair. "Is she engaged?"

"Not yet. She shall have no trouble. She is very beautiful, and rich enough. It is only her first season." Kitty looked at her appraisingly. "And how well she knows her own looks. You see that she has stained her lips with poppy petals, her eyelids with matchsticks—nothing conspicuous, only the few proper touches."

"There is a whole world of women's art cut off to me," Lenox replied. "I often think it must hinder me as a detective in ways I cannot even perceive."

Kitty smiled. "I shall be your partner on matters of female beauty. For the duration of this case, at least. Tell me, though, Charles, in confidence—do you have any suspicions?"

He did not. Not Willie Schermerhorn, not Lawrence Vanderbilt, not even Clark, the scarred old war veteran—for where on earth would he have come by such a flask? Easier to imagine him carrying a parasol.

"Only very vague ones," he said. After a moment of silence, he added, "I have rarely taken to anyone as much as Mr. Hunter."

Kitty's faced filled with happiness. "I am so glad when someone values him—and particularly you, an old friend."

"He is everything I should want a woman I admired to marry."

There was a long pause then. At last, Kitty said, "Perhaps, Charles, I can tell you, as someone I have known for a long time, that my second marriage is much happier than my first was. Indeed, I scarcely believe my luck when I sit down to breakfast each morning."

"I am very glad to hear it—very glad," he said earnestly.

She gestured at a new arrival toward the game of croquet. "There is the young man that Rose Bennett will likely marry, I should say. Winthrop Blaine. He arrived in Newport last night."

Lenox looked and saw a tall, handsome young man, a rose in his buttonhole. He carried himself with the indolent confidence of someone who possesses three of three parts of money, youth, and good looks.

"Is he older brother to Teddy Blaine?"

"The boy with the clubfoot? Yes, he is, exactly. But how do you know about Teddy?"

"I traveled with him here. He is interested in detection."

"Is he! Good. I know they have wondered whether anything would catch his attention. A diffident boy."

Lenox had expected young Blaine, with his owlish curiosity, to have a bit more gumption than to drop away as he had: no visit this morning, no attempt to communicate with him, and now absent from this party. Still, he understood; perhaps there was even something proper in being turned away from this profession of Lenox's.

"I've found him—"

But at that moment there was a sudden change in the party, as pronounced as if it had started raining, yet invisible, at least to the Briton. He felt it so strongly that he broke off speaking and scanned the lawn.

The cause of the interruption had not been lost on Kitty. "Caroline Astor has come," she murmured. She was gazing with unaffected interest at a small assembly near their hostess. "So she shall have the ball despite Lily's death. Let Newport begin its races."

CHAPTER TWENTY-TWO

The tenor of the party changed after the new arrival. The conversation rose a few excitable octaves in volume, fresh wine was brought off its ice and opened. A glass of pressed lemon and Madeira, with fanciful curlicues of orange peel in it, was placed in Mrs. Astor's hand. Kitty said this was known to be the drink she preferred.

"Then she had considered canceling her ball because of Miss Allingham?" Lenox asked.

"People wondered if she might. She is unpredictable."

Just then Mrs. Greer signaled with what she must have imagined was surreptitiousness that she desired Kitty's presence, and Kitty gave Lenox an apologetic look and said she would find him again shortly.

Left to his own devices, Lenox strolled toward the water, where a few partygoers had broken away into groups. The sun was beginning to set, and there were comfortable chairs, chaises, blankets, and pillows laid out here, along with maids to fetch drinks.

One of the people who had also made their way to the water was Lily Allingham's particular friend, Rose Bennett, whose artful makeup Kitty had admired. Lenox hadn't planned to speak to her until an opportunity presented itself irresistibly—she stood up, to a gale of laughter, and started with careful strides back across the lawn, such that their paths must inevitably meet.

"Miss Bennett," he said.

He watched her read him as an older, tedious gentleman, and was surprised to feel a pang in his heart—not because he wished otherwise, exactly, but because it had once no doubt been he who so badly concealed his youthful impatience. "Good evening."

"I hoped to have a brief word with you. My name is Charles Lenox."

She immediately looked him over again. "Oh! The detective?"

"Yes," he said.

"Of course. But could you walk with me back toward the party? My mother will be desperate to know where I've gone."

"By all means," said Lenox.

He offered her his arm, and they moved at a stately pace back toward Greystone and the noise of the tea.

"Have you found anything out about Lily?" she said.

Her voice was calm. But Lenox was seasoned enough to recognize the grief in it—greater than Lawrence Vanderbilt's, he suspected.

"I hope I shall. Not yet. You might help me."

"I should be very happy if I could."

"Were you at the ball at Cold Farm?" he asked.

"Indeed I was."

"How did Lily seem?"

"Very gay, until the middle—after that, though, preoccupied."

"Did she tell you why?"

"No. I wish she had." At that moment, one of her high heels gave way slightly into the turf, and she gripped Lenox's arm, righting herself. "These shoes are seven kinds of hell," she muttered.

Lenox smiled. He had never heard an English girl of Rose Bennett's age swear an oath so unabashedly. Kitty Ashbrook's comparison came back to mind.

"Do you think she was more likely to marry Willie Schermer-horn or Lawrence Vanderbilt, Miss Bennett?"

She thought, studying the ground now as she trod carefully across it. "Probably Willie, in the end," she said.

"But she hadn't decided?"

"No. To be honest, I think she would have liked it best if some-one else had swept onto the scene. A prince, or a count, or even a scoundrel. Someone *interesting*. Neither of them was her perfect dream of a man."

"Was there ever a third candidate?"

"No. She would have told me. She wanted to be in love so badly, Lily. She came close with Lawrence, I think. He is very charming."

"What about Mr. Blaine?" Lenox asked.

"Winthrop!" She laughed. "No. Only men who have something to prove loved Lily. It comes from being so beautiful. Winthrop could barely abide her."

Lenox frowned. "That sounds uncharitable in him."

"Only honest. I've told him many times that she's different, pri-vately. And she is. She was."

Rose looked crestfallen as she said this, having talked herself there in just a few sentences. The naked emotion of the young. "Do you know if anyone ever threatened her?" asked Lenox.

"Certainly not that I know," said the young woman. She stopped. They were close enough to the party—to the flagstone terrace—that she evidently meant for them to part ways. "Is there a suspect?"

"There are a few. Do you have any?"

She looked somewhere over his shoulder. At last, she said, "I don't know. I've been thinking of nothing else since it happened, and truly I don't know."

He took a chance. "So you don't think either Willie or Lawrence capable of it?"

"I don't."

"Of course, they are your friends," said Lenox.

She scoffed. "Willie and Lawrence? Hardly—or I should say, yes, they are, but that would hardly stand in the way if I thought one of them had killed my *closest* friend. My best friend. I suppose Willie, in the right mood—he can be so proud—but even he—no, I don't think either of them can have done it, Mr. Lenox. When I imagine her left alone on that shore all night, my heart . . . I fear it must be a madman. I almost hope it is."

"Has there been any rumor of that kind of person about? Who would it be?"

She shrugged. "Someone from the village, I suppose, or a passing visitor. Or, who knows, one of us here."

"Mm."

"Certainly none of the girls will be walking home from Mrs. Astor's. Those of us who are invited." She gave him a frank, apologetic look, which seemed to conclude their conversation. "Was there anything else?"

"Yes—by chance, do you know of anyone who carries a gold flask with a ruby in the center? No monogram."

"Of course," she said, to Lenox's sincere surprise. "I would know the description anywhere. Lawrence Vanderbilt got it at his eighteenth birthday from his uncle, the Commodore."

Cornelius Vanderbilt: the original titan. "I see."

"Why? Is it missing?"

"Not that I know of. Only clearing up loose ends," said Lenox, with, he hoped, a tolerable impression of indifference.

"Good afternoon, Mr. Lenox. I would be happy to answer more questions about Lily some other time if you like. She deserved better." She squinted away toward her friends by the water. "I do not think I shall be the same again."

They parted then, with amicable words, and Lenox returned to the party.

It went on and on, the tea, a tea that lasted from four into the golden hour when the sun was spread low across the water. If it had been a success before, Mrs. Astor's presence made it a triumph, and it was with a tone of regret that Kitty told Lenox everyone would be scattering off toward eight o'clock suppers soon. She wished she could invite him—should have thought of it, but the notice for her husband's cousin might prove too late now.

"Don't think twice about it, please," said Lenox, who had finally taken a single glass of wine. He wanted to eat at the Paul Revere tavern again anyhow—maybe the Seagull—and write a few letters home. "But I wonder if you could answer two questions for me before I go. It might help."

"Of course."

"Do young women drink gin here?"

She shook her head firmly. "No."

"None at all?"

"No. Although every woman has it in her bedroom—it is the only thing that will bring a stain out of lace, gin."

"Is it!"

"Yes, the cheaper the better, with coffee grounds."

This fact stopped Lenox, who recalled that Lily Allingham had been wearing lace. Had he seen a stain on her dress? He didn't think so. But he might have missed it. "Thank you. Here is my other question: Would a young woman ever carry a flask? A small, pretty one, perhaps?"

There was a bark of laughter from the croquet game, and they both looked over. It was Winthrop Blaine—lording a cricket mallet away from a young woman Lenox didn't recognize, who was reaching for it with something between a laugh and embarrassment on her face, her voluminous skirt gathered in one hand.

"Never," said Kitty, and her tone was so decided that Lenox did not feel the need to press the question further.

They parted again soon thereafter, Kitty being obliged to speak to a very grand woman of seventy-five or so, with wisps of white hair emerging from a black bonnet and a countenance so severe she could have been a judge in chancery. But there was one last surprise remaining at this (from Lenox's perspective) extremely interesting gathering. Just as he was thanking Mrs. Greer for inviting him to attend, he heard a hush behind him, and realized, after a fraction of a moment, that Mrs. Astor was standing there.

Of the people present only Lenox remained unaffected—which was for the best, because he was able to answer, without fainting dead away, when she asked if it could be possible that he was husband to Lady *Jane* Lenox, and, after answering in the affirmative, find himself replying—to the open astonishment of all those around him, an emotion that would soon be supplanted by envy, he sensed—that yes, of course, he would be more than happy to come to a ball on Saturday evening.

CHAPTER TWENTY-THREE

Lenox must have been one of the only guests to leave the tea at Greystone by foot, for he had the pretty, cypress-lined Bellevue Avenue to himself when he departed. Indeed few people seemed to walk here, a town of carriages.

He made his way in the direction of the small western side of Newport. It was modest, but pleasant, housing a variety of shanties, shacks, and lean-tos, some with energetic vegetable gardens and chicken coops, others with that indefinable air of want that means poverty in every nation.

As he went, only one question occupied his thoughts. Did he think Lawrence Vanderbilt was a murderer?

This was what Lenox contemplated as he wound his way up through the streets by the wharf, keeping his bearings by the night's young moon. It was a far cry from Greystone. The smells were strong and various, hearty stews slowly cooking over fires, water running across dirt and stone, and above all the sea, sometimes fresh and clean and sometimes fishy and brackish, depending upon the wind.

Almost every house had some collection of fishing poles and baskets crowded together near their front doors. He nodded at the men gathered in the alleyways, who stood in what he had come to think of as a peculiarly American way: one hand in the pocket of their rough linen trousers, the other with a cigarette; an intimate posture. A few women were outside, too, most engaged in some task—pumping water, hanging clothes to dry, lighting lamps.

It had cooled considerably, and he was glad to stop in at the Paul Revere, which was warm and comfortable, with flickering lamps in its windows and the smell of pipe smoke. He took a table and ate a resplendent meal: roast duck seasoned with onions and carrots, and piled in snug around it baked beans, apple preserves, common crackers, and on the side a slice of cold pumpkin pie.

He leafed through a copy of an old *Harper's* as he ate, mostly full of inside jokes about American politics that he couldn't quite understand, though some he did. The tone was democratic, humorous. His attention was eventually drawn away from it by the pumpkin pie, since it was his first encounter with this comestible, and a very pleasant one. When, thoroughly satisfied, he finished, the saloon keeper came to take his plate and brought him a glass of plum brandy—"on the house, for the British detective."

By the time Lenox left the tavern it must have been close to ten o'clock. The temperature had dipped further still, a taut sea breeze putting some red into the cheeks of passersby. It was nice to see Mrs. Berry's house hove into view, broad and white, with its trim garden. He was tired. He went in, greeted the girl who sat up in the front parlor by night, and asked her to send O'Brian up from the servants' quarters with coffee.

But before he could ascend the staircase himself, a figure emerged from the visitor's parlor. It was Teddy Blaine.

"Blaine! Hello—how are you?" said Lenox.

The young man flushed. He was holding a piece of paper. "Fine, thank you," he said. "Very well. I hope I have not presumed by visiting so late. I have been here some time. I thought you might like to see this."

He took the sheet. "What is it?" he asked.

"A schedule. I spent the day reconstructing Miss Allingham's last hours. I knew enough people at the ball to form what I hope is an accurate picture."

"But this is invaluable!" cried Lenox. "Thank you, Blaine—thank you very much. I had been planning to try to find out as much as I could about her movements tomorrow. You have saved me a whole day."

Blaine's face filled with pleasure. "I fear it may be less helpful than you would have hoped—but I am sure it is accurate, quite sure."

Lenox invited Blaine to sit. "I confess I had wondered if you might have lost your appetite for the art of detection," he said, smiling to soften the words. "I had thought to see you at Greystone."

"Oh! No, not I. I didn't wish to burden you with my presence before I had something to offer."

There was such a painful shyness in these words that Lenox felt a brief guilt. But the schedule was of much greater immediate import, and he read it carefully to himself.

Activities of Miss Lily Allingham, March 13, 1878, Newport

12:00–3:00 p.m. *Lunch aboard the cruising yacht Persephone, belonging to Mr. William Schermerhorn III, upon invitation of his son, Willie, with a party of nine. Subject in high spirits.*

3:00–6:00 p.m. *Rest and preparations at Wales House; Constance Sanders, hairdresser from New York, present throughout (confirmed by wire).*

6:00–8:30 p.m. *Preparations with Miss Rose Bennett, Miss Freya Box, at Cold Farm (cottage belonging to Miss*

Box's family; site of ball). *Several maids present continually. Miss Allingham's behavior unremarkable throughout.*

8:30–9:00 p.m. *Entrance to ball; greeting of hosts; meeting with friends. Numerous witnesses. Miss Allingham still "in happy mood" (Miss Freya Box).*

9:00–11:30 p.m. *Dancing, as follows:*
   1. **Grand March:** William Schermerhorn IV
   2. **Quadrille:** William Schermerhorn IV
   3. **Polka:** William Schermerhorn IV
   4. **Les Lanciers:** Col. Peyton Walker
   5. **Quadrille:** Break for refreshments, seated with Miss Bennett and Miss Box
   6. **Racquet:** Lawrence Vanderbilt
   7. **German:** Lawrence Vanderbilt
INTERMISSION: *Seen departing through kitchen doors; subsequent whereabouts unclear for roughly thirty minutes*
   8. **Les Lanciers:** Absent, whereabouts unknown
   9. **Waltz:** Absent, whereabouts unknown
   10. **Quadrille:** Lawrence Vanderbilt (Miss Allingham described after re-entrance as "distracted," "distant," by friends)
   11. **Sally Waters:** William Schermerhorn IV
   12: **Les Lanciers:** Pledged to William Schermerhorn IV; absent, whereabouts unknown
   13–15: Absent, whereabouts unknown; Mr. Schermerhorn IV dances 14 and 15 with Miss Rose Bennett. Mr. Vanderbilt sits to side with small party, including his sister and two friends. Mr. Vanderbilt described as "inebriated." Mr. Schermerhorn IV as "tight" but "steady."

Post-dance: *Both Schermerhorn and Vanderbilt depart immediately, Schermerhorn on foot, Vanderbilt in carriage.*

4:00 a.m. *Body of Miss Allingham discovered by fishing crew (Messrs. White, Crawley, Tyburn, all local men regularly trawling at this hour along the shore near the Cliff Walk, with confirmed whereabouts the night before).*

"This is first-rate work," Lenox said when he had finished reading. "What time was the eleventh dance—the time of her disappearance?"

"Roughly 11:15. The dancing concluded at midnight."

"Did anyone see her go?"

Blaine shook his head ruefully. "There's a great shuffle between dances—no doubt you are familiar—refreshments, finding new partners. She must have left then. But nobody seems to have seen her actually go."

Lenox thought for a moment. "Did her friends elaborate on her being—let me see—distracted, or distant, as you put here?"

"No," said Blaine. "She didn't seem afraid at all. I asked. But she was preoccupied, perhaps even angry."

Lenox had a a new idea percolating in his mind. "Would it have been natural to leave the ball through the kitchen?"

"No. I had hoped to draw your attention to that, in fact. She would have had to cross the lawn—the large kitchen at Cold Farm is in a separate building. The grass alley between them is where people go to cool off when the Box family has a ball, just outside a pair of French doors. Occasionally there is a proposal there. I would have suspected that, but someone happened to spot her going from the ball through to the stone kitchen house."

"Certainly at the beginning of the night Mr. Schermerhorn seems to have been the favorite. And she danced with him last."

"Yes."

Lenox frowned. "Who is Colonel Peyton Walker?"

"An older gentleman—quite out of the running, a gallant of the war era, a Union colonel. He likes to show a leg with the new girls."

"So he danced with others."

Blaine nodded. "He never misses a single dance, even for refreshment. Famous for it. Hasn't for decades. No chance of his being involved in the murder, I shouldn't think."

"What happened during the intermission?" asked Lenox—but asked the question more of himself than of the young heir, in his round black glasses, intent and serious.

Blaine shook his head. "I tried to find out in the kitchen and couldn't. But much of the staff had the day off."

"We might try again tomorrow," said Lenox.

"Certainly."

Lenox sat back. He was still full, but his mind had sharpened; the coffee (which O'Brian had brought in with a polite nod) clearing away any last haze, the low fire filling him with energy rather than tiredness. Once Blaine had gone, he would stay up late, writing notes about the case. It was often like this when he was closing in on a solution.

"Tell me honestly, Blaine—do you think Lawrence Vanderbilt could have killed her?" asked Lenox.

Blaine hesitated for just an instant. "No," he said.

"Do you say that as his acquaintance, or as a detective?"

"As his acquaintance. I should hardly like to call myself a detective, I have so little experience."

"And what makes you think not?"

"She brought no particularly splendid dowry with her, Lily Allingham," said Blaine thoughtfully. "Vanderbilt likes nice things, and he is only fairly well-off, you know. The Commodore left them full fine, but not devil-may-care. Do you know what I mean?"

Lenox could have named fifty men in London it would have described exactly. "I do."

"I can see Vanderbilt being disappointed she chose Willie, in other words, but not murderous over it. His second pick would be someone like—well, for instance, Miss Bennett or Miss Box would both marry him, I suppose, or any of a dozen other women much richer than Lily Allingham. A Vanderbilt, after all. And women have always found Lawrence attractive."

Blaine paused, and the silence filled with the sound of both men thinking. For Lenox's part, the scenario seemed suddenly all too terribly clear: Lily Allingham had chosen Schermerhorn, and Vanderbilt, "inebriated," and, as the meeting that afternoon had shown him, highly emotional—entitled too—had chased her up the Cliff Walk toward her future husband's cottage, remonstrated with her, and then struck her, either with the flask, on purpose, or while holding the flask from which he had been drinking to console his wounded feelings. In fact it might easily not have been intentional that he killed her.

But then the picture of Lily Allingham's wound, her fallen body, returned to Lenox with tremendous force. Someone had *murdered* that young woman, extinguished her life. And afterward, as far as anyone could tell, rolled her body off the cliff like nothing more than a bale of grass cuttings.

CHAPTER TWENTY-FOUR

I asked O'Brian earlier if he remembered Ireland. "Only being hungry," he said. I told him that was no good and he smiled. "I remember being hungry here, too," he answered, perfectly at ease with the reply. Of course, there are such stories within a stone's throw of King's Cross, but the hedonism in Newport sets a strange backdrop to this one. Today I learned that there is a pair of mating giraffes at Windward Cry, which is the Compton cottage. At Mrs. Astor's house (as I suppose, thanks to you, I shall see for myself on Saturday, if this business is not resolved by then) there is not just hot and cold running water, apparently, but a third tap—salt water.

I wish I could convey with more than these paltry lines, Jane, how much I miss you and the girls.

Lenox paused and looked up. It was late, after midnight, a moonless evening. The air was cool and heavy at once, alien to Lenox in a way that was not unpleasant, or uninteresting. According to Mrs. Berry, who spoke with the irrefutable certainty of one who had passed her life among mariners, there was a heavy storm on the way. Lenox wouldn't have known; his steward on the ship had carefully packed away McConnell's barometer, with the air of a man handling something whose owner was annoyingly oblivious to its fineness, and it still sat in his trunk.

He was outside on his balcony, writing home by candlelight. He had spent most of the evening writing out copious notes for himself about the Allingham case. He was satisfied that he had enough information to solve it, though tomorrow would bring the real challenge: speaking to Lawrence Vanderbilt about his flask. The murder weapon.

Pen still hovering above the paper, he once again gazed at the cottages. Cove Court closest by. Why did the opulence here bother him? Why shouldn't a fur trader from a tenement in New York have as much wealth at his disposal as the Duke of Westminster, if either were to have such an outrageous allotment of the world's material goods?

Perhaps because here he saw with new eyes. If there was one good quality that Lenox would have admitted to possessing in a greater preponderance than most people he knew, even his brother, it was a sense of fairness. He was in no fashion above the common sins of life—deception, vanity, jealousy. But somewhere deep in his soul he had always hated the idea of unfairness. Perhaps it was starting life as a second son. Perhaps not. As to whether it was the cause or an effect of his career, he had no idea, but knew that this bitter indignation had driven him as hard as his own ambition or curiosity, on certain seemingly hopeless cases, to discover the truth.

> I still cannot quite fathom Clara, with her curious eyes, and
> if I do not regret coming to America, I do regret the loss of
> these weeks with her (our miracle child!) and keenly feel the
> anticipation of returning to you all, and seeing once again the
> careful way Sophia holds her. On my last night in London

Again he paused, and he realized he was losing his stream of thought. He would have to finish the letter in the morning. He folded it carefully and tucked it into his inner jacket pocket just as a misting rain started to fall.

He curled the blanket over his shoulders a little more tightly but didn't make any effort to move. (He was an Englishman, after all—what was rain!) In the distance, the sparkling lights of the cottages entertaining that evening reflected a long ways out over the water, shifting in its black glossy surface.

He was picturing that last visit to the nursery before he had left England. Sophia, dressed for bed, had sprinted up to her father when he came to the door. She was six now, boundless in energy, her hair looped in braids so that it would stay kempt while she slept. For his part, he liked when it fell loose and wavy, matching her laughing ways and easy confidence. But Lady Jane scorned the style—said Julia Cameron wasn't welcome to make pictures in her drawing room.

"How is your sister?" Lenox had asked Sophia after embracing her, as she found a comfortable position into which she could curl herself next to him on the settee.

"Will you read me the story of the wolf?" she'd said.

"Miss Huntington can do that," Lady Jane had said.

This was the governess, a sweet, fair young woman of good family, with a soft way about her, deeply unworldly. Jane had been with her on the other side of the room, looking into Clara's crib. There was much left to do before they departed for Plymouth in the morning.

"But wolves aren't *real*," Sophia had whispered to her father, eyes large and serious.

"Wolves are real, but the stories about them aren't," he replied.

"What do you mean?"

"There are wolves, but they can't talk, and they wouldn't hurt you. They would be afraid of you."

"Of *me*?" she said.

He stroked her hair. "Of you," he said.

She contemplated this, nestled next to him. He allowed her the silence, as he always tried to do. Having children had recalled to his mind something forgotten—the weight words held, how a stray sentence from a father or mother could occasionally stay with a child forever, like wax taking an impression. It called for great care.

"What about Clara?" she said. "Would they be scared of her?"

He considered this. "No, I suppose not. But there are no wolves in London," he said, "and as for the country—she is never alone there. Anyhow, she'll be bigger soon."

Sophia thought this over. "I could stay with her."

Lenox looked across the room. Clara looked in no danger of being neglected. Indeed, her governess and mother were presently engaged in an intense conversation about whether she was fat enough.

He had never expected a second child. Sophia had been gift enough—all of heaven in one small human, everything in which he ever needed to believe, he felt. The rightful possessor of every good part of himself. He almost hesitated to concentrate too closely on Clara, by contrast, as if the bounty was so great that he might jeopardize it by claiming possession.

Wolves of all kinds, lurking about.

"She would certainly be safe with you."

"Did Uncle Edmund ever see a wolf?" Sophia had asked.

"Uncle Edmund!" Lenox had said incredulously. "Your father is worth ten of Uncle Edmund at seeing wolves—I saw them by the dozen while Uncle Edmund was sneaking jam roly-poly from the kitchen."

"Did he really?" said Sophia, diverted by the thought of such wickedness.

"He did, too. But I suppose he probably sets eyes on a wolf once in a while." Edmund was, to Sophia, everything to do with the country and its mysterious ways. "If you're curious, we can certainly see a fox when we visit this summer. Maybe a wolf, if Mr. Morton knows where they are."

That was his brother's gamekeeper. She turned her head slightly—not sacrificing her comfortable position. "You haven't either seen a wolf," she said.

"Don't be rude to your father," Lady Jane had said without turning.

Sophia looked up at Lenox. She had crinkly blue-green eyes, and cheeks with just a trace of baby fat left in them. "I didn't mean to be, Father."

"I know, darling," he said. "But you must remember your manners."

"And never speak at table."

He smiled. Her subterfuge was not subtle. It was her great wish to sit at supper with her parents, but she was not allowed. In various ways (like this one) she had tried to manufacture permission for herself, thus far without success.

"When the time comes, no. That's right. Shall we go look at your sister?"

"No."

"Why not? I haven't seen her today."

"I saw her *all* day."

"Not during your lessons," said Charles.

"Oh, fine."

She squirmed off his lap and ran to Lady Jane. Lenox followed. He peered into the crib—farthest back of the four people doing so—and his soul gave its usual little leap at the warm little personage he saw, the thin skin of her sleeping eyelids. The curl of her hands. Her dark, wispy hair. She looked so different than Sophia had as a baby. That had surprised him most.

"May I hold her before we go?" he said.

"Perhaps for a moment," said Lady Jane. "Miss Huntington, what do you think?"

"Of course," said the nursemaid.

He took the baby in her soft eiderdown quilt. She shifted a bit, then settled into his arms. It was a strange, stirring feeling to look into the face of an infant; it erased the world. Any emotion other than love seemed an absurdity.

Recalling this, on his little balcony in Newport, he suddenly made a private vow: that when he traveled again, if he was ever allowed the chance, it would be with all three of them, Lady Jane, Sophia, and Clara. Never mind that it would slow him down.

He tried to hold them in his mind as he went inside, brushed the slight dampness from himself, and changed for bed. But the human mind wasn't built for so prolonged a meditation; and as he fell gratefully into bed and drifted toward sleep, some detail about the dance card, something strange, kept playing over in his mind, never quite within his reach, but close, close.

CHAPTER TWENTY-FIVE

Young Teddy Blaine seemed to take it as a given that his hard work reconstructing Lily Allingham's last night alive had earned him a spot at Lenox's side in the next day's investigation. Nor was he wrong. Early in the morning, the pair set out to make their inquiries at Cold Farm, the cottage where the fatal ball had been held.

"Why is it called Cold Farm?" asked Lenox as they rode down Bellevue Avenue. They were in Blaine's carriage.

"It's one of the older houses on the island. Its first owner was a Welshman named Ceald last century, but over time people started saying Cold Farm instead of Ceald Farm. Some people here still say it the old way. And there's a Ceald, Gerald Ceald, who has a house up-island. But it has been out of that family since at least the war in 1812, probably longer."

"Whose house is it now?"

"The Chambers family. She is a Box. They are from Portsmouth, New Hampshire—in shipping, I believe, very profitably. They bought it over the winter. It was what people called a white elephant, drafty, hard to heat, small rooms, but then, there are not so many cottages in Newport that one can ever go very long without finding a buyer, not now. They will renovate it before long, I suppose. In the meanwhile it has a very fine ballroom."

Lenox thought of the present the Kings of Siam had traditionally given to courtiers who annoyed them: the rare albino, or white, elephants, impossibly valuable, ruinously expensive to care for. But, perhaps influenced by Dallington's reaction to the backlog, he decided this wasn't the moment to mention it.

"How did the Allinghams come to be staying at Wales House?"

Blaine thought, hands on the black walking stick with its silver ring that he carried, at the moment clasped snug between his knees. "The Vanderbilts are always gathering people. Royals, actors. I would guess that Lawrence Vanderbilt asked if she might stay there."

"I wonder if, should that be the case, whether Lawrence Vanderbilt might have felt Lily Allingham was beholden to him."

Blaine considered this and said that he thought that sounded more like Schermerhorn somehow, really, which Lenox thought an astute observation. On the other hand, very young men accustomed to all their wishes being granted could be unpredictable; more than that, were one of the great lurking threats in the world, in Lenox's experience.

They were now passing the long row of cottages between the town and Cold Farm, each busy with deliveries, gardeners, and titivation, each a small universe. This was the world into which Lily Allingham had been poised to gain permanent entry, Lenox thought. It would certainly be an intoxicating one to many people.

At Cold Farm, a startled footman said, "Mr. Blaine—is there some—did you forget—"

"Good morning. We hoped to speak to anyone who was working in the kitchen on the night of the ball," said Teddy.

He had an authority in his voice that could only be assumed so effortlessly, indeed unwittingly, Lenox thought, through years and years of unconscious practice. The footman registered it. He went straight inside to check, and Lenox and Blaine sat down on a picturesque little wooden bench outside the front door and waited.

"I spoke to a young woman named Rose Bennett. She did not think either young suitor could have killed Lily Allingham."

"I don't suppose I do either," Blaine said after a moment. "I think Vanderbilt would confess, actually. I don't know about Willie. I think he might run."

"Run?"

"Yes, perhaps the islands around Florida, or California. He has always loved long cruises. He is more passionately in love with his boat than I imagine he ever was with Lily Allingham."

"So you think Willie more likely."

Blaine shook his head slightly, as if he were troubled. "Not . . . well, yes, more likely, I suppose, but that's not the same as *likely*. Its happening at Cove Court is the only thing . . . but having known him so long, I don't think he could have."

"It might have been an accident," said Lenox.

"If it was an accident, I think he might kill himself, knowing Willie."

Lenox raised his eyebrows. "Goodness. Why?"

"He has very rigid ideas of honor and duty. So do his mother and father."

"I'm glad you're such a close student of your subjects."

"I don't know that I am. I have been around them all my life, that's all."

The footman reappeared and led them with great courtesy to a small stone building that was set about fifty or sixty yards east of the main house. There was a direct path between it and the French doors of the ballroom, and the footman pointed out the marks in the grass where the temporary tented walkway between the two buildings had been built for Saturday night, so that guests didn't have to see food and drink coming from the kitchen. Lenox remarked that it was an odd house, and the footman said that all houses in Newport had been built this way before 1830 or so, because the kitchens had to be cooler. It was a custom brought up to Rhode Island from the south, he added.

A woman in a blue dress and a much-stained white apron took custody of them as the footman withdrew. Her name was Mrs. King. She was about seventy, with fair hair and a friendly face.

"Good morning," she said cheerfully.

Evidently she'd been told or knew who Blaine was, for it was he she looked at, and it was he who spoke. "We are looking into the death of Miss Allingham."

"Dear me," she said, shaking her head. "The saddest thing."

"Did you see her Saturday night?" Lenox asked.

"Yes, I did. I told Welling all about it." She pointed at the stone kitchen house. "There's a secret hedgerow behind the cook's lodge. She was there."

"A secret hedgerow!" said Lenox, his mind filling with gothic possibilities.

She smiled, and two youthful dimples formed in her cheeks. "Not much of a secret—I suppose half the young men in Newport had their first kiss there. Isn't it so, Mr. Blaine?"

No servant in England would have spoken so familiarly (or called the mayor of the town "Welling" that casually) and Lenox felt for Teddy Blaine, who reddened and said that he was sure it was true, yes.

Mrs. King continued. "Very pretty little place to sit. I go out there myself once in a way, if I ever need a moment. Which you do in this job!"

"How do you get there?"

"The only way is through the kitchen."

"Did you see what Miss Allingham was doing there?" Lenox asked. "Who was she with?"

"Nothing like *that*!" said Mrs. King vehemently, as if it had been Lenox, and not she, who mentioned kissing. "She shared a glass of gin with one of the girls who happened to be on a break. Sweet of her, the dear. I think she must have just needed a rest from the goings-on. Oh, how I hate to think of her being dead only a bit later! And just so close, too. It shivers me, it does."

The gin. "When was this?" Lenox asked.

"During the intermission in the dancing," said Mrs. King immediately. "I know because we had to bring in the new punch bowl then. It took four of our young boys to carry it. A piece of ice the size of a hedgehog to keep it cool."

"Was she there the whole intermission?"

"A good part of it. You know how girls are. She fell into chatting."

Lenox had taken his notebook. "I would like to speak with the young woman she was with, if possible."

"Maryanne Morris? You would have to wait till Mr. Chambers's shooting party next week. She's one of the temporaries. Comes in for events only—does the same at other houses. Works most weekends somewhere or other. Very reliable girl."

"How old?"

"Maryanne? I've known her these ten years, so I suppose she must be onto twenty-five by now. The prettiest thing, such a delicate little mouse."

"Too delicate to work full-time?"

"Maryanne? No! I would hire her full-time in a jiff, she looks so tidy in the uniform, only she takes care of her father four days of the week. He was a whaler. Swaps with her sister, a married woman—very respectable—when she has to work."

"How did Miss Allingham seem to you?" said Blaine.

"I scarcely saw her for a moment, but gay enough." Mrs. King sighed. "Now Maryanne is pretty, but Lily Allingham! One of the loveliest faces I can remember seeing my whole life long, that girl had, and she was ever so sweet to the servants. It's the pity of the world."

They went through a few more questions, until Lenox asked the question upon which he was always forced to fall back when he was at a loss. "Is there anything else unusual you remember from Saturday?"

Mrs. King shook her head stoutly. "No. I wish I did."

"No, not at all. Thank you for your time," said Lenox.

"If you think of anything at all, you need only send word for me," added Blaine.

"Of course, sir."

The two men bade goodbye to this estimable woman and walked back along the house's drive, which was laid with crushed white clamshells.

"How long a walk would you say it is from here to the Schermerhorn house?" Lenox asked Blaine.

"The Cove?" They both glanced to their right, where the water lay, ragged with white frills. This was just where Lily Allingham had first ventured up the Cliff Walk on Saturday night. "Ten minutes perhaps? It is only seven or eight cottages."

He had grown unaccountably tense—and then Lenox remembered his foot. Such a walk would take him longer than ten minutes, of course.

"Yes, I thought the same," he said. "Very well. Now for Lawrence Vanderbilt."

CHAPTER TWENTY-SIX

As they drove the short distance to Sea Cloud, Lenox measured the time in his mind. Could Vanderbilt have run up to the Cove and murdered Lily Allingham, then come back to Sea Cloud soon enough to be noticed returning "early" from the ball?

He decided it was possible. Newport was tiny, a tiny village full of enormous spaces, a strange combination. Lenox wondered if this was to be the way of the future, and some city in England was soon going to be marked out as the playground of the very rich, parceled out into monstrously large houses extremely close together. The only thing he felt sure of in his countrymen was that if it happened, it wouldn't be by the sea.

As they were approaching Sea Cloud, Blaine said, "Blast it—I have just seen the time. I promised my father I would call upon him this morning in his office. Could I meet you again in an hour?"

"Of course."

"I'm very sorry—only—"

"Don't mention it."

They decided to meet at the mayor's office in town in an hour and a half. Blaine said he would send around a spare carriage to wait for Lenox—who almost declined the offer out of pure instinct but then reconsidered. They were getting closer to the truth. He didn't want to miss out on a chance because he was on foot.

"Why the mayor's office, out of curiosity?" asked Blaine as Lenox was getting out.

"In case I've arrested Lawrence Vanderbilt," Lenox replied.

Blaine looked shocked. "You can't really intend—do you think—"

Lenox merely gave Blaine a look, as if to say he didn't know; and shut the carriage door.

If this branch of Vanderbilts had been on edge last time, they seemed calmer now. Or at least, Lawrence and Mary did, greeting Lenox once more in the sitting room facing the water. Of course, they didn't know what Rose Bennett had told him about the flask.

Mary Vanderbilt offered Lenox coffee, and he accepted a cup, since it had already been served, was indeed sitting out on a large silver tray, surrounded by dishes of hot and cold milk, ginger biscuits, and dainty sleeves of sugar with the ends twisted into patterns.

Lenox poured a little milk and the contents of one of these sleeves into his coffee, and was grateful for the first warm sip. It was the coldest of the days he had experienced thus far in Newport—something heavy coming on to blow, no doubt, as Mrs. Berry had predicted, something stronger than the mist of the night before.

Mary Vanderbilt made sober but amiable conversation with the detective, until at last it was her younger brother who broke the spell of good manners that had reigned for an uneasy quarter of an hour.

"Have you found out anything about Lily?" he asked.

A great deal of Lenox's job depended on timing, and after the briefest instant of hesitation, he set down his coffee cup, patted his pockets, and then looked at the young man.

"Lawrence, the time has come in this matter when a gentleman must speak honestly, without concern for the consequences."

"Excuse me?"

But Lenox saw that this shot had hit home. Vanderbilt might be flashy by Knickerbocker standards, but he and Willie Schermerhorn had been taught by the same dancing teachers, sat in the same rosewood pews at St. James' Church on East Seventy-Second Street, marched in the same corps of little pre-military chaps parading up and down Park Avenue at the age of ten and eleven in their tiny version of Union grays bought at Brooks Brothers.

Lenox pulled a snow-white handkerchief from his jacket and laid it upon the dark tea table between them.

"What is that?" asked Mary Vanderbilt.

Lenox unfolded the handkerchief. It had taken the impress of blood in a few faint traces: the flask, dented in its body, smashed and bloody at one of its lower corners, the small oval ruby at its center a gruesome joke.

Lawrence Vanderbilt started forward. "My flask! Is that blood?"

"Lawrence," said his sister warningly.

He glanced at her. "It is my flask, Mary. There is no point in saying otherwise." His gaze shifted to Lenox. "Am I to take it that this was involved with the murder?"

"My best surmise is that it was the murder weapon, Mr. Vanderbilt."

"Oh, no," he said, and indeed seemed bereft at the idea.

"Did you kill Lily Allingham?"

Lenox was on guard for some kind of violence; he had a hand near his right boot, ready to reach for the small folding knife he kept there since his old friend Gerald Leigh's case the year before had put him into one or two sticky spots.

But Lawrence was not in a violent temper at all; rather, he began casting about desperately for a distraction, eventually settling on the large chased silver box of cigarettes. He took one and lit it with unsteady hands.

"Of course he didn't," said Mary Vanderbilt.

The detective was not so sure. He waited until Vanderbilt's eyes met his. The gaze held for a moment, and then Vanderbilt spoke.

"Of course the flask is mine," he said. "But I did not kill her. Nor was I present when she died. I know nothing about it. Absolutely nothing."

"Not even how your flask came to be at the scene?" Lenox asked.

"Yes, I do know that, and I can tell you how, if you would be gracious enough to give me ten minutes' time before taking me in to—oh, hell, who would it even be. Welling?"

He ran a hand through his thick dull golden hair. His momentary maturity—a glimpse of the man he might be at thirty-five—had dissolved, and he was a disconsolate schoolboy again.

"Of course," said Lenox.

Vanderbilt glanced right. "Outside all right to talk? It's too hot in here. Mary, join us if you like."

"Oh, Lawrence," she said, and stood up, went around the couch, and slipped her arm through his, clasping her hands tightly as if that would stop him from being pulled away. Her brother merely tolerated it, but Lenox was moved at her gesture of love. Even if he was a murderer, she seemed to be signaling to him silently, he was her brother.

Outside they sat in canvas chairs around a polished wood table. There were seagulls flying overhead, the especially choppy waters muffling their keening cries. Mary had dismissed the servants.

"I gave Lily Allingham that flask at ten twenty on the night she died," Lawrence said. "At Cold Farm. That was the last time I ever saw her."

"Why did you give it to her?"

"She had just agreed to marry me."

Mary cried out something indistinct. "Lawrence!"

"It's the truth, Mary. She'd said yes at last. During the quadrille. I impressed upon her how hopelessly I was—how—that I was—I told her I loved her. I told her I couldn't live without her."

"Why haven't you mentioned this until now?" asked Lenox.

"It was nobody's business."

"She's dead."

Vanderbilt looked furious. "Do you think I don't know that?"

"Surely you must see that the information might have been relevant."

"I do not!" said Vanderbilt.

"So you gave her the flask when the dance ended?"

"In the middle of the dance. It was all I had on me. I wanted to give her something special. I wish I had been wearing a ring, or a pin. But I told her about my uncle's little speech to me when he gave it to me—a kind word it was, too."

"What did she do with it?"

"I can't remember. Put it in her little jeweled bag, I suppose. The main fact was that she had agreed to marry me. I had her in my arms and we were dancing. The flask was the last thing on my mind."

"Did she show it to anyone?"

"I don't know. I don't think so."

"How did her mood seem?"

"Her mood?"

Lenox had memorized the dance card that Blaine had reconstructed from Lily Allingham's activities at the ball. The quadrille was the tenth dance, coming after the beautiful young lady's disappearance at intermission, *after* her friends had described her as "distracted."

And before she had danced the eleventh and twelfth dances with Willie Schermerhorn, then disappeared into the cloudy Newport night.

"What was her mood?"

Vanderbilt seemed to consider the idea for the first time. "I suppose she was—she must have been relieved. Importunate fellows everywhere."

"Not giddy, then."

Vanderbilt frowned. "Not giddy, perhaps, Mr. Lenox, but fully aware of how momentous an event—"

"And she danced with Schermerhorn after you."

"Yes," said Vanderbilt. "He had filled up her dance card early. That is partly why I was so happy. I dreaded the thought, to be honest, that she would accept him that night. This week is the end of the New York season and the beginning of the Newport one. She knew things would be changing."

"Does that mean she was under pressure to get married?"

Even in this grave moment, both Mary and Lawrence smiled in disbelief at the naïveté of Lenox's question.

"Yes, she jolly well was," said Vanderbilt.

"When did you next see her after the quadrille? After you gave her the flask?"

"I returned her to her table—to her friends—and after that I saw her stand up with Schermerhorn. It made me sick with jealousy. But I knew that it would all be over soon; she was telling him about us. So I waited. I went outside and smoked. When I eventually went back inside, she was gone."

"I see. You are sure she told Willie Schermerhorn?"

Vanderbilt looked at him seriously. "Yes. And he was also looking for her. He was asking everyone where she'd gone. It doesn't mean he killed her, too. That was when I went after her. But I chose the wrong direction. I'd give anything I have to do it over again."

CHAPTER TWENTY-SEVEN

The picturesque little town of Newport, when Lenox arrived there not long after this conversation with Lawrence Vanderbilt, was thronged. Near the train station especially there was a great deal of shouting and horse-trading. Messenger boys as well as men of business strode through the streets, almost all carrying parcels of various shape and size.

Lenox stopped in at his rooms to fetch a heavier coat before meeting Blaine. "Good afternoon, Mrs. Berry," he said as he closed the door behind him.

The venerable lady, who was sewing something by the fire, said hello, and asked if he had found it quite busy outside. Lenox replied that it was and wondered aloud if she might know why.

"Mrs. Astor's ball, of course," she said.

"All this is for Mrs. Astor's ball?" said Lenox, surprised.

"Yes. Have you not heard of her?"

"I have, but I—well, I don't know. It would have seemed to me that her ball could not be very different than the other ones."

Mrs. Berry stared at him, momentarily speechless, and then said that, yes, it was different. She started to recount the ways.

"Trains from New York—specials hired to come in, artists, chefs, all kinds of people. Nobody here minds. It brings a great deal of business, and it was a hard winter for fishing. Too much ice in the bay."

"Interesting. Well, I shall be in my rooms for a few minutes," Lenox said. "I am to meet Mr. Blaine in a little while, but if he calls you may send him upstairs."

"Very good, Mr. Lenox."

Lenox was in the midst of writing half a dozen letters, which were strewn across his desk. He picked up the one he had been writing to Graham, his old friend, valet, and running mate in detection during his lean early years. He scanned what he had written. Mostly impressions of this new country. Unable to resist, he sat down, dipped his nib in the inkstand, and finished the letter.

A dispatch after speaking with Vanderbilt. It looks as if Schermerhorn may in all probability be the killer—at least, if Vanderbilt is an honest youth. I suspect he may be. The flask I mentioned above was his, he freely owns. He gave it to Miss Allingham when, apparently, she accepted his offer of marriage. She was killed with it two hours later or so.

If it was not Vanderbilt's hand—if indeed he gave her the flask at the dance—one can imagine the encounter between her and the hotheaded young Schermerhorn: she brandishing the flask as proof that her betrothal lay elsewhere, he seizing it and striking her with it, ashamed and furious. Did he know he was going to kill her? In the end it doesn't matter, of course.

There are strings to tie up. I expect a confession sooner or later. I must go—but look forward to a long-overdue meeting when I am back in London, not two weeks hence, and you are at leisure from the professional activities that I sometimes fear have become all too consuming, all too grueling. Until then, I remain, with a handshake in my heart,

Your friend,
Charles Lenox

The detective blotted this note and cast around the papers on the desk for an envelope. He had tried not once or twice but three times to see his old friend before he left for New York, and it had stung not to receive a call in return, however busy Graham might have been. A little thought flitted through his mind that his friend had grown into a different life, and Lenox felt a quick sadness, hoping he was wrong.

As he was sealing the envelope, the detective contemplated what he had written about returning to London. The first ship he had a berth reserved on was in a week, the next Saturday. He had planned to see so much by now: New York, Massachusetts, the rocky coast of Maine, perhaps Chicago and St. Louis. By this time on the calendar he had been intending to be moving southward, either to New Orleans or Atlanta.

Instead he was still in this town, and momentarily he felt stifled. But he hadn't even seen Partridge, the town's primary police inspector, a single time since that afternoon on the beach; usually in such a case his footsteps crossed the police's at a dozen different junctures. For that reason alone he was glad he was here—that, and also his conversations with Kitty and with Rose Bennett, which had brought home to him, despite her immense temporary power, how young and inexperienced Lily Allingham must really have been, just nineteen, after all, both blessed and cursed by her beauty, a well-designed curse, perhaps the best-designed curse. How could she have known what she wanted at such a tender age? Vanderbilt,

Schermerhorn, some other gentleman, even solitude; whichever she had chosen, she would have known exactly as much about the world as every nineteen-year-old, which was at once a good deal and so very little—in some respects, absolutely nothing.

These ruminations were interrupted by a knock at the door and the entrance of O'Brian, who brought with him a letter and two newspapers.

"Good day," Lenox said. "Is the letter for me?"

"Yes, sir. And you are in the newspapers, sir—I took the liberty."

"Am I? Thank you."

"Look—here, and here," said O'Brian helpfully, and Lenox felt a surge of affection for the charcoal-haired lad in his thin breeches.

There were three items all told in the two papers, the *Herald* and the *Times*. Two were long stories about Lily Allingham in which Lenox was mentioned. He read them with some consternation, for they bore the unmistakable signs of journalists warming to a story.

The third reference to him was in a column called *Society Squabbles*, which reported acidly that Mrs. Astor had been overheard inviting Lenox to her ball—a surprise that had elicited "curiosity" and "no little frustration" in the "witnesses" to the moment, per the article's writer, who was identified as J. Gossip Gadabout, a name which Lenox, with his years of practice in detection, strongly suspected of being a pseudonym.

He set the paper aside. He had suddenly remembered that he didn't have proper evening dress here.

"Oh, hell," he muttered, and looked about, as if a tailor might appear from a wardrobe or behind the door. But none did. Another item to add to the day's agenda. Perhaps he would skip Mrs. Astor's ball, he thought. His heart was already heavy in anticipation of the inevitable confrontation with Willie Schermerhorn. If it ended as he feared it would—if the case was over in an hour or two—he could send his regrets to Mrs. Astor, leave for Boston, and do his best to meet the great Mr. Ralph Waldo Emerson. There was still time.

In fact, Schermerhorn proved the subject of the letter O'Brian had been bearing with the newspapers.

> March 16, 1878
> The Cove
> Newport, RI

Mr. Lenox,

I would be exceedingly grateful if you might apprise me of any new discoveries regarding the terrible incident that occurred close to my property. I ask not in the hope that you will take a fee—I apologize again for the offer—but out of concern for the girl. Please call on me here any time. My son, too, is very eager to have whatever news you may be able to impart.

> Your humble servant,
> *William Stuyvesant Schermerhorn IV*

Lenox's eyes lingered on the phrase "close to my property." It was all very well for Schermerhorn to try to distance his family from the murder, but it had been flush up *against* his property that she died, very likely on it; and Lenox wondered, uneasy thoughts stirring, if the father already knew about his son's guilt and was merely now in one of the later stages of mitigation. He supposed it was even possible that the older Schermerhorn had killed Lily Allingham himself.

He wrote back that if it should prove acceptable he would call on Mr. Schermerhorn at 2:30 that afternoon and dispatched O'Brian with the letter.

This done, he rounded out two of the other letters (one to his brother, one to Thomas McConnell) and addressed them, then left them with Mrs. Berry's grandson to be stamped and mailed. At just after noon, Blaine did arrive, and the two of them took his carriage the short distance up Bellevue Avenue—through even denser traffic than had been crowding the streets an hour before—to check in with Newport's mayor.

CHAPTER TWENTY-EIGHT

Lenox came from a country whose fashionable manners were largely determined by just a few hundred people. It was said the Prince of Wales could walk along Pall Mall without any risk of being recognized because so many gentlemen had copied his appearance—his clothes, his smart beard, his regal pace and posture. The exactitude was almost scientific. Once, after a bout of rheumatism, the prince had taken to shaking hands with an arm pressed tightly to his side. Within a week it had been the only acceptable way to shake hands in society.

America was different. Even in the level and open way Mrs. King, the cook at Cold Farm, had addressed them there had been an intimation of her bedrock knowledge that before the eyes of their nation, Lenox, Blaine, and she were equals.

Yet, here, too, what counted was inevitably what could be counted. Lenox saw that when they went to visit Mayor Welling.

The local government worked in a large white house on Bellevue Avenue, not far from Mrs. Berry's. It was also home to the town's historical society. It sat in a tidy row of prosperous-looking shops and houses, beams exposed in the brickwork facing the street, bunting in the pattern of the American flag strung across their upper windows.

In front of the tavern next door was a weathered man missing an arm—one sleeve was pinned back to his shoulder—and next to him a tin cup and a small but vivid painting of the whaling accident that had brought him to his current predicament: a man flying from a small boat, splayed, and about to be pinned against a larger ship by a right whale with a diabolical fury on its face.

Lenox dropped a coin in his cup and followed Blaine next door to the Mayor's office.

It was a spacious room they entered, with desks that had nameplates for each of six city counselors, though only Welling was here. The mayor, standing with an open newspaper, a cigar between his thumb and first two fingers, saw Lenox alone, initially. Blaine had paused outside to clean his shoes. Straightaway Welling put up his hands, though his demeanor was friendly.

"We're very busy today, I fear," he said.

Then Blaine opened the door.

Instantly Welling's whole conduct changed, his meaty face breaking out in a new kind of smile, and Lenox understood that of course it was Blaine's family that allowed Newport's prosperity, the leavings from their table that made this fine row of houses and Welling's thick, well-made worsted suit possible.

"Mr. Blaine! Fancy seeing you here! Mr. Lenox, if you'll excuse us—"

"Oh, we're together," said Blaine.

Welling didn't falter. "Then you must both join me for a cup of coffee—piping hot, too. Stevens!" he cried. "Bear a hand! Three cups of coffee, please!"

There was a loud response, possibly containing words, from behind a door to the rear of the room, and Welling, apparently satisfied with it, gestured toward the office that lay just off this central room, his name in silver lettering upon the door: MAYOR JOHN WELLING.

"How long have you been mayor, Mr. Welling?" Lenox asked as they sat down in a small, neat room with a view of the street through wooden slats.

"Nine years, sir," said Welling. "A very good nine years for Newport, as I know Mr. Blaine will agree."

"I was only twelve when they began," Blaine pointed out.

"Ha! True. You wasn't there when we overturned the restriction on playing ball sports on the town green, in '75. That was quite heated." He smiled again. "It was the last scandal we had, I think."

"We had some questions about Lily Allingham," said Lenox. "We were wondering what you—or really Mr. Partridge—might have found."

Welling gave him a doubtful look. "Found? Well—Mrs. Astor's ball being tomorrow, things have—"

"I am assisting Mr. Lenox in his investigation," Blaine said.

"Are you!" Welling slapped his desk. "What a fine thing to do, Mr. Blaine. A credit to Newport. We all regret the girl terrible—an inexcusable thing."

"We've heard you've been spreading it about that Miss Allingham might have fallen," said Lenox.

"Only that it was a possibility. Only that it was a possibility. She was handled rough—inexcusable, that—but our fellow says that could have been *incidental* to a fall."

Lenox was starting to despise Welling. "So he thinks the fall could have killed her? Caused that wound?"

"I don't know. That will be in his full report."

"Who is the coroner here?" Lenox asked.

"Dr. Fitts. A dab old hand."

At that moment a tall, handsome gentleman entered the room

without knocking. He wore white socks up to his knees in the very old colonial American fashion, as Lenox had noticed some men still did here, and held a tray of coffee cups on one arm.

"Coffee," he said, glancing around and nodding courteously but briefly.

"Thank you, Stevens."

He set down the tray, which had small pots of cream and sugar on it, and then pulled some papers from a pocket. "Crime report and afternoon newspapers."

"Very good. Set them there." Stevens withdrew, and when he was gone, Welling said, confidentially, "Took the war hard, Stevens. He was only sixteen when he went in. Soldier's heart. The town found him a place—a right hero he was in those battles, so they said. Awful things they saw. We saw."

"You served, Mr. Welling?" said Lenox.

"That I did, sir."

Lenox glanced after Stevens, striding away across the broad room. He knew the term, at least by report. There were numerous veterans of the civil war here, it was said, who had a strange lingering emotional aftereffect, what medical men referred to as *soldier's heart*. Apparently it meant nightmares, long periods of diffidence, and even violence on occasion; mingled with the strongest recollections of the war at random, even inappropriate moments.

Welling was pouring the coffee. "What was on the crime blotter today?" asked Blaine.

With one hand, Welling riffled through the sheets Stevens had left. "Looks like a fight at the docks and a break-in up-island. About the normal run of affairs." He took a sip of his own coffee. "Ah. That's the stuff."

"When was the last murder you had?" asked Lenox.

Welling frowned. "That's hard to say. Three years ago there was a bloody fight between two fishermen. One of them took a fever and was sick for some weeks, and he went, eventually. I don't know you could properly account that a murder, though. Old Bradford Ellingboe."

"And before that?"

Welling blew on his coffee. "Not in my time. Oh! That's not true. Warwick Ondine shot a man over cards at Creve Coeur. That's one of the cottages. Southern gentleman—came up and reported the death himself in this very office, as calmly as you can please, dressed all in white. Said he'd do it again. That was six years ago."

"I remember it," said Blaine.

"He sold his place out to a New Yorker, fittings and all, and headed south again before the law came after him."

Lenox frowned. "Surely he might have been arrested at home in the South—murder, after all."

Welling shrugged. "It was a matter of honor. The dead man's family agreed, said it right in an open letter. He had been cheating at cards—ten people saw it. Blind drunk, the poor fool. A Frenchman, you know how they are."

"And otherwise? Smaller crimes?"

Welling sipped his cup. He was right on this subject, anyhow: It was good and strong, putting a spark in Lenox's spine. Much better than what he had been given at Sea Cloud by the Vanderbilt siblings.

"You met Mr. Clark, I believe," Welling said.

"Indeed I did."

"A right hard horse, Mr. Clark," said Welling, and gazed directly at Lenox.

The message was clear, if less direct than Welling's look: There were too many ladies and gentlemen of astronomical wealth, each with a fleet of staff, for crime to be a problem in Newport.

"Given how rare it is, I wonder that Miss Allingham's death is not more remarked, then," said Lenox. "The town seems to be going on much apace."

Blaine and Welling exchanged a glance. It was Blaine who

spoke. "You must think of yourself as being on the floor of a stock exchange, I think, Mr. Lenox," he said. "Any match that could be arranged at Mrs. Astor's tomorrow evening would be worth millions of dollars."

Lenox was from a country where ten thousand pounds was considered a fine fortune, and the word *millions* still threw him, though he had heard it used often enough in New York and Newport; but to think of the whims of two youths of twenty determining how those millions were transacted still slightly took his breath away. He wondered if he had underestimated money as the possible motivation for this murder.

"People are very conscious of Miss Allingham's death, you may trust in that," said Welling.

"Are they?"

"There will be no women traveling unaccompanied this summer on Newport. There are a dozen other people looking into it just as you are." Lenox detected a slight triumph in the mayor's look. "Good men, too."

So that was why the mayor could sit here calmly sipping coffee. All across this small island, apparently, there was a concerted, silent effort to root out the murderer. But was this true?

"Where was the break-in?" he said.

"The break-in?" asked Welling, puzzled.

Lenox pointed at the sheet Stevens had brought in with the *Newport Beacon* and the *New York Daily Caller*. "Last night."

"Oh." Welling drew the sheet toward him again. "Mrs. Walliter's, from the looks of it. Smashed back window. Nothing taken."

"Who is Mrs. Walliter?" asked Lenox.

"She has a boardinghouse for young women. Occasionally a constable will go up there to see to a rejected suitor making trouble. A broken window is about ordinary."

"Ah. I see. And the fight?"

Welling consulted the paper again. "Two men at the Seagull who fell out over right of way on a fishing route, it says. One was . . . oh—Josiah Franklin. He's reliable for a fistfight every six weeks or so. Usually it's not reported. A good man when he's not in his cups. But I see here he took after a young stripling—Walcott, out of Hyannis. No surprise it got bloody."

Lenox filed these names away in his mind. "Is Mr. Partridge in?" he asked.

"Ah!" said Welling, and with a meaningful look he tapped his nose. "He's out on his shoe leather working the case, too, never you mind. He's a deep file, old Partridge. You'll see. He might even get there before you, Mr. Lenox."

Welling chortled and took another sip of his coffee. Lenox looked at the clock. It was 12:40. He felt suddenly uneasy—sensed, in an old, primitive way, that there was something he had missed. Even that there might be violence yet to come in this matter.

Out on the porch, the old mariner was still there with his tin cup. A carriage pulled by four horses was passing, with ROTONDI FLORISTS, 29 ORCHARD STREET, NY printed on the side. Through its windows Lenox could see hundreds of bouquets of flowers. It occurred to him again that if he meant to stay for the ball he must find a tailor, quickly.

CHAPTER TWENTY-NINE

Lenox, after considering his options for a moment, peered up and down the street, up into the stormy sky, too, and said to Blaine, "I'm going to the fishing town up north."

He nodded in the direction opposite from where they stood in the center of Newport, from the cottages. "May I ask why?" said Blaine.

"It's the only part of Newport I haven't seen," said Lenox.

Thoroughness wasn't the whole truth. Sometimes instinct took over in a case like this, and even if the mystery of Lily Allingham's death ended at 2:30 that afternoon, when they met with Willie Schermerhorn, the mystery of her last hours was still tugging on him.

"Shall I accompany you?"

This was awkward; Lenox intended to walk. "Actually I was hoping you might do me a different service."

Blaine took out a pocket-sized leather notebook, and Lenox felt a quick fondness for him. "You need only name it."

Lenox had seen Blaine's effect on Welling. "I wonder if you might be able to track down Partridge and apprise him of what we know. Lawrence Vanderbilt's confession. It will sugar the pill to have the news from you—besides which, he may have information we do not, and which he would share with you but not me."

Blaine finished writing, and said, "Of course. Shall I see you at two thirty, then?"

"Yes, by all means."

Blaine nodded. "Thank you again, Mr. Lenox, for allowing me to follow along with you."

"Of course," said Lenox. He had determination, Blaine, lurking behind his shyness, his politeness, and his impossible reserves of wealth and prestige. Lenox thought of saying something, but time was short. "You have done very well."

They parted, and it was alone that the detective walked the mile to the tiny fishing village at the northern tip of Newport, covering the ground briskly—the temperature having stayed chilly.

He studied the crowded houses as he approached them, planted along an outcropping, each a fiftieth of the size of one of the cottages, yet home to souls equally divine, if you believed what you heard on Sunday mornings, as those in the cottages. The village was rather picturesque—the houses clustered together, small and mostly made out of weathered old boards, paint peeling off many of them, a dozen or so boats and skiffs hull-up on the shingle by the water. Buoys in the water and a strong smell of fish. The whole scene was set in front of the choppy, unhappy sea, which rippled this way and that in slashes of sharp white.

Just as he arrived, it started to rain. The sky had very suddenly (by his Sussex boyhood reckoning) resolved from gray into a series of huge dark storm clouds. He checked his pocket watch—one o'clock, a minute or two after. He pulled his hat lower, put his hands in his pockets, and looked around. There were lanterns above a number of doors now, glowing yellow even at this midday hour. They knew the weather. One, a few steps down a narrow alley, had a picture of a small boat at sea on it, and he took a chance and stepped inside.

It was a cozy place, a tavern. "Afternoon, sir," said a stout man behind the bar.

"Good afternoon. How are you?"

"Still haven't heard from Mrs. Astor." The man laughed at his own joke. Lenox smiled and sat down at a table. "Anything to drink?"

He was cold and wet, pondering even now whether he dared steal into the second seat in front of the fire. "I would be very grateful for a cup of tea. Coffee, if you don't have it."

"We can manage tea."

"Thank you."

"Have a seat by the fire if you're wet. Jeffries won't bite."

Jeffries was apparently the rumpled man already sitting by the fire, who said "Mmm" from behind his pipe and beneath his fisherman's hat. When he returned his stare to the fire, his eyelids, briefly stirred into greater openness at the mention of his name, began to grow heavy again.

Lenox noticed that over the fireplace there was a pair of crossed pistols and a banner that said 7TH RHODE ISLAND INFANTRY. A crisp copy of a daguerreotype stood above it on the mantel—Mr. Lincoln, Lenox saw, that unmistakable face, deep-eyed and wise, revered on both sides of the Atlantic.

One thing he hadn't anticipated when he sailed—well, aside from coming to Newport at all—was how recent and present the Civil War would still seem in America. He thought of Clark's face, the new black ribbons pinned next to the plaque in the Union Club every day, of Stevens, bringing the mayor coffee, and of soldier's heart.

Lenox grew so lost in thought that he didn't notice the keeper of the house approaching. He set down a pot of tea and a cup. It was bitter stuff, but hot, and with enough sugar it went down gratefully.

"Anything else?" the barman asked after a reasonable interval.

"I would take a glass of wine."

The man smiled, his lined old face crinkling up. "That we have too, I think." He glanced at the fat casks underneath the front windows. "Something to eat?"

"What do you recommend?"

"There I'd have to think, me. Most'd say the stuffies."

Lenox nodded, though he had no idea what those were. "That's fine," he said.

"Fair play. Won't be long."

The man withdrew. To Lenox's left, something stirred in front of the fire and readjusted itself: a dog! A mastiff, or at least kin to a mastiff. Edmund had mastiffs. Lenox's heart gave an absurd leap, and he went over and put a hand to the old hound's nose. It sniffed, slowly and solemnly, and then pressed its great head comfortably into Lenox's shoe and closed its eyes, adjusting infinitesimally along its curled body, sage creature. Lenox scratched the dog's ear for a few minutes, letting the fire heat his own skin until it tingled before giving the dog a final rub on the back and returning to his table.

A glass of ruby-red wine appeared, and soon afterward his— it would seem—stuffies. There were a dozen of them, and when Lenox picked one up he discovered it was in a hard shell. This must be a clam, he realized, and he was glad he hadn't bitten straight into it; though he'd heard of little else besides seafood since arriving in Newport, it sometimes seemed. His stomach growled—a delicious scent of onions, celery, toasted bread, and the sea steamed up from the plate. He took a small experimental bite, which was enough to convince him that the smell was true to its source, and soon enough, ravenous, he had eaten the whole plate.

The barman came to fetch it when he was done. "Wonderful," Lenox said.

"Ah, good. Never seen 'em do a hungry fellow wrong yet."

"I suppose they're from Rhode Island?"

The man frowned. "You hear of 'em in Pawtucket; but not Providence; and Boston, never. So I should say they're local, like."

Lenox didn't understand a word of this. "I see."

"Was there anything else?"

"I was hoping to call upon Mrs. Walliter," he said.

"Well, you've as good as done it."

"Excuse me?"

"I'm her brother. She lives next door." The barman gave Lenox a more intent look. "What is it you're needing from her?"

"I'm investigating the death by the cliffs."

"Oh, you're that limey. Miss Allingham. Yes. Mighty sad, that. And the rich folks'll have their summer anyhow, won't they?" He heaved a sigh. "Fair enough that you've come, of course. I'll tell Emily you're by. That's Mrs. Walliter. It might be a few minutes, mind."

Lenox thanked him, once more surprised that knowledge of his presence on the island had preceded him, but glad in this case, and settled in to wait. The gentleman with the low hat and the long pipe had fallen asleep. The pipe had burnt out yet remained lodged firmly in the grip of his mouth—a sailor's trick, that.

It was only when there was a tap on the flagstone floor that Lenox started and realized that *he* had been close to slumber himself, there in the comfortable chair, the rain pattering outside and a good meal in his stomach.

A small, pretty, elderly woman in a bonnet and a calico dress was standing behind Lenox with the barman. The detective rose.

"Mrs. Walliter? How do you do?" Lenox asked. "Thank you very much for coming to see me."

"I only have a moment."

"Of course. Let me get straight to my point then. You run a boardinghouse?"

"Aye, that I do. But poor Miss Allingham has naught to do with it."

"No, I didn't think so. But I understand you had a break-in last night."

A look of consternation passed over Mrs. Walliter's face. "So we did. Some fool young fellow, I make it. I tell all of the girls that they may always accept callers in the parlor, as long as myself or someone else is present. But will they listen? Will they ever."

"Then you don't think it was a burglar?"

"In Newport? No. Any stranger would have been told us about a while since. I heard you were ten minutes here before our George came to fetch me."

The barman, caught, shifted a little bashfully. "Was anything taken?" Lenox asked.

"No, nothing."

"Which window was broken? A front one?"

"A side one." She exhaled dramatically. "It will cost six dollars just the glass, and Chapman won't cut it down for less than another two."

Lenox paused, thinking; and then he played the hunch that had brought him up to this part of Newport.

"Can you tell me, Mrs. Walliter—is one of the girls who stays at the boardinghouse a Miss Maryanne Morris?"

She looked surprised. "Why, yes," she said. "She's been with me three years—nearly a daughter, Maryanne. The sweetest, prettiest girl. It was her window that was broke."

CHAPTER THIRTY

A sense of urgency surged in around Lenox's fatigued faculties. However dozy he had been a few moments before, he was wide awake now. Whoever committed murder on this island three nights before was still here, and had tried to break into the room of the servant with whom Lily Allingham had shared one of her last conversations. It was impossible that it could be a coincidence.

"Where is Miss Morris now? Was she in her room?"

"No," said Mrs. Walliter, taken aback by the intensity of Lenox's tone. "She's gone to see her father. Goes from Tuesday to Thursday each week."

"But it's Friday."

"She wrote yesterday and said she might be another day or two. She's a dutiful daughter."

"Yes, I'm sure it does her great credit. You're sure it was she who wrote?"

"Goodness me, yes. Lord, the takings on! Yes, Jack Fillaby saw her only this morning over near Portsmouth, anyway, told her all about the break-in. She was taken right aback, our Maryanne. Coming home by train even now I should think. So you see, all's well that ends well."

Lenox forbore from informing Mrs. Walliter that nothing had ended, well or otherwise. "Then no one was in the room when the window was broken?"

"No. Her sister sometimes stays with us—a very genteel girl, married, ever so complimentary of the breakfast we have. Which I do say it's humble, but there's as much in eggs and oatmeal as a person could—"

"And you're *quite* sure nothing was taken?"

Mrs. Walliter looked a little put out now by Lenox's forcefulness. "Yes—I saw the room myself. I came across it this morning and looked through."

"No one saw the person who broke in?"

"None of the girls did, no. I assume if someone had seen it from the street they would have told one of us by now."

Lenox glanced over at George, who was back behind the bar, polishing glasses. "Could you ask your brother to spread the word that we are looking for the young man who did it? Anyone who was seen out last night."

"I suppose," said Mrs. Walliter. "But this can't possibly have anything to do with Miss Allingham, can it?"

"I fear it may. Regardless, as concerns Miss Morris, I cannot vouch for the young woman's safety as long as she is alone."

Mrs. Walliter looked horrified by this statement, and her brother, who had been eavesdropping with no great pretense of concealment, concerned.

But it was the man by the fire who spoke. Jeffries. He rose up out of his seat, his eyes just visible beneath his soft-brimmed cap, his pipe still in his mouth. The mastiff was immediately on its feet, too, and Lenox realized this man must be its master.

"One of the girls at the boardinghouse, Emily?" he said.

"Yes. Old Duckie Morris's daughter, up Portsmouth."

"I know him."

The man nodded, looked hard at Lenox for a moment, and then

turned and left, his dog heeling closely, two-thirds of a glass of beer still on the table.

"That makes me feel better," said Mrs. Walliter, more to her brother than Lenox. "Criminy though!"

"Who is that gentleman, may I ask?" said Lenox.

She looked as if Lenox had asked who King Henry the Eighth was. "That's Captain Jeffries."

"Who's Captain Jeffries?"

"Who is he! And him cousin to most anyone you care to meet. Which he's lived here every day of his life, I suppose. Well, except for the war. Grew up on the deck of a boat."

"He's a captain?" said Lenox.

"Yes, in the navy. He stole back New Orleans for the Union. They gave him every medal and ribbon they could find, too," said Mrs. Walliter triumphantly. "He even met Mr. Lincoln. There's a letter from him in the captain's desk at home."

Lenox had thought of the cottages as the likely providers of the army's officer class, but he was wrong, out, America deceiving him again. "And I take it what he meant was that he plans to look after the young woman?"

"If she's alive, she'll stay alive now that he's concerned in the affair," said Mrs. Walliter. "Oh, but what a turn of events! That poor Allingham girl, and now my own Miss Morris, who's like a niece to me, so she is!"

"There, now, Emily," said her brother, who had come around the bar holding a soapy glass, and patted her on the arm.

"I knew it all along, you know," she said worriedly. "I knew it would wake snakes—all these rich ladies and gentlemen coming to Newport. I said it twenty years ago, when it was fields down there. Fields."

She looked miserable, and though Lenox tried to comfort her, he was in a rush, and as quickly he could he gave the barman a few dollars and asked to be sent for the moment Miss Maryanne Morris had returned.

"Just send word, please. I shall pay any expenses, cabs and the like."

Mrs. Walliter nodded unhappily. "I shall. I shall. Oh, but I only hope she's all right!"

"The captain will look after her," said her brother. "If anyone can, he will."

Lenox asked if he could see Maryanne Morris's room himself. Her landlady said she thought usually not—it didn't seem genteel—but given the circumstances—and after some brief moral haggling with herself, led Lenox next door to a small blue house, less handsomely furnished than Mrs. Berry's but equally clean.

After they had gone down a hallway whose walls were adorned with prints of children trying, comically Lenox supposed, to ride various horses, Mrs. Walliter said, opening a door, "And here is her room—there, you can see the window. I've put wax paper and oilcloth over it, to keep the wind out, and you can't ask much fairer than that."

"No," Lenox murmured.

The room was a study in simplicity: a narrow bed, its counterpane pulled tight, a small plain desk with no drawers. A chest, a mirror. A single candle on a bedside table.

The one drawer in the room that locked, a tiny one in the bedside table, was ajar. "Is this drawer usually locked?" Lenox asked.

"It is. I gave her the key myself on the day she moved in. For valuables."

"I take it you didn't open it today?"

"Oh no."

There were fresh scratches around the keyhole. He looked in the drawer and found a few trinkets, including a silver commemorative spoon from Niagara Falls, a lock of hair in a miniature white envelope, and a bundle of letters tied in ribbon. With only a mild pang of compunction, he opened these. They were all from Miss Morris's brother, whom at a cursory glance Lenox saw was off seeking his fortune in California. None was recent.

He looked around the room carefully, trying to think. Outside the storm thundered on. He could sense his appointment with the Schermerhorns ticking nearer in his pocket, but they would have to wait if need be. The whole thing felt as ominous as the banks of clouds in the window—dark, obscure, dangerous.

After a moment of thought he lifted the mattress, which was very light, but found nothing on the pine frame underneath. Nor was there anything beneath the bed, or in the two hat boxes in the small closet, or in any of the pockets of Miss Morris's clothes.

Then his eye fell on the window that had been broken into. It had a thick dark ledge at the bottom and top. He reached up to the top ledge, and his hand ran over something soft.

He pulled the object down. It was a brown velveteen case, about the size of a deck of playing cards. He opened it, and what was inside caused Mrs. Walliter to gasp: a string of huge, glittering diamonds, on a white gold chain.

He very carefully took it out. To his inexpert eye the diamonds looked real. The hallmark did, too—*Louis Comfort Tiffany*, it was signed. A local jeweler? No—it said New York in the lid of the case. On a pendant near the clasp of the necklace there was a small engraved flower, and the letters MM. For Maryanne Morris, of course. Yet she was a temporary maid! While if its diamonds were real, the necklace was more valuable easily than the entire house in which it was kept.

"Have you ever seen this?" asked Lenox.

"Goodness, no!" said Emily Walliter with the conviction of a woman who hadn't missed a Sunday morning at church in sixty years.

"Did Miss Morris have a beau?"

Mrs. Walliter, who had clearly never experienced such an unnerving day, shook her head passionately. "None. I allow visitors in and out with my key—none. There was some talk a while ago of her marrying, as I recall. But nothing came of it. She's enough work at the moment looking after her father. He's far gone, that one, poor old gent."

"Thank you, Mrs. Walliter. That is extremely useful. Thank you very much."

Lenox's mind was moving. He wondered first whether this was the object the burglar had been seeking, if indeed they had come to the room looking for some *thing*, rather than for Miss Morris herself. He hoped that was the case—that she was not in personal danger, that it was a mere matter of greed.

Could Lily Allingham have died for this necklace? It would have been the tenth finest at the champagne tea he had attended at Greystone, but of course they weren't at Greystone; people killed for far less than the necklace was worth in cities across the world, not just the United States.

Lenox put the case in his pocket and told Mr. Walliter he would look after it, leaving his name, address, and Mrs. Berry's card as collateral. He was surprised this worked—but then, it emerged, Mrs. Walliter had known about his presence in town since the very day he arrived, her cousin was the stationmaster, and as for Mrs. Berry's, certainly it was about the town who was staying there, and some of them had even heard, though no doubt it was false, that he had been invited to Mrs. Caroline Astor's own cottage . . .

Lenox spent another fifteen minutes combing through the room. He tried every trick he knew—beneath the pretty patterned paper in the drawers, behind the mirror, a dozen places he knew—but found nothing.

He checked his watch. He would have given ten guineas to speak to Maryanne Morris long enough to find out what she had been discussing with Lily Allingham during the ball—but it was time to go see Willie Schermerhorn, and there was a good chance, after all, that the explanation would come from him.

CHAPTER THIRTY-ONE

Just before Lenox had departed Britain, a new heir had been born to one of Scotland's great clans. He would inherit Britain's oldest unbroken succession of titles and lands—not the War of the Roses, not the Battle of Hastings, neither the dominion nor the fall of the Romans had touched it. To mark the birth, a chain of bonfires had been lit along the country's entire border, with riotous quantities of food and drink provided for their makers. According to a letter from an astronomer in the *Times*, the bonfires had been bright enough that they were likely visible from the moon, which had tickled many letter-writers' and magazine essayists' fancies.

As Lenox approached Cove Court in his hired carriage, he saw something like the equivalent of those bonfires in America: stationed at every door and window, motionless in the driving rain, hands behind their backs, heavy dark slickers giving them an intimidating uniformity, were hired men, guardians of the ancient and venerable Schermerhorn family.

Lenox had read a bit about them in Mrs. Berry's copy of *Who's Who*. Landfall in 1651 at New Amsterdam, the quick establishment of a thriving textile trade on Broad Way, the family's consolidation and survival through the English takeover (when the city became New York), and now, as 1900 approached, a century of gentlemen and women living in the highest echelons of power, influence, and privilege. The elder Schermerhorn's grandfather had outfitted a regiment in the Revolution; his father had been one of the founding members of the opera.

Standing on the top step at the entrance to Cove Court—it was 2:33—was Mr. Clark, his battle-scarred face solemn. He was polite ("Good afternoon, Mr. Lenox") but impersonal. He led Lenox down the dark front hallway, with its sweeping staircase to the left and on the right an infinitely gloomy grandfather clock clicking away the seconds between two severe portraits, presumably of Schermerhorns who had long since joined the majority.

"Going to the Astors'?" asked Lenox of Clark.

Clark went so far as to smile at this. "Not in the capacity of guest, sir."

Here, whatever America's mores, the *sir* remained intact. In this case it sent a chill through Lenox for some reason.

The study looked as it had before, though there was rain lashing at the windows, and Mr. Schermerhorn the Fourth, the current patriarch, was openly sipping a glass of whisky this time.

"How do you do?" asked Lenox.

Schermerhorn looked tense. "Yes. Very well. Ugly weather. Should clear by evening they say."

"You seem to have increased the security around Cove Court."

"Necessary protection. Tricky time."

He muttered this last bit, as if to himself. "Is Willie joining us?" asked Lenox.

"Yes." Schermerhorn glanced at his watch. "He'll be here any moment."

Lenox took a seat. "I am in no rush," he said mildly. Everything inside him was calling to get out of this situation, and while perhaps he ought to have listened to that instinct, he was trying, instead, to change it, to soften the dread mood within these walls. "Would you mind if I glanced at this copy of today's *Times*? I've yet to see it."

"Of course," said Schermerhorn, and, briefly remembering himself, said, "What can I offer you to drink?"

"Tea, if it's not too much trouble," said Lenox.

"Not at all. Not at all."

Something like normalcy soon returned to the room. Lenox was thinking of those bonfires still, for some reason—now, though, as a chain of clues.

As far as he was concerned, the case had all along presented three central mysteries. He had written them in his notebook on the first day he had been in Newport. He pulled it out now and glanced at the page, though without lingering over the words; better that he should be reading the *Times*.

- Who was Lily Allingham with when she died?
- Why did she leave the ball early?
- Why was she at Cove Court—in the opposite direction from her own house?

He thought he could make a plausible guess about the second of the three questions, but the first and third were still a mystery. The first was the crucial one, of course. Yet it was the third to which Lenox kept returning in his mind again and again, trying to puzzle through that strange night.

Once more he made himself entertain the possibility that the older Mr. Schermerhorn had killed Lily Allingham. There seemed to be no plausible motivation, yet he had been extraordinarily tense during the past few days. It could always be love, of course, that he had been the one who loved Lily Allingham. They said there was no fool like an old fool.

Looking around the room, Lenox saw pride. The coat of arms,

the tapestry, the old portraits, the painting of the Battle of Albany, the heavy monogrammed silver inkstand: Every particular of the room spoke first and foremost to pride. If he had killed Lily Allingham, it was because she had insulted his pride.

Almost by accident, pondering this, Lenox stumbled across his name again in the newspaper. This time the reference was highly favorable—it even called him the world's leading detective, which certain partners within his own agency might have grounds to dispute—and again mentioned his invitation to Mrs. Astor's ball.

Next to it was an article (*"The mountain shall come to Muhammad! Archie Blaine, the retiring patriarch of the great family that bears his name, has deigned to visit his seventy-room Newport cottage on the occasion of the ball of the year, planning however to arrive in town and depart on the same day, unfortunately for local trade"*—and so forth) that reminded him Teddy Blaine ought to be here. Perhaps Clark was keeping him out; if any man would dare close the door in a Blaine's face in the town of Newport, Rhode Island, it was likely James Clark.

The door opened and two maids came in with tea. Lenox thanked them with a smile, made himself a cup, and, for all the darkness of this moment, the tension of waiting for Willie Schermerhorn to arrive, felt his body relax when he took a sip.

Another fifteen minutes passed. Lenox read—sometimes feigned reading—while Schermerhorn paced, occasionally going out into the hall, then returning with an awkward nod to his guest.

It was just before three when Lenox began to grow uneasy in a new way. At a quarter past the hour, the door burst open, and Clark, soaking wet, stood there.

"What is it?" said Schermerhorn.

Clark didn't say anything, merely strode purposefully across the room and handed Schermerhorn a damp, folded piece of paper.

Schermerhorn read it, and seemed to pale.

"No," he said to Clark. "Is it true?"

Clark nodded. "Yes, Mr. Schermerhorn."

Schermerhorn stood there, the paper twisted up in his hand, forgotten, a look of horror on his face. He made for the door, grabbing a heavy cloak from a stand as he went, and after that, stopped, returned to his desk, rifled through a drawer, seized some object Lenox didn't have time to see, and ran from the room.

Lenox stood and followed, astonished. He half expected Clark to stop him, but nothing at all kept him from matching the pace of Schermerhorn, who had run out into the driving rain and was headed directly toward the Cliff Walk.

For a panicked instant Lenox feared that he might jump. But of course it wouldn't kill him, and anyway he didn't. Instead, he took out whatever he had fetched from his desk and stood there with it. Lenox, nearing him, saw what it was: a glass, a telescope.

"What is it?" he called.

Even now he could sense Clark, fifteen or twenty yards away. He realized the town's gossip might not be right that Clark had killed Lily Allingham—but it was right to fear him. Lenox's own animal senses were always reminding him where Clark was.

Schermerhorn didn't reply. He was standing stock-still, with the glass to his eye—another handsome object, needless to say, of polished brass and silver.

Lenox followed his gaze but couldn't see anything. Despite the rain it was fairly clear now, the sky white, not so black and tumultuous as it had been. But it was still too dark to make out whatever Schermerhorn was looking at so closely through the glass.

Then he saw it: a small boat, richly outfitted, of white paint and dark wood. Lenox squinted but couldn't make out the name on its portside stern. It was bobbing on the waves, sailing steadily away from them, away from Newport.

"Whose boat is that?" he asked Schermerhorn at last.

"My son's."

CHAPTER THIRTY-TWO

I think I know the person he's left with," said Lenox.

"With?" said Schermerhorn, lowering the glass for the first time. The boat was beating up—well-handled, you had to give Willie Schermerhorn that.

"He's a good sailor."

"The best."

Lenox doubted that, but sympathized with the father who would make such a claim. "Mm."

"Who is he *with*?" Schermerhorn asked urgently.

Lenox did not wish to be the person under questioning here, for practical reasons. "Perhaps if we are to stand sentry over his departure," he said, "you could ask one of your servants to fetch me a coat."

"Very well, who is it? Please!" Schermerhorn said. At the same time he was signaling, and two people were there almost before his hand was down. "Fetch wet-weather things for Mr. Lenox, please—my hat as well."

"Thank you," said Lenox.

The thanks had been for the two men who were already beating a hasty path back toward Cove Court, but it was Schermerhorn who told Lenox he was welcome.

He studied the ship again for a moment, and then, as if admitting to himself that he could not be out there upon the waves with it, turned, lowering the glass, and said, "Please, Mr. Lenox, tell me the plain truth. Did my son kill Lily Allingham?"

"Until a few moments ago, I was almost sure that he had."

"And now?" said Schermerhorn.

Lenox paused, and then very slightly turned his head. "I do not believe so, no."

The relief in Schermerhorn's face—in his whole body—was so profound that for a moment he looked as if he were going to slump to his knees. "Ah! I knew it. I knew he couldn't have."

The confidence of these words was belied by the reaction, but neither man mentioned it. "Can you tell me what happened at the yacht club?" Lenox asked.

Schermerhorn looked baffled by the question. "The yacht club? With Willie, you mean? It was—not nothing, but it was—" He shook his head. "One of the servants at the club struck another one for being insolent. Willie intervened. The result was not ideal. The senior servant was injured in the altercation. He ultimately left Newport."

"Your son intervened in defense of the servant who had been struck?"

"Yes."

"Of what race were these men?" asked Lenox curiously.

"Both were Negroes. Why?"

At that moment the cavalry returned—umbrellas, chairs, jackets—and Lenox and Schermerhorn waited almost a minute in silence while all of it was unfolded, offered, and so forth, before they were alone once more.

They were still standing, but now beneath the cover of four large white umbrellas, a space big enough that they could have had a small luncheon party here if they were inclined.

"I would be grateful if you would look at something for me," said Lenox.

"Look at something?"

"In your study this morning, I noticed your family's coat of arms again. Very handsome. It was on your stationery, too."

"Thank you, though I fail to see the relevance."

"There was a phrase on it—and two flowers."

"Yes. Tulips, two. One standing tall in Holland, the other in America."

As Schermerhorn was repeating this family saw, Lenox was taking a box from his pocket. He opened it, and even in the gray light of that stormy day, the diamonds on the necklace glittered.

He turned it carefully in his hand so the inscription would be visible. "Is that a tulip?" Lenox asked.

Schermerhorn studied the necklace. Something almost gentle came into his voice. "Yes, it is," he said.

"The MM," Lenox said, "stands for—"

"Maryanne Morris."

Lenox glanced up from the necklace to the small man, with his stiff posture and carefully debonair salt-and-pepper hair. "The name is familiar to you?"

Schermerhorn didn't reply. Instead, he stepped out from the cover of the umbrellas and went to the very edge of the Cliff Walk, where he held the telescope up to his eye. He remained there for a long while, long enough that Lenox finally put the necklace away, sat down, and dried himself off with one of the stack of towels that had appeared on a table—all of them warm and dry, thanks to some ingenious servant's careful work.

The rain beat steadily down on William Stuyvesant Schermerhorn the Fourth long after the little ship had escaped the visibility of the naked eye; at last, apparently, it sailed even beyond the powerful reach of the telescope, for Schermerhorn lowered it, and for some time stared at the part of the sea where his son had been.

"So," he said, as he walked slowly back and took one of the towels for himself. "My son is to marry a housemaid, raised in a fishing shack."

But there was little anger in his voice. He was too relieved that Willie was not a murderer. "It would appear so," said Lenox.

For the first time in a while, Schermerhorn met the detective's eye. Some of his self-possession was returning. He already seemed slightly put out to have exposed his feelings to Lenox so unguardedly. "Will you be so kind as to tell me what you know?"

Lenox had closed the soft brown case in which the necklace was resting, but was still holding it in his right hand. It was small enough to fit snugly there.

"Would you have been happy if your son had married Lily Allingham?" asked Lenox. "You only have one son, one heir, I know."

"Yes, I would have been delighted. She's from a good family—they would not have had to worry about money—and she would have been an ornament to Cove Court, of course, a young woman as beautiful as that. But I have always told Willie that he must marry as he chooses—within reason."

"I take it that your caveat precluded Miss Morris."

Schermerhorn replied, curtly, "Yes."

Lenox nodded. "It's the same in my country, of course. A bad marriage can have ramifications for years—generations, if it's unlucky enough."

Schermerhorn leapt at the olive branch. "Yes! Oh, I tried to tell him, I tried, but one's children . . ."

He had trailed off, and Lenox had to nudge him. "Yes?"

"Eh? Oh." Schermerhorn took out a flat gold case and lit a small Cuban cigar. "It all happened two years ago. Centuries ago, in the life of the young, with their balls and parties. Miss Morris was a maid at one of ours. Willie, I will say, did not merely try to—he courted the young woman."

"I see."

"Finally she assented to his proposals. He came to me and said he loved her and planned to marry her. I forbid it, of course." Schermerhorn looked troubled for a moment. He tinkered with a gold cigar cutter. "Clark went up to see her, arrange about her father's medical care."

"And Willie?"

"Willie spent the rest of that summer with his cousins in Madaket."

"Evidently the affection did not die."

"He said at the time that he would obey my wishes. But he also said that his heart would never change. I attributed it to—oh, youth, I suppose. I encouraged him when he told me about the Allingham girl. I might have had some cavil before Willie's episode with Miss Morris, but Lily Allingham was a life raft as far as I was concerned."

An ornament for Cove Court. Lenox about had the measure of the father. He was cautiously impressed that the son had greater scope of mind, if worse manners. Lenox had noticed something strange about Willie Schermerhorn at their very first meeting: real, credible grief for Lily Allingham, but along with it a strange, occluded sense of triumph, perhaps resolve. Now he believed it to have been the clarity that sometimes comes to those adjacent to tragedy. Willie Schermerhorn had heard of Lily Allingham's death and with a new viewpoint on the crucial matters of life had cast his future immediately and irretrievably with the woman he loved. Maryanne Morris. All of his actions bespoke that priority.

And Lenox knew what certainly must have happened. Lily Allingham had gone out at the intermission of the ball and sat with Maryanne Morris for half an hour. No doubt she had coaxed the whole story out of the maid—heard, Lenox would guess, that Willie Schermerhorn and she were in contact still.

Then she had gone inside and broken off her engagement to Willie during the evening's twelfth and thirteenth dances. Their engagement to be engaged. This would explain her mood, her distractedness.

It could also have explained her death—but Lenox did not believe that Willie Schermerhorn killed Lily Allingham. He didn't think he would have been stupid enough to do it at Cove Court, or hurt enough over the rejection either, not when his heart clearly belonged to another woman.

"What did Clark report back of Miss Morris two years ago?"

"She would take no money," said Schermerhorn. He had the good grace to sound uneasy. "He returned a second time and pressed her, but she would not move. Something was done for the father, as I said."

It was not Lenox's place to ask what Schermerhorn would do now, though the answer was clear enough. His son was too precious to him to lose. The second tulip; the heir to all those coats of arms and stories about when Manhattan was still forested.

Lenox told him, briefly, what his own conception of Willie Schermerhorn's and Maryanne Morris's past few days had been. There was her delayed return, to give them time to go, as well as, most significantly, the absolute bareness of her room. No young girl alive could keep only a bundle of her brother's letters for company at night.

It had of course been Willie who had broken into her lodgings and removed all the traces of their connection—whatever letters, trifles, and presents she had from him still. Apparently he had not known the hiding place of the necklace.

"A cleverer man than I would have seen the flower and thought of the tulip immediately. But it took me until this morning, entering your study again and seeing the coat of arms, to connect the two."

Schermerhorn listened carefully. The rain was quieting when at last he said, "I underestimated you." There was a long pause. "Why did Willie do that, though?"

"I have been wondering. I assume it was to protect Miss Morris's honor. He knows he is the suspect in a murder, and must have known what her family would think if she disappeared, and in her room her sister or her landlady had found all of your son's declarations of affection. They would assume he had seduced her."

"He'll sail down to Key West and marry her there," murmured Schermerhorn, already adjusting to the new facts of his life. "But wait—if not Willie, thank God, who killed Miss Allingham?"

Lenox shook his head. "I don't know."

CHAPTER THIRTY-THREE

It was five o'clock by the time Lenox left Cove Court, only a chilly drizzle falling from the sky now. He had the night free. He was glad; for one thing, he had to find a blasted suit of clothes if he really meant to attend Mrs. Astor's ball; for another, he needed to sit and think.

For if indeed Willie Schermerhorn was innocent, who did it leave in the running? An unlikely bunch, Lenox thought as he rode up Bellevue Avenue. Vanderbilt—Clark—a madman—the old gallant colonel who had danced with all the young women that night . . .

He strode into Mrs. Berry's and was immediately warmed by the fire blazing in the parlor and the potbelly stove burning brightly near her chair, two cats stretched on the rug in front of it.

"Goodness," said Mrs. Berry, taking in the state of Lenox's clothes.

"Yes—it's wet."

"We've a few stages of dry left before we get to wet, by Newport standards—but let me fetch you—here, that's better." She had come up and was patting him dry with a towel. "I was wondering when you'd return. You have all sorts of letters and wires. And a parcel, too."

"A parcel?"

"From New York," she said.

He thanked her and took the towel to dry himself further, climbing the stairs as he did; not a moment after he had opened his door, O'Brian flew in, holding a plate of sandwiches in one hand and a pewter tankard by the handle in the other.

"Hot spiced cider," he said. "With a tot of rum. I told them you'd be hungry."

"Ah, thank you," said Lenox, and smiled a real smile. "Thank you, O'Brian."

He had taken off his boots with the bootjack and replaced his stockings, but he was otherwise still damp all over. He ate anyway, with the wind whistling and the light fading through the glass doors that looked outside. As he did, O'Brian took his wet things and set them to drying, rekindled the fire, and arranged Lenox's letters alongside the large parcel that had been haphazardly piled outside the door.

Lenox, for his part, merely chewed and drank mechanically, his mind occupied with Lily Allingham.

Before he'd left Cove Court, Clark had ventured out to the cliffside with a letter a servant had found on Willie Schermerhorn's bedside table, written to his father and explaining his actions. Based on what the father was willing to disclose—it had been a letter of several pages—his tale had largely matched Lenox's guesses. The letter also declared again his innocence from the murder of Lily Allingham—and his regret over it, too, at leaving before it was resolved, and for her parents.

"I could have loved her if we married, an outcome that this time last week I was sure would occur," the lad had written, "but I have only ever been in love, or will be, once."

By the time Lenox had left, Schermerhorn was already talking about a grandson. Resilient creatures, humans; even very rich ones.

Lenox finished the sandwiches, put the plate down with a happy sigh, and sat back on the horsehair sofa, listening to the rain, watching the fire. It occurred to him that most crucially what *hadn't* changed with Willie Schermerhorn's departure, the single fact he must bear in mind with new attention, was the location of the girl's death. She had died at Cove Court. Why? He fell into such a deep rumination over this that in fact he fell asleep, the warmth of the room cocooning him—and he stirred with some embarrassment, until he realized O'Brian, bless the boy, had withdrawn, covering him with a loose-woven blanket first.

After allowing himself a moment to get his bearings, he stretched up and out, properly awake. The plain round clock on the mantel told him it was 7:30 in the evening. He changed into a passable suit of clothes. When this was done, he turned his attention to the letters and package waiting for him.

One of the letters was a formal invitation to the ball—very elaborate, handwritten in looping calligraphy so clear it could have been typeset, and accompanied by a small watercolor of Newport (he would give that to Sophia), and a pair of solid gold cufflinks, with an image of the Astors' cottage engraved on each.

The second was from Lily Allingham's parents.

> March 19, 1878
> Wales Farm
> Newport
>
> Mr. Lenox,
> My wife Cora and I have returned here to gather our
> daughter's and our own belongings before we depart Newport.
> We should be glad to see you at your convenience.
>
> Sincerely,
> *Creighton Allingham*

Lily Allingham's father. Lenox grimaced. He felt the loss—the daughter who had been four and seven and twelve, and now would never grow older again, not though the world should carry on forever. It was sharp, it hurt, to see the handwriting of this gentleman, his adherence to forms of courtesy that must, after the death of a child, of any loved one, have seemed so meaningless to him. Yet what could one do?

In formal language, Lenox wrote a reply of thanks and asked if they would be available the next morning.

Another letter was from McConnell, and he checked to make sure it contained no pressing news before setting it aside for later; another was from Blaine, who apologized profusely for his absence from Cove Court, inquired about the case, and explained that he had been kept back on family business. He was sorry—and wanted to know what could be done to help the next day. Then there was a letter from Polly, and since she wrote to the point as a habit, Lenox read this through, after which he was apprised of the basic state of affairs of the agency, and learned that for whatever reason poor Dallington was still stumbling through Plato. "And it puts him in a foul mood," Polly added—which he smiled at, for he could hear her saying it, and she seemed very far away.

There—none of the letters were urgent. Finally, he looked at the package. It was indeed from New York, and Lenox opened it without knowing what to expect. On top was a note, however—not in the author's hand, perhaps, but unmistakably in her tone:

Have someone help you with the tie if you can.—Jane

Lenox's face broke into a smile. He unfolded the carefully packed clothes inside the package, breathing a sigh of relief—he had brought a fine black suit in which to dine out, but here were a long dark tailcoat and trousers, a white shirt with a winged collar, a white grosgrain bow tie, and a pair of gleaming black shoes, all in his sizes.

He had no idea how she'd known he was invited to the ball, let alone arranged this shipment from New York while in London, but he folded the clothes up again carefully and said a silent blessing yet again for the day he married Lady Jane Gray.

O'Brian must have heard Lenox moving about, for he returned. "Get anything for you, sir?" he said.

"I'm all right, thank you. But would you kindly ask Mrs. Berry when the telegraph office is open till?"

"Of course, sir," said O'Brian.

Before he'd left, Lenox had asked Schermerhorn if his son could make it down to Florida without stopping. He'd thought it over, and said that he thought so, in a pinch. It might be hard in heavy weather to pilot such a large vessel single-handed, but Willie would hide the bad weather out.

"If I know Willie," he'd said, "he'll slip into Bay Head and pick up Joe Collins and Sam Warshauer. Two reliable old hands. They could sail the ship in their sleep."

Lenox had asked about the telegraph office because he wanted to send word ahead to Bay Head this evening. He had a question for Willie—nothing to detain him, if his plans were to proceed to Key West, or indeed to the Cape of Good Hope—but a question, which Lenox thought could be vital . . .

O'Brian returned and said the wire operator would be there for another half hour. Lenox quickly scrawled out messages to be left at the docks at Bay Head for Schermerhorn and each of the hands his father had named, making clear that he only needed a brief answer and paying the reply postage on all three. O'Brian took them to be sent, as well as the letter to the Allinghams.

At last, all his social and animal business concluded, Lenox sat down at the small secretary near the fireplace. He had a carafe of water, brought by Mrs. Berry's grandson. He trimmed the wicks and lit the two lamps himself, so the room was bright. Through the window the detective could hear the strains of music, some concert, a string quartet; and soon he fell deep into a trance of concentration. He went over every stray note he had jotted on a receipt about Lily Allingham, every thought about the case he had written for himself to consider later.

He wrote and wrote, until at last he had a clear and concise vision of the case, which laid out every particular he knew; then he went over this, crossing out, amending, until it was perfect.

When he was done making a fair copy of this, it was midnight. He rang for O'Brian, who had been sitting outside the door, looking through the society papers, and if the red pattern on one of his cheeks was any indication quite possibly sleeping.

"Is there anything left to eat?" Lenox asked. He was bleary-eyed and tired but more contented. "I don't want to rouse Mrs. Berry."

"There's a steak in the kitchen, which she said to make free of taking, sir, after heating it up on the little black stove that's hot all night."

"Perfect. If you don't mind fetching me that, and a half bottle of wine. I shall be up late. I must think. I've been very slow, I suspect."

"Oh, I doubt it, sir!"

Lenox smiled ruefully. He crossed the room and took the cufflinks he had just received from the Astors. "You can take these if you like—or perhaps your mother might make something pretty of them. No, no, no need to thank me—just the food, if you don't mind. Leave it outside and knock. I'm famished, really I am. Then get some rest."

"I can bring the food in, sir."

"That's all right. I'll get it when I can. As I said, I need to concentrate."

CHAPTER THIRTY-FOUR

On the morning of Mrs. Astor's ball, Newport was full of more commotion than Lenox had seen even in Manhattan. He'd thought the little town was crowded the day before, but that was nothing—today quiet Bellevue Avenue was like Fourteenth Street, with horses crowded together outside every store, newsboys running among the crowds hawking papers with the latest news of the invitation list, and every few minutes someone, for private reasons, sprinting pell-mell up or down the street.

Lenox took this in from Mrs. Berry's, standing next to the swinging porch chair with his hands in his pockets. He had been up very late—very late, working from the initial document he had drawn up. It had been years since he had worked quite so closely with his own memory, for he was alone here, other than Blaine, who was barely in the infancy of his training.

So it was that Lenox had taken the time to write down from scratch every name, associating freely in his loose scrawl as he described to his own satisfaction all the people in this interwoven little community, even writing down his conversations from memory, a skill at which he had once excelled, and which he found, pleasingly, he still had.

"Anything going on today, do you think?"

Lenox turned and saw the mayor, Welling, on the street beneath the porch. He smiled. "You must be very pleased."

"Aye, she handles well in a breeze, Newport." Welling laughed. "I've too many errands myself to linger—but enjoy yourself tonight!"

This stray remark was only the first indication of the day that things had changed for Charles Lenox in America. Everywhere he went that morning, eyes seemed to be on him, including the newsstand and the chophouse where he sat outside at a sunny table and ate a plate of eggs and toast (with a pot of risibly weak tea, to which he added a double order of extra dry leaves at half-a-penny a pinch). As he was passing up Bellevue Avenue, a well-dressed young man carrying an absolutely enormous white box that said *Worth* nearly snapped at him, until seeing his face, when he made his obeisance and moved on—and Lenox was compelled to weigh the unhappy idea that his image had been in the newspaper.

Bellevue Avenue was impassible by carriage toward the cottages, and so he decided, at about nine, that he would walk the mile to see Creighton and Cora Allingham.

They met him on the front step of Wales House, a small but sweet cottage toward the tip of the island, with much of the land given over to stables. Horses roamed freely, grazing. Lenox wondered that they never ran. Two groomsmen stood not far off smoking.

"Mr. Lenox?" said the mother.

She was very pretty herself, about forty-five, with blond hair that was beginning to lighten, and large piercing eyes. Her husband was a careworn but dignified and handsome gentleman in a linen suit. Like so many here, he wore the rosette of his regiment from the war.

Neither parent seemed as inconsolable as they had a right to: manners, the great bulwark against outward grief, prevailed. They invited Lenox very politely to a shaded stone terrace overlooking the water and gave him a welcome cup of tea, much better than he'd had with his breakfast.

"Thank you for coming to see us, Mr. Lenox," said Allingham.

"On the contrary," said Lenox gravely, "I am grateful to you for making time to see me. I know these must be most difficult days."

There was a pause. Mrs. Allingham looked away. Lenox had assessed them, partly from Blaine's account, and thought he knew who they were, what in England would be called squires, or in Scotland lairds, land-owning country stock. Perhaps a little over their flight here amidst the opulence of Newport's first families, however. It was Lily—her beauty—that had lifted them so high.

"Where are you from?" Lenox asked.

"We live in New Jersey most of the year," said Allingham, "upon a gentleman's farm I acquired there after the war. We have always spent time in the city, however—my brothers both live there, and are in society a great deal. I myself prefer the countryside."

"But moved into the city when Lily was preparing to come out."

"Yes. It was clear that she had a chance to make a good match. The boys who live near us are fine young men, of course, but not cut of the same cloth."

"I always had a secret wish that she might marry Ned Braeburn," said Mrs. Allingham, more to her husband, or perhaps even herself, than Lenox. She turned to the detective. "He was a sweet boy. Ever so handsome. He graduated from the University of Pennsylvania and has set up as an engineer in Philadelphia. But what is an engineer in Philadephia to a girl with her head full of yachts, and Newport, and balls, and—you were nineteen once, Mr. Lenox!"

Lenox smiled. "When I think of how I might have handled being the apple of society's eye at that age, I feel a sort of horror. Though there was no risk of it, I can promise."

Mrs. Allingham smiled gratefully. "Exactly. And as her parents—

you only love them, after a certain . . . but oh, we must have made mistakes, because . . . if only—"

"It's all right, Cora," said Mr. Allingham, and put a hand gently on hers. "I'm sorry, Mr. Lenox. The grief is still very new."

"There is no need to apologize at all. Mr. and Mrs. Allingham, do you know who Lily intended to marry?"

They both nodded, and the husband spoke. "Willie Schermerhorn. She settled upon it a few weeks ago, and I think told him of her decision. Lily was already speaking about her trousseau, their honeymoon in Italy, the ruins in Rome."

"She needn't have even gone to that ball at Cold Farm," said Cora Allingham miserably.

"It sounds as if she was very happy."

"Oh, yes."

"But it wasn't announced yet?"

"No," said Mrs. Allingham. "Willie wanted to speak to his father formally, though Mr. Schermerhorn knew—he was very gracious to us, invited us to stay at the Cove for the whole length of the summer, though we have been happy here at Wales Farm until this week."

"I don't know that her mind was wholly made up, either," said Allingham.

"Creighton!"

"It's the truth." The wind increased in intensity for a moment, flattening the grass, causing the horses to look up, then died down. "Lily was so caught up in the world here—I don't know what she might have done had she lived. Anything."

For the first time, perhaps, Lenox realized how powerful their daughter must have seemed to the Allinghams. All their lives, she had listened to them, taken their instruction, followed their principles, and then suddenly everything had changed, and it had been she who was telling them what codes they must follow, which families counted, how one ought to behave. It must have been bewildering.

"Did Lily wear a ring?" Lenox asked.

"Several," said her mother. "She received—oh, dozens, from these gallant young boys here."

"But no special one?"

"Yes, one. She had a gold ring that we gave her on her fourteenth birthday. It had a pattern of lilies—after her name." She blushed. "You're a detective—I shouldn't have said that, I suppose—but since you asked."

"Did she wear it on her third finger?"

"Yes. Why?"

"I could tell that she had been used to wearing a ring there, and there was none near where she—lay. But perhaps she had taken it off that day."

Allingham looked unsure. "Perhaps. I cannot recall the last time I saw her without it."

"Can you tell me about the day and evening of Lily's death?" he asked.

They gave him a detailed account, much of which he already knew: an early ride on horseback with Rose Bennett, lunch on Willie Schermerhorn's yacht, preparations for the ball, and lastly the event itself.

Lenox asked them about Vanderbilt. They knew him vaguely, as one of the many boys (their word) who had often been mooning around their daughter. Keen to ingratiate himself. But they could offer no insight—probably knew him less well than did Lenox himself, in fact.

He condoled with them again before he left. He asked whether they planned to stay in Newport or return to New Jersey. Mrs. Allingham answered that they were thinking of taking a year and going to Munich; her sister lived there, she said, and her five nieces, and she might be of some use, while Creighton, she said, could finally write his memoirs.

The gentleman nodded, though to look in his eyes was to doubt that such a project would ever come to fruition. One sensed that it would take years in Munich, if not longer, for him to begin to understand what had happened three days before.

Lenox thanked them and strolled back up Bellevue Avenue, brooding the whole way about Sophia and Clara. He would have traded his ticket at Mrs. Astor's ball to be spirited back home for five minutes, he thought. When he returned to Mrs. Berry's, he stopped in at the telegraph office first, but they said that neither Willie Schermerhorn nor any of the other recipients had replied to the wires the office had transmitted the night before to Bay Head. He went back up to his room, thinking of the last thing he had told the Allinghams, that Lily's death had at least been painless and quick. He felt guilty, for he had no idea if it was true.

CHAPTER THIRTY-FIVE

Back in his rooms, Lenox discovered Fergus O'Brian standing in a ghastly, graying black suit and a frilled white shirt, his face bright as a beet.

"What are you dressed up as?" Lenox asked, amazed.

"It was Mr. Berry's suit, sir," the lad answered in a choked voice.

Lenox surveyed him critically. "Was Mr. Berry the filing clerk on a pirate ship?"

O'Brian strained to get his voice above a hoarse whisper. "I don't know, sir."

Mrs. Berry returned at that moment, beaming. "Here it is! His own tie. Only the slightest bit frayed—the frayed bit will tuck right under, too." She held up a black tie that looked as if it had been made during the presidency of John Adams. "Doesn't he look fine for the ball, Mr. Lenox? Such a handsome young gentleman."

"Very," said Lenox. "But you might want to loosen the collar slightly. It will be inconvenient if he dies of apoplexy."

"Wasn't that just the next thing I was going to do?" said Mrs. Berry. "This is a fitting."

"Oh, a fitting. Of course. Carry on, then."

O'Brian gave him a despairing look, and Lenox performed for

him the small charity of unbuttoning the top button of the shirt, to the boy's visible relief. Mrs. Berry was mending a tear in her late husband's tie and didn't notice. Better to ask forgiveness than permission.

Lenox went down to sit on the porch and read the papers. They were full of Mrs. Astor, even the front page of the *New York Times* offering a small preview of its longer story on the front page (GREAT BALL TO BE THROWN IN NEWPORT; THEME STILL SECRET) and a list of confirmed guests' names inside, Lenox's own among them.

Why had Mrs. Astor invited him? Perhaps simply because of Lady Jane; perhaps some combination of that and his exoticism, a dash of flavor. Well, he could pay her back there: For his own part, he was mostly going because he wanted to observe these foreign creatures at their pinnacle, on their finest behavior, in their most rarefied habitat.

Lily Allingham's name, he noticed, barely appeared in any of the papers, though one or two had articles (MYSTERY LINGERS OVER BEACH DEATH). It was difficult to keep a story going without new information. All the phrasing—even "beach death," rather than "murder"—might have been written by Welling, someone whose priority was to keep the information out of the public eye.

Lenox sighed. He had been sure someone would emerge from his late-night scrawlings, some definite thread.

And it was there, too—he sensed it, he could *feel* the truth of the case. But the facts still lay just beyond his grasp.

It might be, he thought, that there was too much to consider, too much crowding in around his line of vision for clear sight to be possible. At loose ends for once, he decided that he would take an hour or two away from the case, from the ball, too, and call upon Kitty Ashbrook.

He found her and Mr. Hunter sitting together in a gazebo, enjoying the breeze and reading, with iced tea on the table. They greeted him happily, the only people he had found on this island whose motives were clearly amiable, and he accepted a glass of the tea with curiosity. ("One of the traditions Newport has retained since it had a more southern population, I believe," said Kitty.) It was undrinkably sweet, he thought, though not quite bad once the ice had melted down.

They had not been invited to the ball, and though they did not quite give up hope yet—Mrs. Astor was infamously unpredictable—both seemed resigned.

After begging their discretion, Lenox told them (indeed, it had been hard to keep to himself) the details of Willie Schermerhorn's dramatic flight. They listened intently. Hunter seemed doubtful of the lad's prospects for happiness in marriage. For her part, Kitty was delighted.

"Tell me," he said suddenly, after they had been discussing one for some time, "did you ever notice Lily Allingham wearing a ring?"

"The gold one? I did."

Lenox's pulse quickened slightly. "Did you! When was the last time?"

"The day of the ball, I believe—yes, I would have noticed if it were gone. She told me about it. Her parents gave it to her."

"The day of the ball? You're sure?"

"All but sure. Why?"

Lenox looked away across the green fields toward the sparkling blue water, lovely and soft. "I'm not certain," he said. "Tell me, if I told you that it was Vanderbilt who killed her—Lawrence Vanderbilt—what would your reaction be?"

"Surprise," she said. "I wouldn't have thought him violent."

Hunter agreed.

"Quite," Lenox murmured.

But of course, it might easily be one of those murders—quite a few were like this, in truth—with an element of mischance, less a concerted effort to kill than death as a horrifying outcome of a terrible but less murderous act of violence. Of course, the outcome was no different. It left so much unclear.

Before long Hunter had to leave. He was dining with a senator from Delaware. He and Lenox parted with a friendly handshake and an exchange of sincere hopes that they might see each other before long on one side of the pond or the other, and Kitty was left alone to entertain Lenox.

"You've had a long year or two since last week," she said sympathetically.

"Yes," he said.

"Yet you've been invited to Mrs. Astor's ball! I have friends who sailed for Europe on Thursday to avoid admitting that they hadn't been. Trip booked for months as insurance—thousands of pounds—and there they sit, despondent, in the first-class dining room of some luxurious ocean liner, wishing for all the world that they might have torn up their tickets and been in your place."

"They sound like fools."

She laughed. "Perhaps. But whenever I think that of someone, I try to remember that I, too, have been a fool, and could easily be one again."

This was what he had most loved in Kitty Ashbrook, he realized: her ability to see the world differently than he did, and often more acutely. Looking at her, it was hard not to remember his lost competition with Lord Cormorant. Where would he and Kitty be sitting now, if this were their twenty-fourth year of marriage? London, probably, or perhaps the countryside. He would have chosen no other path—and she, too, seemed at peace, Hunter a sound chap to his end teeth. But that didn't mean another path had never existed. Lenox looked at his old flame and felt a distant chime of their love, his old admiration, the passionate melancholy he had felt in those quick-blooded days.

"You're quite right," he said, "and I've no doubt the things I'm foolish about are ones I don't think foolish."

"Would you stay there for a moment?" she said. "I was going to ask you to take something back to England for me."

"Of course."

She walked inside. When she returned, she was holding a slim leather case. "What is it?" Lenox asked.

"I cannot quite recall myself," she said, opening the case.

It was a piece of paper. She removed it delicately—it was obviously very old—and scanned it. At the bottom both saw a name hard to miss: Queen Elizabeth.

"It has something to do with Cormorant," said Kitty. "I think it was the grant of their land and titles, perhaps. I have never been able to read the old script. Every *s* looks like an *f*."

He laughed. "It's true."

"Besides which," she went on, in a more subdued tone, "I do not look back with great happiness on the time of that marriage. I was sorry for my husband's death. He was too young—it was a loss. But I will not pretend that my life since has not been happier. He was a cold, arrogant man, Cormorant. He had good qualities, to be sure. He gave me this on the night we married. I thought then that we might be very happy indeed."

She ran a gentle finger over the paper.

"To whom shall I take it?" asked Lenox.

She looked up. "I don't know. Cormorant's cousin, I suppose, his heir—though they say he's a drunk. It would really be ideal if there were some parson in the family, or some . . . but I have been gone so long. Has young Elijah Cormorant grown into something respectable? He was fourteen last I saw him, covered in spots, but very sweet. He went to your school. Now he would be thirty."

Lenox nodded. "Leave it in my hands."

"Ah! How I hoped you would say that. Thank you, Charles. It has weighed on my mind. You are doing me a great service."

"Then it was worth it to have come to America."

She smiled and withdrew her hand from the paper, where it had lingered. "We sail to Cape Cod tomorrow, where Hunter's people spend their summers. Perhaps I shall not see you again?"

"I could call to visit before you go."

"You would be welcome. But if you do not find the time, let me tell you how glad I am to have seen you."

"And I you."

She looked him in the eye. "Charles, I will speak openly. If I ever hurt you, I'm heartily sorry for it—I grieve it. I truly do."

He could not say that she had not hurt him, for she had. But he was a gentleman. "Oh! That is long forgotten, Kitty. Besides, every moment we spent together brought me joy," he said.

"Ah!"

"And I hope, if this is going to be a leave-taking after all, that the next time you are in London we may see each other, too."

She brightened. "Oh, yes! I shall be so curious to meet Lady Jane—the most glamorous woman in London—I shall tremble before her, I fear."

"No," said Lenox. "She will be all too delighted with you, and with Hunter, too. She loves a good American to quiz."

Kitty laughed. "Excellent. It's settled. Next year, or the year after at the very latest."

"A deal," he said.

They talked on for some time. When Lenox left, he had the leather case. Kitty rose with a smile and squeezed his hand. It was a queer feeling to go, a goodbye of more than one kind. When he looked back at Kitty from the distance of the avenue, he saw her seated again, staring out to sea, and the thought struck him, from where who knew, that for the first time in a long while she was no longer Lord Cormorant's wife, or even the young woman Lenox might have loved, but simply, and finally, herself.

CHAPTER THIRTY-SIX

There were more sightseers than partygoers at Wave Run, the Astor cottage, that fateful night. But the sightseers, too, drank champagne.

They were standing across Bellevue Avenue from the 90-room mansion, which massed into the sky above the rounded edge of Ochre Point. Welling's police lined the way to keep the peace, but Caroline Astor was less anxious about their presence. Footmen came out at seven o'clock on the dot and passed around crystal flutes with A etched in regal scroll around the base of their fragile stems. Following behind them, servants came around with jeroboams of champagne, bottles as large as four regular ones, and poured the golden liquid into any flute that was held out; and people could drink very quickly. It was the true old champagne, made from the same grapes planted by the monk who had spent his life obsessively making wine two centuries before, during the Sun King's reign, perfecting his method, Dom Pérignon.

It was the first hint of how much grander in scale the evening was to be than Lenox had conceived. Or no—perhaps the second, because at 6:30, having just changed into his new suit, he had had the surprise of hearing Mrs. Berry's grandson call out that there was a carriage for him.

Lenox hadn't ordered a carriage until 7:15. "Please tell the driver he's early," he called into the hall.

"It's from Wave Run, Mr. Lenox."

Lenox looked through his window and saw four fine sable horses waiting patiently, harnessed to a sleek carriage, with a coachman who could have been plucked from Thackeray atop its box.

Lenox made a few last adjustments and then asked Mrs. Berry's grandson to cancel his own carriage before making his way outside with O'Brian, who was staggering a little behind him in his suit, which was much too narrow in the legs and much too broad in the chest.

At least his collar was fixed. "You look splendid, O'Brian. Shall you ride on the cart?"

"Very good, sir," said O'Brian miserably.

"You can stay behind here if you prefer," Lenox said.

But the boy didn't want to miss the ball, or the company of the servants outside it. They even received the same food as the guests, according to Mrs. Berry, and some years there were party favors for them.

Four horses just for him; four hundred guests. Call it a thousand horses deployed across Newport and its environs, Lenox thought as they rode south. Astonishing.

As the carriage pulled close to the Astor mansion, Lenox saw the sightseers first, then the house.

Wave Run was the first of what Blaine had said were to be many new cottages. It was beautiful—of that there was no question at all, Lenox (having anticipated a lack of taste) ceding the point in his mind immediately. It was cream colored from the outside, with an immensely complicated series of balustrades, arcades, terraces, balconies, and promontories, like a rajah's palace. It contained more windows, people said, than any house mankind had previously produced.

The effect ought to have been overcrowded, but the stark backdrop of the sea and sky made it look, instead, rather marvelous, like a ship built to sail to the stars.

There was a long walkway between the front gates and the house, where several carriages were already jostling one another in friendly fashion, as across Bellevue Avenue the continually growing crowd of spectators watched on.

Lenox dismounted from his carriage with a thanks to his driver and started up the walkway, which had dozens of sculptures made of ice lining it, all scenes from Greek and Roman myth, he slowly perceived, a huntress Diana, Hercules wrestling a lion, and numerous others.

A gentleman with large white mustaches who happened to be strolling up the carpeted path at the same time as Lenox said, confidentially, "Can you guess the theme?"

"Ice?" said Lenox.

The man frowned at this attempted witticism and turned away, looking for his wife. No evening for frivolity, it would appear.

As Lenox neared the door, he accepted the offer of a glass of "Mrs. Astor's punch," which two gentlemen behind a bar prepared for him from scratch, squeezing and zesting what seemed a dozen different citrus fruits over ice and clear liquor.

It was delicious, and disorientingly strong. Indeed Lenox was half-drunk by the time he got to the house's front door, where an infinitely discreet personage in a white suit and sapphire-blue ascot took his name, glanced at a coterie of assistants to confirm that Charles Lenox was not someone impersonating Charles Lenox, and then, at last, ushered him into the great party.

Almost the first person Lenox saw in the large, graceful anteroom to the ball was Mrs. Astor. He bowed, a little unprepared— not far from flustered.

She was more than equal to the moment, however. "Mr. Lenox," she said, curtsying and placing a hand in his, "how kind of you to come."

"I am most grateful for your hospitality, Mrs. Astor. May I say that your dress is beautiful?"

She smiled. "Thank you. I got a new one, you know."

He laughed. He liked her instantly, upon this second meeting, though he also knew he had been read well, and that to another she might not make sport of herself. Indeed, of everyone Lenox had met in America she was obviously intelligent—awareness, thought, the motions of the mind, all these shone from her ordinary, rather mild face. In a sense she was not dissimilar from Disraeli, really.

She must have been in her forties, he supposed. She introduced him to her husband, Mr. William Backhouse Astor Jr., who seemed as bewildered as Lenox to find himself in circumstances of such overwhelmingly precise opulence, and comforted himself by taking snuff at what seemed like ten-second intervals, sneezing all over himself on each occasion.

"And do you know my cousin? His name is William as well," said Mrs. Astor.

It was Schermerhorn. He was resplendent, the little fellow, in a gray evening suit, with only a silver tie pin for decoration; the picture of Knickerbocker restraint at this particular ball, where Lenox had already seen a dozen women float by in his peripheral vision wearing jewels worth enough to subsidize a mission to the Arctic Circle.

Lenox bowed. "We are acquainted. Though I was not aware you were related, Mrs. Astor."

"My wife is a Schermerhorn by birth," said Mr. Astor. He looked around proudly, as if defying anyone to contradict this claim, and then pinched some snuff between his fingers from his silver box. "Ain't that right, William?"

"Of course it is," said Schermerhorn, irritated.

Astor looked satisfied at this confirmation of his marriage into the Dutch aristocracy, and took the snuff. The inevitable sneeze followed, during which Lenox studied him for an extra second;

whatever was left in his bloodline of his grandfather, John Jacob Astor, the great constructor of the family's fortunes, seemed to have mellowed beyond recognition.

"Your own suit looks very fine," said Mrs. Astor in a quiet voice.

"Thank you! It is new."

"I know. I wired your wife."

Lenox laughed out loud. "You have scouted me, the pair of you—I am undone. Thank you very kindly, Mrs. Astor."

They chatted a few pleasant minutes longer, until she had to greet a new fleet of guests and begged to be excused. It was perhaps her special charm that as she went, Lenox had the feeling he had made a friend.

Lenox and Schermerhorn were left alone. Lenox asked with sincere interest about the house, and Schermerhorn first reluctantly and then more enthusiastically began to describe Wave Run's building to him as they drifted through the vaulted round entry room, which had parquet floors and whose furniture was all in a beautiful shade of walnut, with dark blue upholstery. There were servants in every direction, yet never in the way; strings playing in the corner; an infinity of food, but tactfully recessed into the parts of the room where it could be perused without attracting notice.

"I hope you have been well?" Lenox asked Schermerhorn as they neared the vast doors which would lead into the rest of the party—the true party.

"As well as can be hoped, given the circumstances."

Lenox paused for a moment, hands behind his back. "Did you ever hear of Viscount Palmerston?" he said.

"Of course," said Schermerhorn. "He was your Prime Minister."

"Yes, exactly. Twice, in fact. At any rate, I have long remembered something he said to me once: 'Lenox, only three people have ever really understood that Schleswig-Holstein business—the Prince Consort, who is dead; a German professor, who has gone mad; and I myself, who have forgotten every detail of it.' Then he laughed."

"I'm not sure I'm familiar with the Schleswig-Holstein family," said Schermerhorn.

Lenox stood there rather awkwardly, his anecdote a failure. Suddenly it occurred to him that Schermerhorn wasn't very *bright*—his whole mental world lay within the parameters of his identity, those tulips, the Battle of Albany, Cove Court.

"I suppose what I mean to say is that nobody remembers these intricacies after the fact."

Schermerhorn looked at him sidelong. "Oh. You would be surprised," he said.

"Tell me, will Lawrence Vanderbilt be here?" Lenox said, hoping to change the subject.

Successfully: Schermerhorn looked appalled. "No."

"I see."

"The Vanderbilts are—" He searched for the word, and, with the confidence of a very rich man, didn't even consider speaking until at last he found it. "New."

"I see."

"Tell me, Mr. Lenox," said Schermerhorn, "I am afraid there is still talk about Willie on the winds. Do you know yet who killed Miss Allingham?"

Lenox replied that he did not. If he had been in a surlier mood, he would have added that the exculpation of Willie was of less moment to him than the solution to the crime.

A servant presented him with a fresh glass of punch, and Schermerhorn with a new whisky, and the conversation moved on.

CHAPTER THIRTY-SEVEN

It was the Blaine family who interrupted the slightly tense conversation between Lenox and Schermerhorn: four guests, all of different mien, fresh from being greeted by Caroline Astor themselves.

"Good evening, Blaine," said Lenox in a collegial tone.

Blaine blushed, looking happy to be recognized, and said good evening. He had on the same round black glasses that he always wore, and in manner seemed his usual diffident self, but he was dressed well, in a dark suit and a silk top hat. He still carried his battered old walking stick, though even this had been beautified, polished as well as could be, the gold ring that joined its pieces shining anew.

"Allow me to introduce you to my father, Mr. Lenox. Father, this is Charles Lenox, who is in the States from London. He was once a Member of Parliament. He is a detective now."

Blaine's mother and Schermerhorn were speaking, and Lenox, in a flying glance, classed them together. Blaine's mother had a lovely profile; like Schermerhorn, she was small, vain, and seemingly motivated largely by social interest, her eyes darting around the spacious room.

Blaine's father was a more unusual specimen. He had a large, powerful-looking head, mathematical somehow. He never seemed to quite meet one's eye—but not in a shame-faced or rude way, more as if it would have caused him pain. What hair he had left hung in a low fringe over his collar, and one could see the veins flickering in his muscular temples. He had no passion for niceties. Blaine's mother made up for that, as did her very obvious protégé, the sunnily handsome young Winthrop Blaine, the chap who had been teasing all the girls at that tea at Greystone.

Lenox spoke highly of Teddy Blaine's abilities to his parents—unsure of whether anyone was paying attention, though he suspected that very little passed by the elder Blaine, or indeed for that matter, on a different level, his wife.

The detective, sipping his punch, was curious about Blaine's father, who had left Georgia with eighteen dollars at the age of twelve and was now one of the richest men in the world. Nothing drew him out, however, until Lenox mentioned that the Astor house was a very lovely setting.

"I suppose—I don't care for balls," said the elder Blaine.

"How do you prefer to pass your time?"

"Reading."

"What do you like to read?" asked Lenox.

Archie Blaine considered the question. "I like this fellow Eliot. *Middlemarch* is my idea of a good book."

Apparently this was a strange enough reply that the other Blaines, as well as Schermerhorn, looked over. "You've been reading novels, Father?" asked his elder son.

"Yes, I have," said his father. "I used to do sums in the evening, but now they tell me I must have culture—and I don't mind, except I refuse to read Carlyle."

"Heavy going," Lenox said, diplomatically.

"Trash," Archie Blaine said, less diplomatically.

At that moment, all the clocks chimed eight o'clock in perfect unison. A rare feat, Lenox reflected, but no doubt they had all been set by the butler's pocket watch just moments before the party to guarantee it.

"Supper," said a servant, whose attire would not have shamed a meeting of the House of Lords. Lenox hoped poor O'Brian wouldn't encounter him in Mr. Berry's antique suit.

As a low chatter resumed and they all drew toward the doors, Lenox had a chance to observe the people in the room.

The women were dressed in what at least seemed to him like quite precarious gowns, great shifting piles of tulle, silk, and taffeta. He knew from Lady Jane (and now from experience) that no lady here was allowed to show an inch of flesh in the daytime, while at night the standards were different, and indeed Rose Bennett had on a pink gown whose decolletage revealed her ribs, a daring, fantastical sort of garment, Lenox would have said.

She was with a group of friends, one in a high-necked blue gown but with her arms bare and different diamonds on every finger, another in a dress of yellow and white with a small bustle, an allusion to the fashion of Lenox's own boyhood, but so different, so much less frumpy, that he smiled to see it. He could picture Lily Allingham laughing conspiratorially among them. His heart gave a quick ache at the thought.

He found that he had accidentally fallen into the conversational firing range of young Winthrop Blaine. "So you've met the whole clan!" the young man said.

"Yes, with great interest. I understand you yourself are just back from Harvard."

"I am." He lifted a small cigar to his mouth and looked over at Lenox. "You know, I think we all appreciate the time you have given my brother. But I would warn you that he is a queer sample. He has been strange his whole life, Teddy. It's for your own sake that I mention it."

"I think he would make a good detective."

"Yes? Perhaps so. I fear you have a tender nature, however."

"Not unusually so, I would have said. Believe it or not, I am known as a competent judge of character in my part of the world."

The young man put up a conciliatory hand. "I do not doubt it for a moment. I only said something because he is my brother—I felt bound in duty. But I leave the field to you."

"Tell me, how did your father start out?"

Winthrop Blaine looked surprised. They were shuffling slowly toward the doors, the scent of perfume on the air, the chatter getting louder.

"He worked at a general store in Poughkeepsie," said Winthrop Blaine. "He still owns it. I've been there several times, as it happens—the field expeditions of our youth. He slept under the counter when he was starting out."

"And saved his money, I take it."

"Worked, I think, more like—he did not marry until he was forty-eight, you know, Father. He had been working ceaselessly until then. By the time he was sixteen he owned a partial share of the store. By the time he was twenty he owned a railroad. By the time he was thirty he owned Little Rock and half of Arkansas. And now apparently he reads novels."

Winthrop Blaine had a strange look on his face as he recapitulated this story of success, somwhere between strong pride and equally strong embarrassment, and Lenox looked at him with a new curiosity. He wondered why the Blaine family was considered acceptable here, yet not the Vanderbilts, who were just as rich.

"A remarkable person," said Lenox.

"Ah! Yes, I think so. Yet those of us less remarkable are luckier, I sometimes reflect. History shall never know my name, yet I venture I am happier than most of those whose names it will."

This was a more interesting observation than Lenox had expected from Winthrop Blaine. "You must know Lawrence Vanderbilt."

"Lawrence? Indeed I do. And perhaps I should take this opportunity to say that he could not have killed Lily, not in a million years. Not in ten million."

"You are friends?"

"Friends? Not quite. We do share a set. And we are very old acquaintances."

"What makes you so certain of his innocence?"

Winthrop dropped his cigar into a gold ashtray on a plinth near the doorways. "I just know him."

That was unconvincing on its face, of course, but it did carry a strangely powerful conviction. "Who do you think did it, then?"

The young man shrugged. They were entering the dining room. "I do not know. A madman, I would have thought. What table are you? Ah—I thought so." Winthrop put out his hand. "We part ways, then. Good evening, Mr. Lenox."

Lenox shook his hand. There was not so much harm in the fellow as he had thought. "Mr. Blaine."

The detective paused after they had separated and allowed himself a minute simply to stare. For it was wondrous to behold, the room, the party, the supper. He wanted to remember every detail so that he could write to Jane. In the dining room there was a suite of eight enormous paintings by Rubens, which hung magisterially above a dozen large round tables, each one of them its own glittering splash of beautiful silver, gold, and crystal.

What was the theme? That had been the great subject of the papers—but Lenox wondered if there was one at all. Beauty, perhaps; every second person was a beautiful young man or woman, and he had to give Mrs. Astor credit, for they made up a greater proportion of the gathering than he would have expected, given how prized the invitations were, but also quite unconsciously added to the evening a gaiety, a sense of possibility and enthusiasm and mischief, some of them looking deliriously happy to be there. You wanted that, Lenox saw, glancing over at Caroline Astor, who was having a friendly, fast, and evidently devastating word with a servant, who went pale and nearly sprinted toward the kitchen.

The Greeks and the Romans, of course, he suddenly saw—all the Rubenses were of Roman myths, and the ice sculptures had been, too. So the paintings, by the most expensive of all history's artists, were *specific to the evening.* Lenox, who had thought he was beyond astonishment, was astonished.

"Wire, sir," said a footman behind Lenox.

Lenox turned, curious. "For me?"

"Yes, sir."

"Thank you for finding me."

"Your valet Mr. O'Brian was adamant that you would wish to see it," said the young man without inflection.

"He was quite right. Thank you."

The footman bowed. "Sir."

It was with some distraction, when he was alone again, that Lenox looked at the little envelope, with its familiar *Western Union Telegram* lettering in the upper left-hand corner.

The truth was that he had known for ten minutes or so who had killed Lily Allingham, he realized. Perhaps that was why he had paused on the edge of this room. He surveyed it again, with a heavy heart, thinking of what he must do. Then he tore open the wire. As he expected, it was a reply from Willie Schermerhorn. He read it, and now he was sure.

CHAPTER THIRTY-EIGHT

Caroline Astor had done Lenox a very good turn in seating him. To one side of him was an awful bore, it was true, an old, deaf gentleman, much interested in birds, an Astor—but this fellow had a close friend in this passion to *his* direct right, a tall woman who rather looked like a crane herself in fact, and they amused each other to no end discussing egrets, long-eared owls, and other birds they had seen.

Meanwhile, to Lenox's left Mrs. Astor had placed the perfect guide to the evening, a very Virgil.

His name was Belmont. Society ran on fellows like him—men who took real pleasure in company, who discussed the affairs of others inveterately but not maliciously, bore no grudges, could play a hand of cards, sit a horse, and make themselves agreeable toward any lady without being impertinent. He knew everything about the opera, and as for ancestry, Lenox doubted whether anyone alive could have matched Belmont's elaborate knowledge of the lineal relations of the people inside and outside of the room.

As they ate macaroni *parisienne* (anyone trying to count the courses would have found his or her mind outpaced by the shuffling servants, appearing in graceful waltz with new dishes before the most recent had even been investigated), Belmont told Lenox enough that soon he felt he might actually understand Newport.

"They live at Briar Hall," he was saying, nodding toward a radiant young woman with an older gentleman. "Married a month ago."

"Is she the *parvenu*, as it were?" Lenox asked.

"The opposite. He made his fortune in fur. He had his study carpeted in hundred-dollar bills when they met."

"What a bother to clean."

"Whereas she's a Minuit, but one of the poor ones. You'll be pleased to hear she's renovated the house and given him a new study. It's the largest house on Thirty-Fourth Street now, I think."

It was the rare party at which almost everyone seemed genuinely happy. Of course, this was partly because there were something like a dozen glasses for various wines and spirits at each setting, filled with precision by the army of servants who flowed through the room as smoothly as water over a creek bed.

Lenox sipped but did not drink; his attention was sharp. The food was of a perfection too rich for his taste, but superb to be sure, and he wasn't even tracking all that was lost on him—the real gold foil around each croquette which opened to reveal a different poem etched inside, the tinkling stand of silver bells in the center of each table with the guests' names, each on an individual one; an endless flow of small touches, dozens, hundreds of them—but he would have to read in the papers what they had been, so little of his attention could they claim from thoughts of Lily Allingham's murder. His small, beautiful silver sculpture of Ariadne, a thanks for coming from Mrs. Astor—ha!—had already been packed and sent to his boardinghouse, a footman discreetly informed him when he realized he had lost track of it. Belmont's Hermes was gone as well, they realized. Goodness! How could anything be so well managed! It put the Egyptians to shame; and as for England, she looked like a country of the most bizarrely simple tastes, positively Shaker, side by side with this pageantry.

At nine—shortly before the main course was to be served—
Lenox managed to cross the room to where Teddy Blaine sat between a very beautiful young woman in a pink gown and a very
plain one in a blue gown. No doubt he was meant to pick one of
them to marry, Lenox thought.

"Do you have five minutes to spare?" Lenox asked Blaine in a
quiet voice when the ladies' attention was momentarily distracted.

"Of course."

"There is a small study two doors to the left down that hallway
by the musicians. I shall be there at nine fifteen."

Blaine glanced up at one of the clocks and nodded. "Shall I make
my excuses to be gone for the rest of the evening?"

"No, no," said Lenox hurriedly, and then, nodding to confirm
the rendezvous, went back to his table.

On his way, however, he was stopped by the greeting of Rose Bennett. After complimenting her earrings and her hair, his minimal
duties as a gentleman on such an evening, he asked her a question,
received the answer he expected, and after thanking her, moved on
through the room.

He was tense with concentration now, and running over all the
factors of the case in his mind even as he offered phatic nods to
Belmont's anecdotes and observations. Clark, Miss Morris, Vanderbilt, the telegram, Cove Court, Lily Allingham, Creighton and Cora
Allingham, Wave Run, Blaine, Mayor Jack Welling—tightening and
tightening the thing in his mind, indeed almost hoping it would col-
lapse. But it did not.

He excused himself just at the arrival of the first dessert course—a
towering confection agleam with honey and sugar—and went to
meet Blaine.

He had found the little room quite by accident earlier in the evening. It was presumptuous to commandeer it, but he had no other
choice. There were servants passing up and down the hall, but if

any wondered why he was going into a private room belonging to the Astors, none asked.

And indeed, the room was strangely denuded of personal effects, as if specifically set out for just such a use. There were rows of leather-bound books here, likely bought by the yard, pages still un-cut; on the desk, an inkstand and plenty of paper with the house's name and likeness on it; in the windows, stained-glass images of old Knickerbocker New York. Maybe this was all purposeful, Lenox thought—in such a large house, no doubt often filled with people laboring under responsibilities of national importance, a room like this was a convenient one to lend to others.

Blaine had the same thought when he entered, closing the door quietly behind him. "Good evening, Lenox. A good private spot to have found."

"It is, too," said Lenox.

There were two soft fawn couches facing each other, the room's only other furniture, and Lenox sat down on one of their arms.

He looked at the aspiring young detective, who was leaning on his walking stick, still studying the room, and waited for his gaze to settle back on Lenox.

Finally it did, and Lenox spoke.

"Why did you kill Lily Allingham, Blaine?"

Theodore Blaine started, and then fixed his eyes on Lenox with an expression of disbelief. "Excuse me?"

Lenox had been in this moment on many occasions before. "I know it was you," he answered in a voice of practiced softness. "But I would like to know why."

The smile dimmed on Blaine's face. A moment before, he had been prepared to discuss the case with Lenox, perhaps run some useful errand. But that person was gone. And somehow, without any visible change, all the power of Blaine's family's money had returned to his posture. Standing there, he looked quite debonair, handsome even, and exuded the power of his position.

"Know what was me, Mr. Lenox?" he said.

"Could I see your walking stick for a moment?"

Blaine's pale skin went a mottled red. "My what?"

"Your walking stick."

"Certainly not. Are you making sport of me because I am hobbled? For shame."

"Of course not," said Lenox. "Sit, if you would prefer—but I would still like very much to see your walking stick."

Blaine tightened his grip on the scratched and battered black cane. "My father gave this to me after my accident. I've had it since I was nine."

Lenox had assumed Teddy Blaine's disability had been with him since birth. Interesting. "I would only like to look at it for ten seconds. It does not seem much to ask."

"Why on earth should you need to look at another man's cane?" Blaine asked, and gave an ugly laugh.

"Come, now, Teddy," said Lenox. "I cannot pretend to know your exact motivations—"

"This harassment is too much," said Teddy, and from his position near the desk, closer to the door, stood to go. "I am disappointed, I confess. I had hoped you might be a mentor."

"You—"

"But of course you're no more than another busybody, looking to take advantage of my father's money."

"I am not, Teddy. And my patience is growing thin."

The sudden anger in Lenox's voice caused the young man to hesitate.

"What is it you think you know?" he said, looking back. In that instant, Lenox saw—thought he saw—a terrible malice course through Theodore Blaine's face, before it reverted to its usual diffident, impassive expression. "Something about Lily Allingham? And *me?*"

"If it is all so preposterous, you will let me see your cane."

"No!"

The cane was half-hidden at Blaine's side now. "Remind me—when did you propose to Lily Allingham? Over the winter, I believe?"

Blaine's face was no friend to him—it became mottled again, raw and angry. "That was all a mistake. Who told you about it? It was a mistake."

"One, I suppose, that must have hurt. It sounds as if she wasn't very discreet about the rejection of you. And no one likes to be laughed at."

Blaine was crimson now. "A gentleman's private affairs are—"

"*Every cripple and scrounger in New York*, those were Willie Schermerhorn's words to me. I should have realized sooner that he meant them literally."

"That word—"

"But you did propose to her?"

"I have never killed anyone."

Lenox rubbed at a tiny mistake on the couch's upholstery. "My real question, Blaine, is why you came and found me."

He looked up. At this question there was—even now—a gleam of triumph in Blaine's eye. Didn't he know the whole thing was up?

The young heir went to the door. But not, as Lenox had imagined, to leave. Instead, he locked it. Then he pulled a small revolver from his jacket pocket and placed it, thoughtfully, on the desktop, leaving a hand on its grip.

He looked up. "I was curious how good you were," he said. "That is why I came to you. Not bad, I suppose. A bit slow. Here—would you like to look at my cane after all? Not many people ask."

CHAPTER THIRTY-NINE

Lenox took the ebony walking stick from Blaine, who had picked up the gun.

"Lily Allingham's ring," Lenox murmured, looking closely at the gold band that joined the two pieces of the cane. There were lilies dancing in an endless loop around it, just as Cora Allingham had described.

"Yes."

Lenox returned the walking stick to Blaine. "You took a souvenir from the scene then. You will know from my research it is not an uncommon thing to do."

Blaine shrugged, smiling faintly. "How did you spot that it was hers?"

"Your walking stick had a silver band on it when we met."

Blaine clapped his hands together, with seemingly sincere delight. Like all of his kind, Lenox thought—cold-blooded killers, not hot-blooded ones—he was in the end desperate to talk. "You really are a detective! I should never have guessed you would notice something so small. When I dropped off my cane to be repaired with the new ring, I assumed I would be the only one who ever noticed the little joke. What a pity."

Lenox stared at him for a long beat. "Just to be clear in my mind, then, you and I met at Delmonico's. But the same night you slipped up here, killed Lily Allingham, and returned in time to meet me at the train station the next morning."

Blaine nodded. "Yes, just so," he said, after the briefest pause.

That admission meant he was going to use the gun, Lenox knew. His job now was to buy himself time.

"Shall I tell you how I put it together? You must be curious—here at the endgame."

"Yes. Please do. Would you like to smoke?"

He felt weary to the bottom of his soul. Why had he imagined he wanted to come to America? What sort of game had this boy entrapped him into playing?

"No, thank you," said Lenox.

Blaine lit one. "Then please, continue."

"Ah. Where to begin. Let me think." Lenox frowned at the floor for a moment. In truth he was thinking about his position—when they would be missed from the party. "One question, first—what if Schermerhorn had not sent for me? I assume you wanted it to be me who investigated, after all—to match your wits against mine?"

"I would have received a wire with the news when we arrived in Boston," said Blaine. "I think I could have convinced you to come to Newport."

"Yes. No doubt you could have," said Lenox. Then, mostly to himself, "I have grown arrogant."

Blaine looked bored. "It can't only have been the ring."

"No. Of course not."

"Then what?"

"Your meeting with your father was a misstep."

Blaine winced. "Ah. Yes. I realized that one at the time, but you didn't seem to catch it."

Lenox remembered the article (*"The mountain shall come to Muhammad!"*) breathlessly announcing that the elder Blaine, the great tycoon, would be coming to Newport on the day of the ball, that very Saturday morning.

But Teddy had used a meeting with his father as an excuse the day before that.

"I might have been telling a simple fib to cover up for some other reason," Blaine said. He sounded almost as if he were on the stage in a debating society. Lenox ignored it.

"I should have seen from the start how scarce you made yourself—how many of our meetings and my steps in the investigation you missed, from that very first day onward. I assume now it was because you thought someone might have seen you the night you killed Lily Allingham—Vanderbilt, Schermerhorn, anyone really—and wanted to lie low."

"Yes. I had to appear at the ball at Cold Farm briefly, unfortunately, for my plan to work."

Lenox thought of the telegram in his pocket. He would hold that back—if he were shot, it could tell its own story.

"It was surprising, in retrospect, how you took the lead in our conversation with Mrs. King. But I suppose you were ready to cut her off at the pass if she happened to be on the verge of saying anything about you being at the ball or knowing Lily."

Blaine nodded. "Yes."

"And you told her to get in touch with you, not me, if she remembered anything else, I remember." Lenox stared at Blaine. "But I am only speculating. Tell me the thing in your own words."

Blaine grinned. "You're quite good, you know."

"Good?"

"For an instant there I thought we were only talking! It's an impressive skill. I must remember it."

"So you really mean to be a detective, Teddy?" said Lenox.

"And using my first name. Clever. I shall remember that, too. But it won't work on me—I don't feel what other people feel. All that rot."

Suddenly Lenox remembered what Winthrop Blaine had said. *My brother has always been different.* Lenox had assumed this was intra-familial snobbery, but it had been a real warning. Fair play to the boy. He must have been trying and failing to alert people against the machinations of his pitiable, retiring brother for many years now, felt that scorpion sting himself.

Blaine's father, with his overpowering intellect and drive allied to his shy manners; his mother, with her artificiality, glitter, her pressed cheer: Together, they had created this hideous mind.

"What other people feel?"

"In other words," said Blaine, who was now comfortable enough that he took another small cigar from the spring-loaded silver box on the desk and lit it, "all that sentimental tripe—feeling close to you, or as if I owed you something, or less inclined to kill you because you use my name. Still, as I say, a clever thought."

"What did you feel for Lily Allingham?"

Blaine carefully blew away a scrap of glowing paper that was clinging to the tip of his cigar. It settled to the rich, intricate Persian rug between them and died. "It is banal to say it, but I had never seen a more beautiful girl."

"Then beauty is not lost on you," said Lenox.

"No."

"And you asked her to marry you."

"Yes. A Blaine, offering her a hand in marriage! She would have been a princess of New York."

"Perhaps she laughed at the idea," said Lenox. "Or you were angry that she might have—behind your back. I know that she could often be rude."

Blaine shook his head furiously. "Be quiet!"

Lenox obeyed this order. At length, it was the younger man who broke the silence.

"She didn't laugh. But she ought to have been more polite. A little nothing like that. She barely stopped to say no."

"Hm."

If Blaine had noticed Lenox's methods for encouraging people to talk before, his vigilance had wavered, for he went straight on now, as if he were with an old and sympathetic friend.

"A rejection I could have stood!" he said, standing up from the desk and turning distractedly away in his zeal to be understood. "But for *Schermerhorn*—good lord, that proud, puffed-up, inconsequential little dullard. Now that I could not abide."

"I take it you hoped that he would stand accused of the murder," Lenox said. "That is why you lured her to Cove Court."

"Yes." Blaine puffed on the cigar. "First I arranged for her to learn about Willie's previous attachments I assumed that might loosen his grip on Lily. I had not given up."

"Maryanne Morris. How did you know about her?"

"Everyone on this blasted island knew. Everyone my age. It was a joke. But Lily was stupid. Once she found out, she broke with Willie. Thus far my plan had worked, you see."

"But then, instead of choosing you, she chose Vanderbilt," said Lenox. "She showed you the flask to prove it."

"Yes!" said Blaine, shaking his head with disbelief. "Vanderbilt, of all people—as flashy, as stupid a man as you could care to meet. She was throwing away her life anyway. If I helped hasten along the end, I see no way I can be blamed for that."

"Did you plan to kill her all along?"

Blaine shrugged. "If she had consented, I would have married her. As it was, I decided that she and Willie could both go."

So he had gone into that late-night meeting at Cove Court planning either to marry or murder. "And the flask?"

"She showed it to me, as you said. After she broke off with Willie—ha!—I had a note slipped to her, telling her to come up the Cliff Walk. I sent it on very fine paper, with a diamond ring. I knew she couldn't resist that. A little mystery. Silly girl.

"It was the perfect time. Nobody about, a cloudy night. I told her again that I would marry her. But she wouldn't listen. She had been crying. In fact she was drunk, Welling was right about that, Maryanne Morris had shared a glass of gin to console her.

"I asked again. I gave her a very fair chance to accept me. Anyone who was there would have to admit that. But she wouldn't listen.

"It was no trouble to get her near the edge of the cliff. I had a chunk of rock in my pocket, but then she showed me the flask and it was too—well, it seemed perfect, put Vanderbilt in the mix as well. A perfect crime, really. That was how it struck me as I was walking away down the beach, back home. I was quite satisfied, if you must know. I'm trying to remember whether I wanted to murder her, as you ask. I suppose I did, in a way. You see, I'd been reading about you for so long."

Lenox felt sick. "About me."

"Yes. The great detective. And when I saw you were coming to New York! The papers full of your arrival, everyone at the opera talking about your old triumphs . . . well—I have always been fascinated with crime, you see. I had to know for myself what I would be up against. I knew if she wouldn't marry me, I had to kill her to meet you."

Lenox already saw that he would carry this knowledge heavily in his heart for the rest of his days. But there was no time to consider it at the moment, not when this might be his last day itself.

"And now?"

"And now I have met you," he said. "I admit the ring was a step too far, but it's been such a lovely few days, you see, having a secret no one else knew, and I thought about coming to the ball, opening the season, and knew I had to have the ring on my cane. Ah, well. More's the pity. But was there anything else? My father, Cold Farm . . ."

"There were one or two other details."

"What?"

"They don't matter, Teddy. It's over."

Blaine smiled faintly. "Yes, you're right," he said. "It is."

And with a powerful stride forward, more powerful than Lenox would have expected he could make, he drove something deep into the right side of Lenox's body.

Lenox was sitting on the sofa's edge, and for a moment felt nothing. Had it been a fist? But Blaine was rather weak! How could he expect that to work?

Except that then Lenox experienced a sudden, rushing loss of focus, quite unlike anything he had known before. He stumbled backward and fell onto the floor, clutching his ribs, hitting the sofa on his way. He looked down and saw that there was blood where his hands had gone to his side.

Blaine was walking back toward the desk, saying something. Lenox strained to listen.

"The gun would be too loud. As it is, this will make for a good mystery—the person investigating Lily Allingham's death, murdered himself. I look forward to investigating in fact. My first case. Welling will make no trouble."

Blaine had stubbed out his cigar and was approaching the detective again now, dragging his right leg. There was something gripped in his hand, and Lenox's whole being recoiled from it, the wound in his side giving an awful wrench at the sight. Then he saw: It was a long, very sharp knife, which Blaine was gripping so hard that his knuckles were white.

With his last energy, Lenox groped in his boot for the knife Jane had given him. He pulled it out. Even then all he could do was slash feebly at the air, it was enough to drive Theodore Blaine and his knife back for an instant, though how far Lenox had no idea—a foot, twenty feet, to his swimming vision it was all the same.

He slashed again. He couldn't quite remember where he was. Still, he parried the air, using all his strength in his left arm—his right was strangely useless—did he *have* a right arm—oh yes—he glanced down—of course—oh blast it all he had forgotten that of course—sensing the approach of a dark large shape, he swung his left arm wildly, just in time to drive Teddy Blaine's face back an inch or two—he swung it again—but then the light around him was turning black—he was spent, utterly spent—he thought of home—and finally, against his last shred of will, he fell into that void only the mortally wounded have known.

CHAPTER FORTY

Was he in Amsterdam?

Lenox realized with some relief that yes, he must be in Amsterdam again, for the room in which he finally opened his eyes was a quiet comfortable brown one, with hunter green curtains pulled close over two vertical slits of late evening darkness. Yes, Amsterdam. When had he come here though?

The next time he woke he realized it wasn't Amsterdam but Haarlem, its neighbor. He could tell. The good old dark wood, the slightly damp air. The northern country. The lowlands. He was looking forward to seeing the canals again, the men in their odd hats. He liked the paintings very much. But why had he come here? And now it was midday, too—but he was in bed. That was wrong. He struggled up and felt a blinding heat, and then heard a voice saying something, and felt a blessed coolness on his forehead. Then he was asleep again.

It was when he woke up the next time that he remembered for the first time that he was, of course, in America. There was candlelight playing on the walls and two people were hovering above him. One of them smelled like mothballs. That was all he had time to register before there was a sharp needle in his arm, and then relief coursing through his wracked body . . .

Until at last, on the sixth day, the fever broke, and he opened his eyes in the very early morning to see a figure slumbering in the armchair next to his bed.

It took him a long moment to realize who it was. He had assumed it would be O'Brian, possibly Wyatt. But he was wrong.

"Graham?" Lenox said hoarsely. "Can that be you?"

But his voice was so out of use—so soft—that the chair didn't hear, and before he could try again, Lenox fell back to sleep.

At last, at around four o'clock that afternoon, he woke up to a living world. There was a nurse changing a pitcher of water, and two doctors standing and talking in subdued tones next to his bed. The light was watery and clear, rather beautiful—New York light.

"Ah! The patient awakens!" said one doctor, smiling. "How do you feel, Mr. Lenox?"

Lenox was still, even in his deteriorated state, detective enough to know from the man's tone that the news was good, that he was going to survive. Without answering, but with some inner spring of relief loosed by the revelation that he would not leave Jane a widow, not leave his daughters fatherless, he fell asleep again.

It was that evening at around seven o'clock that he woke up and felt real clarity for the first time. He almost thought he must have imagined Graham, but there he was, sitting at the bedside.

"Graham?" said Lenox.

Graham drew a little closer in. "It's very good to see you up, sir," he said.

"Theodore Blaine—"

"Yes. It's all over. It's done."

Lenox's whole body relaxed. If Graham said it was over, it was over. If he said it was done, it was done. So.

Lenox and Graham had known each other for thirty years now. Lenox found himself brought to the brink of tears by thinking that his friend had come all the way across the Atlantic. It must be the wound—he chastised himself, and let his head roll away from

Graham, the effort of holding it up exhausting, so that if tears had appeared in his eyes no one should be able to see them. Ridiculous, after all; the knife wound costing him his sanity.

Graham was a compact, sandy-haired person, who for many years had been Lenox's valet. Latterly he had gone into politics and shot through into the firmament of that profession's stars in Britain, making himself as indispensable to the nation as he once had been to Lenox.

Lenox fell asleep again. When he woke, it was in a panic. "Theodore Blaine?" He pushed himself up onto an elbow. The pain in his side went hot with flames. "Teddy Blaine? You must—"

Graham was still there, and patiently talked Lenox out of his confusion. When the detective had taken a ginger sip of water and lain back, Graham told him the story in a quiet voice.

"There was a chap named Clark listening at the door the entire time. He has given the police a full account of every word the two of you exchanged."

"Clark," said Lenox, momentarily unequal to this information. "James Clark?"

"And of course, there was the telegram."

The telegram. He had forgotten. But he could bring it into his mind as clearly as if he had just opened it, which he thought must be some kind of good sign, the telegram he had received that night from Willie Schermerhorn, sent in at Bay Head, New Jersey, by the Western Union lines:

> Was younger Blaine who told Lily about Maryanne
> STOP But he has done me a favor STOP Tell father
> letter coming STOP Mind made up STOP Cannot
> deny love STOP WS

Blaine had made numerous small errors, but only this telegram and the ring tied him definitively to the murder. Lenox was pondering this when he realized he had closed his eyes and was again nearing sleep.

But there was so much to say—to know, to ask. He adjusted himself so that his side would hurt a little less, but as soon as that was done, rather than pursuing the conversation further, he fell asleep once more.

It was fifteen days after Mrs. Astor's ball when Lenox first rose to his feet again.

The knife wound had penetrated his torso just beneath the last rib on his right-hand side, tearing into his liver and his gallbladder according to the best of the doctors, a phlegmatic young professor at the college of medicine in Philadelphia.

"You are fortunate the knife did not touch the peritoneum," he had told Lenox, when the detective was at last fit enough to sit up and understand, "or indeed the stomach."

"Am I?"

"I suppose you must be the judge of that. We would not be having this discussion if it had."

In truth, Lenox probably rose from his bed too early—but Lady Jane had arrived the evening before with Sophia and Clara, and he couldn't bear to let them see him unable to move, even if it was only a few creaky steps he managed. Sophia was old enough to be worried, and Lenox realized, with a sad fall in his heart, that she was creating a permanent memory, that she would never forget their sea voyage to see her injured father.

He tried to make up for it by good cheer now.

"Did it hurt?" she asked him.

He was in a smoking jacket near the window. Graham had helped him dress, for the first time in a dozen years. They were in a small, sweet white house on Washington Square, with daffodils growing wild in the little yard in front of it.

"I suppose it must have!" he said. "I can't quite remember."

"Can I see it?"

He opened his jacket to show her the padding of bandages beneath his shirt. "It's all freshly dressed up now—like a doll, you see."

She nodded, though she looked confused. Later that day she and her governess began making bandages for her own dolls; not white, like Lenox's, as Sophia herself pointed out seriously, but blue, because that was the only material Miss Huntington had. Lenox said he thought it would do just as well.

It was Graham who had arrived from England first, of course, and in the last six days, preceding Jane's arrival, they had spent more time together than at any point in the last decade. It was amazing how rapidly they fell back into their old bachelor routines though: at seven (once Lenox was conscious again) Graham would come in with newspapers and a wax paper bag of savory pastries from the baker on Washington Square while O'Brian made tea. Then they would sit in the second-story bedroom with the papers, occasionally commenting to each other on stories, breaking to delve deeper into a subject, while gradually birdsong, light, and the scent of Washington Square's high birch trees filled the quiet room on the second floor.

"Take me through it one more time," Lenox said almost every morning.

Then the sometime butler would tell Lenox the story of his survival again.

It had indeed been Clark who broke into the study and saved Lenox's life—Clark, whom Lenox had suspected, along with his master and various others (even Rose Bennett!) as he made his speculations, before his focus had resolved itself onto Teddy Blaine.

He wrote to thank the Union veteran. He had also asked why Clark was at the ball. There had been a brief response from Schermerhorn's man, apologizing that he had not entered the room sooner—he had been listening carefully, he replied, and neither Blaine nor Lenox's voice had led him to believe they were close to any kind of physical violence until the last possible moment.

This was true, of course; Lenox specifically remembered not acknowledging the gun.

He had been at the ball, Clark said, because a young woman had been murdered on his master's property; he had followed Blaine and Lenox to eavesdrop on them. In his reply to Clark, Lenox acknowledged the force of the first point and said that he could hardly blame Clark for the second.

He had been almost dead when Clark entered. According to Graham (who had pieced together the story), it had taken Clark no effort at all to disarm Blaine, and indeed the ball—Lenox had seen the papers!—had suffered no interruption.

Still, only quick action by Clark and Caroline Astor had saved Lenox's life. They had sent for doctors, who had dressed the wound, and then suggested that for his own sake Lenox be taken to a hospital in New York.

The Astors' best horses had driven him, unconscious, into the city, where a team of surgeons had sewn him up before daybreak. Almost immediately he had broken out in infection—the long period of his confused impressions during brief bouts of wakefulness that he was in Holland. Doctors had been called in from Cambridge, New Haven, and Philadelphia, according to Graham—before Graham's arrival, it had been Mrs. Astor and O'Brian supervising affairs, an unlikely twosome.

All of them had agreed that the infection was too intense to survive. On the fifth night, one of the nurses, a young woman named Lucinda Carraight, had poured alcohol onto the bandages after the doctor had left. She only admitted it after Lenox began to improve: her uncle's trick, she said, never known to fail. Whether it was this old superstition or luck, he began to get well.

His recovery was of course welcome, but it was agonizingly slow. He was usually at his best after breakfast. Two strong young men would (humiliatingly) carry him in a fireman's lift downstairs and place him in a wicker wheelchair, after which Graham would perambulate him, tolerating Lenox's irritable complaints about the unevenness of the pavement, the brightness of the sun, the loudness of the infernal birds, around Washington Square.

Following these outings, Lenox slept most mornings. He was in fair shape for lunch, generally, but beyond that his energy was nil.

He wanted to be on his feet—to figure out where Teddy Blaine had vanished, curse him. But it was too soon. He had never been so humbled before his own body. The effort to lift anything with his right arm was excruciating, and even to shift in his bed, or swallow food, was sometimes enough to cause him to close his eyes and breathe evenly, in an attempt to stave off the pain.

It was Caroline Astor who had wired Lady Jane on the night of Blaine's attack. She had warned that the doctors were not sure whether Lenox would survive. Jane had spread the word to one or two people, as she eventually told him when they were alone, Sophia and Clara asleep upstairs. She had arranged to sail the next afternoon but one with the girls.

Yet even by then, she said, Graham had already been aboard the fastest ship bound for America, the mail packet, having left behind only a letter on his desk at Parliament, which wasn't discovered by his panicked aides, who were suddenly forced to cancel dozens of meetings and speeches, until he was already part of the way across the Atlantic.

CHAPTER FORTY-ONE

Soon enough Lenox was walking around Washington Square Park under his own strength. He cut a feeble figure, moving at a snail's pace, generally leaning on Graham's arm. For long stretches the most pleasant thing to do was sit upon a quiet bench and bask in the nourishing sun, eyes closed—which was all to the good, for he could not make it much farther than a few hundred yards from his front door without running short of breath.

He grew to love the little house on Washington Square. Caroline Astor had let it to him for two weeks at first, a term now extended to two months by Graham's offices, the length of time the doctors agreed Lenox must wait before attempting to travel.

Finally—if not on any schedule he had planned—he was seeing America.

"People are being terribly kind," said Lady Jane one morning over breakfast, sorting through the post. "I have had two notes from Alva Belmont just this week."

She was at a circular table with a pretty white lace cloth, a tea-cup and a piece of toast with blueberry jam in front of her. It was from Maine; and she had already ordered two dozen jars to take back to London. Lenox was in a softer chair, in the corner of the room, reading. He had found that right now he could tolerate only Sir Walter Scott.

"Who is Alva Belmont?" he asked.

"You sat next to her brother at the Astor ball."

"Oh." He paused. "I do not see that as a very profound claim on our friendship. She wants to gawk at me."

Lady Jane glanced up and smiled. "Only someone who loves you as much as I do would want to gawk at you in your present state."

He chuckled, though it hurt his ribs. There had been complications recently with his wound, unhealthy discharge; too much exercise. "You might be surprised."

Inevitably, word had trickled out into society about the confrontation at the ball. For a week, true, the stories from Newport had all been about what Caroline Astor served for dessert, whom she had excluded from her invitations, the engagements that had been decided by the end of the night.

But soon there were other, more troubling rumors abroad about that evening, and while they were too unclear to appear in the papers—and Blaine's father too powerful for most journalists to risk his wrath—these rumors were nevertheless busily multiplying across New York.

Lenox had accepted no visitor yet except for the Allinghams. To them he had told the unvarnished truth about Blaine. All others, with the exception of a visit from Mrs. Berry, in her best bonnet and bearing a new quilt as a present, he had declined; even Caroline Astor, grateful though he was to her, he preferred to write.

Lady Jane had been more sociable. But the real triumph had been Sophia and Clara's—with Miss Huntington, the girls had set out to discover the various parks of New York and seemed to return each time with tales of new playmates. The trip had turned into a delight for them: American children had much worse manners, Sophia said, which turned out to mean that they were not stiff or formal but ran about in heaps and had the kind of fun Sophia always longed to have. If her parents, even her governess, indulged her, perhaps it was forgivable.

Lenox had fallen back into *Rob Roy* when O'Brian entered the room. "A visitor, sir—or rather, quite a lot of visitors."

"Excuse me?"

"It is mainly Mr. Blaine, sir. The elder one," he added hastily, realizing it might have sounded as if Lenox's assailant was returning to finish the job of killing him.

"Who is with him?"

Jane had gotten up and was peering outside. "A small army." Then she corrected herself. "Not that small."

Reluctantly, Lenox roused himself from the chair, went to the window, and peered through the slats toward the park, which was a lovely green in this morning hour, dappled with shade.

There was Archie Blaine, it was true, standing, staring at nothing in particular, smoking, and with him perhaps twenty people, some of whom looked like business associates, others whose notable qualities looked to be more in the physical than the mental line.

"If he is still here in fifteen minutes, you may show him into the lower parlor," said Lenox, and sat down again.

Teddy Blaine himself had vanished. His knife, his walking stick, his limp; he had taken all three and since remained invisible to the law, which had been seeking him. No one knew whether he was in China or California or a boardinghouse on Broadway.

It was an uneasy feeling. Only the two intimidating guards stationed at the doors by the Astors made Lenox feel secure.

The elder Blaine waited him out, and in due course the two men sat opposite each other in the lower parlor, a small room furnished for card playing. They were alone.

"How is your health, Mr. Lenox?"

"Improving, thank you," said Lenox.

Blaine missed the coldness in the detective's voice. "I'm relieved to hear it." He glanced up and around the room they were in. "This is a very fine house."

"To one such as yourself it must seem modest."

Archie Blaine smiled and met Lenox's eyes, albeit briefly. "You could only say that as one who has never lived truly modestly, Mr. Lenox. I never knew a floor could be made of anything but dirt until I was ten."

At the moment Lenox was uninterested in this line of conversation. "Where is your son, Mr. Blaine?"

"I don't know."

"You must think me stupid."

Blaine shook his head impassively. "No, I do not. You pieced together what he had done. Nobody else did."

"But you will not say where he has gone."

"I know that he is safe somewhere and is being watched. I could have a report on his every step within ten minutes, should I choose. But I have asked not to be told anything directly just yet."

"So that you do not have to tell the police?"

"No. Because I would be tempted to tell the police."

Lenox waited. Mr. Blaine, though, was immune to this trick, happy to sit in silence for some time. He was one of the most peculiar people Lenox had ever met, somehow—not in his dress, or even his conversation, but in the way that it seemed to Lenox that he was living in an entirely different world. Making money was evidently very easy for him; making sons rather harder, bewildering even, perhaps.

"Then why have you come to see me?" said Lenox at last.

"I want to know what I can do for you."

"Do for me?"

"You seem to have good quarters—family close—good care." Some of the best doctors had been sent by Blaine's people in fact, no expense spared. Lenox had been unconscious; sometimes in his ill-humored moments, now, he imagined turning them away. "What else can I provide?"

"The question insults me, as I'm sure you know."

Archibald Blaine looked at him, startled. This time the coldness in Lenox's voice must have been unmistakable. "Insults you? Oh—because it's money. I see. No, I am not trying to buy your coopera-tion, Mr. Lenox. I am distraught at what Teddy has done to you."

"Less distraught than I am, or the Allinghams, I would have to imagine."

Blaine nodded at the justice of this, but did not reply directly. "I also wished to explain."

"Explain?"

"About Teddy. He has always been troubled, my younger son."

"You don't say."

"The difficulty is that he's exceedingly bright."

"Yes," said Lenox. "I saw that for myself."

"I hoped that a good education might salvage him from his worst tendencies. It has not, obviously. I see that now. One imagines—well, a marriage, a career, such things can settle a person. I was even ready to let him become a detective, though it would have half killed my wife."

The great mogul had apparently forgotten that he was speaking to a detective—and for that matter, one who did not hold Blaine's wife in especially high regard, based on their brief acquaintance.

"Were you?"

Blaine leaned back. Outside he had smoked incessantly, but he was unhurried now, his full, immensely powerful attention on the matter at hand. "I ventured into his bedroom at home for myself yesterday. I wanted to confirm what my men had told me."

"And?"

"There were hundreds of articles about you in his desk, on his walls. Hundreds."

Lenox felt that chill again. "About me."

"My son had ample means to pursue his interest, alas. A clipping agency in France sending news of you from Paris. London was easy."

Lenox shifted in his seat. He winced, wishing his skin and flesh would knit again, whole. He had taken his body for granted. Well—he would not make that error again.

"Was there anything about Lily Allingham among his possessions?"

"Eh? Oh—quite a bit. Yes, quite a bit. She was a subject in many of the society columns, of course, and he tracked her assiduously."

Despite hearing this, though, Lenox felt a guilt that went deeper than his mere mind, that went somewhere into his soul. He had come on this trip—had embarked on this very career—so confidently, and now he wondered whether this had been the inevitable outcome of that choice: the obsession of a madman, an innocent person's death.

"You asked if you could do anything for me. I would like to see the materials Teddy gathered."

Blaine hesitated, then nodded. "I shall have them sent over by the end of the day if you really mean it."

"I do. I would also like to know where Teddy is."

"I'm afraid I cannot tell you that."

"Then I and my family are in danger."

"No. Not now, not ever."

The words were uttered so decisively—with such might of wealth behind it—that Lenox was, in fact, reassured, though he did not let on. "Then I may ask one more thing of you."

"Anything."

"I would like to speak to Winthrop."

Archie Blaine looked surprised. "Win? He's sailing in Wellfleet, I believe. But certainly, certainly. I will have him visit you as soon as he is back in New York—indeed he shall come down directly, if it is not in his plans."

Suddenly, Lenox realized that he might not have one of the world's ten richest men sitting in front of him again. It was vanity to throw away the chance. So he said that there was one more thing, too.

"Anything within my power," said Blaine.

"I have a young valet here, an Irish boy named O'Brian. I know there is a bias against his race in America, but he is extremely intelligent and kind, honest too, and his mother and younger brothers and sisters rely on him. When I leave, I would ask that you find him some employment."

Blaine inclined his head. "So it shall be."

"I don't mean that I would beg a place in service for him, Mr. Blaine. I think he has higher capabilities than that. He—"

Blaine held a hand up. "You have my word. His way is made. On this one subject, at least, you may put your mind to rest. I am sorry that I cannot do you the same service on the matter of my son, Mr. Lenox. Most sincerely sorry."

CHAPTER FORTY-TWO

S lowly Lenox's strength returned, until by the tenth of June he was able to walk the full perimeter of Washington Square.

"You told me I would never do it," he said to Graham triumphantly.

"I never said anything of the kind," replied Graham.

They were back in the little house. Though the weather was mild, Lenox was drenched in sweat from the exertion. "Hm. Perhaps you implied it."

"I certainly did not."

Lenox frowned. "Fine," he said. "Have it all your way."

Other parts of his usual life were emerging from their dormancy as well. He was in correspondence with the gentlemen he had intended to visit in Boston, New Haven, and Chicago, and every afternoon at two o'clock, he and Jane took a drive through a different part of New York, occasionally stopping at a shop or to see a view. He liked how the two rivers here in New York hugged the city into them. He decided the city's sin and its virtue were the same: ambition, crowing its song from every corner. In London, the clerks were clerk-like, and the street sweepers held out little hope for more, but here everyone seemed to think they might one day be an Archie

Blaine, and this faith hummed in the city's private conversation with itself, in the gait of the carriage horses and the keen eyes of the newsboys. A different world.

He described it in his letters, which he wrote each morning over a long, idle breakfast. Graham was in Washington, D.C., now, taking meetings—Lenox suspected he would return home to England soon—and Lady Jane was in avid, nearly hysterical demand.

For his part, Lenox was content to read (he had graduated from Scott to a volume of Cicero, sent with a note of condolence by Mr. Hunter, whose wife had also written to express her concern) and occasionally answer a letter. He wrote most often to his brother, who had tried to come, but having a much later start than Graham and Lady Jane—he had been in Madrid on Parliamentary business—had been told that Charles was out of the woods by wire, and that he must stay behind in case they needed anything prepared at home before his arrival.

> I have a few moments of occasional sociability these days. We saw Eddings last night. He was very curious about my adventures in Newport, and saddened when I said that I never need to see it again—though I would visit Mrs. Berry's happily enough.
>
> Jane dines out occasionally, but I am so much work that in the daytime she only sees two people. One is Miss Esham, a woman with whom she was at school for a year as a ten-year-old. She lives in very humble circumstances, working as a governess—her father was part of that breakup over the India funds, and through no fault of her own she was left penniless. The other is Caroline Astor. I told Jane it was beneath her to succumb to snobbery and she nearly had my head off at the suggestion. Still, I suspect her. Maybe I have become too American. The three of them are having tea today. How that shall go the lord alone knows.

I confess I wish you were here, Ed—or say, rather, that I wish we were sitting across a table from each other over a bottle of wine at Lenox House! I regret having spent so little time there recently. Indeed, I have found myself reaching back in the most unaccustomed ways, recently, and wishing that mother could be here, and father. Molly too. Last night I dreamed I was playing chess with Deere. It seemed very real. When I woke I had a moment of strange, bitter sorrow.

But I refuse to bargain my way into a tremulous and regretful old age just yet. I am not even 50 (ha, ha, you old-timer). That is why I have taken a decision of which I hope you will approve; it is to leave my profession. Polly and John will do very well with the agency, and as for myself, there must be something to which I could usefully turn my hand. I am curious to discover what it may be. In the meanwhile my life must be with my family, you among their number. I see that the Wallace murder is going to trial. It will do so without my interest—I skip the articles I see about it, and nearly the first thing I did when I was myself again was ship across the file Disraeli gave me to Dallington. He will handle it as well as I could have, likely better.

Lenox finished this sentence and sat back to look out at the park, which was dotted with a few elderly gentlemen strolling through the midmorning sunlight.

He wondered why he had written to Edmund about his work, and nearly scratched it out. He thought back to Archie Blaine's visit. Why had it troubled him so? Perhaps because, Lenox reflected now, they were akin, the father and son—two people with odd, inveterate intelligences, uncommon ways of looking at the world.

The fact was that he thought of Teddy Blaine almost continuously, running over their interactions again and again in his mind, searching for clues he might have seen earlier. The thought haunted him that he had been the inspiration for Blaine's crime. And he had been so credulous! Was it because Teddy Blaine was, as Lenox once had been, a son of the upper classes interested in becoming a detective? Perhaps it was that easy; perhaps he had been blinded by Blaine's flattery. Embarrassing to consider, that.

A few afternoons later Lenox had a shave, dressed himself pains-takingly, and rode the short way downtown to Trinity Church, one of the city's oldest churches, at the corner of Wall Street and Broadway.

"I will walk the last block," he told O'Brian, who was on the box.

"Are you sure, sir?"

"Quite sure."

The memorial service for Lily Allingham was badly attended. Or perhaps the church was too large—but no, he counted the pews, measured their width with an expert eye, and it was undeniable, the number of people was paltry. He hoped the few who were there had at least really loved her.

Trinity seemed the size of an acorn compared to Westminster Abbey, or St. Paul's, or Notre-Dame. Yet he was sure he had heard that it was the tallest building in America. New York, he supposed, was of its nature a low-slung place, as some cities seemed to be, no building too high, the skies open on every avenue. He hoped, walk-ing slowly but evenly up the aisle toward an open pew, that this young city might stay that way.

"Hello, Mr. Lenox."

He turned and saw Rose Bennett, wearing a black gown. Even in mourning dress she was in the bloom of youth, her skin fresh, her delicate hands clutching a piece of paper.

"Good afternoon, Miss Bennett," he said.

"I hope you are recovering. They say you are."

"Me? Yes—quite well—very well." He smiled. "Thank you for inquiring."

She hesitated. "Can I ask what happened? That night? Can it be true that it was Teddy Blaine who stabbed you?"

"Yes."

She shook her head wonderingly. "I've known him since I was four."

"May I ask what the rest of the night was like for you?"

"It went off like a dream, I must say. There was one loud shout in the hallway—Mr. Clark, they tell us now—but it didn't stop the party for more than ten seconds. Please don't take any offense."

"Of course not."

Lenox couldn't help asking if she had heard any word of Teddy or his whereabouts. She shook her head. "I remember when he offered to marry Lily. She didn't give it a moment's thought, barely mentioned it to me—rich as he was. She knew Willie was in hand. And if not him, Lawrence."

"Did she say anything about Teddy at all?"

Rose Bennett considered the question. "She said that after she gave him her answer, he asked for a ring or a lock of her hair to remember his love by."

"Did she give it to him?"

"I don't know. No—I don't think so. It wouldn't have been like her. She could be difficult. She was so very—I don't suppose any of the portraits capture it, do they? At every party a dozen men fell in love with her. A dozen—I am not exaggerating. Some women have that quality."

"Some men, too."

"They are not thrown my way very often," said Rose Bennett, and smiled.

"No, they are rare, I'm sure."

"She had such large eyes, Lily. And a beautiful mouth. She could put on any kind of rag and it would fit her as if a team of seam-stresses had been working for a week. Oh, I don't know! She could certainly be cold-hearted, but she could be so kind, too. She was kind to me. She listened to every word I ever had to say about my own silly life, and in all the time I knew her she never for a second lorded it over anyone that she was so beautiful—except for men. And they deserve it, for all they have, I sometimes think. Only if she had been plain she would be alive."

Tears had started to spill from Rose Bennett's eyes, though her voice hadn't changed.

"She was nineteen," said Lenox. "All of the difficult edges would have softened, I hope, and the good parts of her come to the fore."

"Perhaps. She didn't have enough of a chance to become herself."

"No. Blaine took that from her."

She nodded, wiping the tears away furiously. "Yes," she said. "Good day, Mr. Lenox. Tell your wife I think I have never seen a lady dress more beautifully—will you tell her that? I saw a glimpse of her the other day, going into Mrs. Astor's house."

"Of course I will," said Lenox. "I hope you will call upon her yourself before we leave New York."

"Oh! On Lady Jane? On both of you, excuse me—yes, with great pleasure—I will leave a card this afternoon, if it is not too forward. Or perhaps tomorrow morning would be more suitable. Yes, tomorrow morning. Thank you, Mr. Lenox."

When the memorial was over—the paper in Rose Bennett's hand had been a reading from Psalms, Lily Allingham's favorite book of the Bible—Lenox exchanged a few words with Creighton and Cora Allingham before leaving them to their closer friends and stepping out to the churchyard to see the stone that marked their daughter's life.

Making his way toward it, he saw names on other gravestones that he knew from his sojourn here, names from Cove Court and the opera house and the cards left for Lady Jane in increasing numbers every day. (He had attracted no such following, as he had observed to her the night before over supper.) These gravestones had lichen and moss on them, but most were legible. Stuyvesant, Jay, Schermerhorn, Crane, Lamb, Waldorf, Baker, Ridley, a dozen others.

Whatever else they had done, they had come to this country early, these men and women, when it was far from certain that it should become what it had become—when the gamble of it all was far from decided. He credited them for that. Newport might be a very paradise on earth for their descendants, but none of these men and women had set eyes on it.

He looked at Lily Allingham's name for a long time, then let his gaze travel to each tree in the churchyard, each building on the stately avenues around it. For the briefest of moments he thought he glimpsed New York as it must have been long before. There was the beautiful weak light, so unlike London's, and there were the unfamiliar songs of birds in the trees; in the middle distance, the clumsily cut streets where the first shops and houses had appeared. The whole thing fell still, legible, before his gaze, how it must have seemed to those first New Yorkers, those earliest immigrants to America. It lasted only a second.

CHAPTER FORTY-THREE

One sunny morning in the third week of June, Lenox and Graham were walking near Washington Square together when Lenox saw William Schermerhorn the Fourth, out for a drive.

He had the finest team Lenox had seen in New York, not excluding those of the Blaines and the Astors, four immense bay draft horses with shining coats and a sprightly step. They wore little cockaded bouquets. A fellow would have been laughed out of Berkeley Square for that, but here it was rather more usual than unusual.

"That is the man who asked me to come to Newport," he said to Graham, nodding toward the carriage. "I rather wish he had not."

They were nearing the carriage, and Lenox lifted his hat and said good morning. But there was no response—Schermerhorn didn't even glance down!—and Lenox, astonished, stopped and turned.

"Did you see that?" he asked Graham. "He cut me dead! Good lord, I call that very discourteous."

"I believe he was with his mistress, sir," said Graham.

"What?"

"They tell me it is the custom here that one's wife, or any other lady of good reputation, sits on the right hand of the driver—while if he is with his mistress, she sits on his left, so that his friends will know to ignore them."

Lenox was incredulous. "Are you sure?"

"I only know what I have been told, but I believe so."

"Then I have been discourteous. Though really, what a Bartholomew Fair it is—his mistress indeed! And I am supposed to know that, and respect the fact enough to—and he a pure hypocrite over his son's marriage, too!"

In fact, young Willie Schermerhorn could not have stood higher in New York's estimation than he did now. To the surprise of many (and the dismay of some), the papers were besotted with Mrs. Maryanne Schermerhorn, the principled young maid from Newport who had married into one of the great cottages. Reporters had been to visit her old room at Mrs. Walliter's; Willie Schermerhorn was considering a run for congress; and the sole time Lenox had caught a glimpse of the pair, she had been wearing the diamonds that had until so recently resided on the ledge above her window in her spartan room at the boardinghouse.

"Different customs, I suppose," said Graham.

"That's coming it pretty high, to call a mistress a custom, Graham. Goodness me."

Graham smiled. "No doubt you're right."

They resumed walking. Graham was departing for England at the end of the week, and beyond thanking him, there was nothing more to be said unless Lenox wanted to verge into the sentimental, which he knew Graham would like even less than he. Still, it seemed an awfully meager return for such generosity of friendship. As long as he lived, he would never forget the feeling of safety that had washed over him when he realized Graham had come—that it was Graham's familiar quiet figure in the armchair next to his bed.

He would find a way to thank him. It would have to go on the lengthening list of things he had to do, a sure sign that his health was improving. At the top of the list, of course, a list private to himself, was the last task he had in mind in his career as a detective: finding Teddy Blaine. That, at least, he was determined to do.

As they walked they discussed the Schermerhorn family, and then the subject moved to Lawrence Vanderbilt and his flask—it must have been returned to him now, Lenox supposed, ghoulish though the idea was—and soon, for the first time in the six weeks since he had been stabbed, he found himself talking about the case again, describing for Graham in humorous detail the different cottages, recounting his first meeting with Blaine and then with Clark, the taverns they had in Newport and the food and the drink and all of it.

They had gone nearly twenty blocks by the time the story was told, and had to take a taxi the rest of the way home; but Lenox felt lighter for having told everything to Graham.

"Did I tell you I sat with Winthrop Blaine for the better part of an afternoon?" he said in the taxi.

"No," said Graham, who had been in Washington when Lenox met the young man.

"He was quite blunt. He said his brother had always been peculiar."

That didn't quite cover the facts, actually. What Winthrop Blaine had said was that he had known his brother was different their whole lives. As a child of four and five, the elder brother had said, Teddy had taken pleasure in the pain of animals, including Winthrop's own dog. He had played cruel pranks on the servants up until the age of around twelve, when his interests had grown more occult, stranger, and the rest of the family had largely left him to his own devices.

They discussed this, and then they discussed, again, Lenox's decision to change professions. Graham had been there during Lenox's earliest days as a detective; he knew what it had cost.

"Perhaps your outlook will change when you are home again," he said.

"Yes," said Lenox. "Perhaps."

But he doubted it. He was tired, and thirsty, and his side hurt. "You could stand for a conservative seat. It would distress Disraeli."

"Then it is almost worth it. But you and my brother have both shown me for an amateur, I fear. No—it will be something new, I suppose. I am almost excited to see what it may be."

As their carriage crawled across Tenth Street, the conversation turned to politics at home. They had spent hundreds of hours since Graham's arrival, and throughout his careful attendance at Lenox's bedside, discussing the intricacies of life in Parliament. It was a world Lenox had departed but whose language and characters he still knew intimately, and it had been a solace to put his mind on something objective. Now they ventured into a complex discussion of the new Farming Bill and how the votes for it might be whipped.

They were deep in this conversation when they arrived at home. For her part, Lady Jane was in the pretty blue drawing room on the second story of the little house.

She saw, the moment he stepped out of the hansom, that Charles had walked too far that morning. She winced, standing at the window. He thought he hid it, but there was a difference in the way he stood when it hurt. Oh, the foolishness! The wound might open, become infected again—and it was impossible to say anything to him, he had been so irascible, so reluctant to accept help, so angry with himself . . .

In her hand was a note from Kirk. He said he believed Kidgerby was "finally ready, ma'am," but that he would stay until their return, obviously; and then he went on to note several of Kidgerby's flaws, before concluding that perhaps he had better stay at least two weeks, or a month to be safe, after their return, and then closing with a positively troubled postscript about Kidgerby's inattention to the rotation of the bottles in the house's wine cave.

Two more weeks. Lady Jane found herself fonder than she had expected to be of America, but she missed home. Or perhaps she missed the time before Charles had almost died; before that awful sea voyage, wondering every day whether he was still alive, sitting with Sophia as she colored in drawings of tigers and palaces for her father. Give Jane back the quiet routine of Hampden Lane, and the endless disruptions to that quiet which London always managed to provide, and she would be happy.

She watched Sophia run down the steps to her father, and she watched Graham subtly position himself so that the impact of the embrace would hurt him less. She watched Charles take the girl into his arms. She permitted herself just a moment of pure happiness, seeing that, the mild light on their faces as she studied them, Charles's thin and drawn, Sophia's laughing and pugnacious. But just a moment. When it was gone, she turned inside—for of course there was much to do, and experience had made her a practical sort of person; and she knew that whatever else you might think you know about life, something else always came next.

ACKNOWLEDGMENTS

This has not been a very normal past year or so, as some of you reading this probably noticed, and that was true even of something as
infinitesimal as the writing of this book. So I'm especially grateful
to the people at St. Martin's and Minotaur, who were full of ideas
and passion even when no one on earth felt like working another
minute—or at least, I didn't—and who are why this book exists.

They brought so many amazing qualities together as they adjusted to working from home: the leadership and (sorely tested)
optimism of Andy Martin, the discernment and sense of humor
of Kelley Ragland, and the generosity and good company of Sarah
Melnyk, without which I don't think I would have made it through
the last Lenox book, let alone this one. Martin Quinn's creativity
and strength are a genuine inspiration to me.

My editor, Charles Spicer, has been almost unbelievably patient
and kind this year, and as ever a superb editorial voice, his presence
felt on every page of this series. I owe his excellent assistant, Sarah
Grill, a really good present. David Rotstein, James Sinclair, Cathy
Turiano, David Lott, Louise Collazo, Susan Groarke, Anne New-
garden, Paul Hochman, Kayla Janas, Dori Weintraub, and Sally

Richardson have also been instrumental in bringing my words to the page, and I'm extremely grateful to all of them.

My thanks are infinite for Elisabeth Weed, and not just for the ice cream. Dennis and Linda, I can't wait to hug you again; Tim and Jenny, you too. Thank you to my mother for everything, but especially for our daily conversations while I wrote this book. My sister Julia was at my side during tough times this year, and I owe her special thanks, along with Isabelle, Rosie, Henry, Teddy, and Jamie, my amazing family. Annabel, since I have your permission— love you bigger than the whole universe! And Em, thank you for everything I have, because you are the person who gave it to me.

Timothy Greenfield-Sanders

CHARLES FINCH is the *USA Today* bestselling author of the Charles Lenox mysteries, including *The Last Passenger*. His first contemporary novel, *The Last Enchantments*, is also available from St. Martin's Press. Finch received the 2017 Nona Balakian Citation for Excellence in Reviewing from the National Book Critics Circle. His essays and criticism have appeared in *The New York Times*, *Slate*, *The Washington Post*, and elsewhere. He lives in Los Angeles.

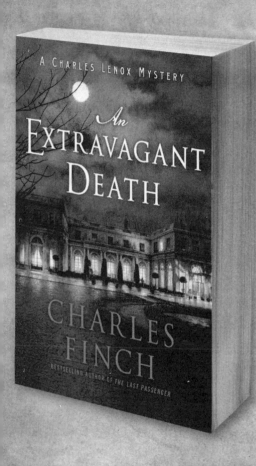